PRAISE FOR
THOSE PEOPLE BEHIND US

"Juxtaposed against the bright and sunny Southern California sky, this multigenerational tale takes a deep dive into the minds and motivations of a seemingly harmless neighborhood as it strips back each dark and complicated layer, piece by piece."
—**Suzanne Simonetti**, *USA Today* best-selling author of *The Sound of Wings*

"Thoughtful and riveting. Camarillo trains an astute yet empathetic eye on the residents of one Southern California community in the year 2017, dissecting the mental and emotional cracks in our foundation at the brink of the Trump era."
—**Shelley Blanton-Stroud**, author of *Copy Boy* and *Tomboy*

"A fascinating and perceptive read about growth, acceptance, and understanding people different than yourself."
—**Diana Wagman**, author of *Spontaneous* and *Extraordinary October*

"Mary Camarillo deftly weaves the lives of these five very different people together, revealing their personalities with skill and sympathy. You'll wonder about your own neighbors—those people behind us—and whether you should make more effort to get to know them better."
—**Anara Guard**, author of *Like a Complete Unknown*

"A town that could be anywhere in America."
—**Leslie A. Rasmussen**, author of *After Happily Ever After* and *The Stories We Cannot Tell*

"Mary Camarillo captures a suburban beach community with such precision, you feel you are eavesdropping on real people's lives, with all their dreams and disappointments, faults and frailties. Camarillo allows her characters to express their differing views and leaves it to her readers to draw their own conclusions."
—**Debra Thomas**, author of *Luz* and *Josie and Vic*

"Peyton Place with a twist of Trump."
—**Eduardo Santiago**, author of *Tomorrow They Will Kiss* and *Midnight Rhumba*

THOSE
PEOPLE
BEHIND
US

THOSE PEOPLE BEHIND US

A NOVEL

MARY CAMARILLO

SHE WRITES PRESS

Published 2023
Printed in the United States of America
Print ISBN: 978-1-64742-565-4
E-ISBN: 978-1-64742-566-1
Library of Congress Control Number: 2023906756

For information, address:
She Writes Press
1569 Solano Ave #546
Berkeley, CA 94707

Interior Design by Tabitha Lahr

She Writes Press is a division of SparkPoint Studio, LLC.

For my father,
Lewis Parker

CHAPTER ONE

KEITH NELSON

Keith watches a skunk family march down the middle of Summertime Lane, their eyes glowing zombie red in the streetlight. It's 5:20 a.m. and the battery on his cell phone is almost dead. He can smell himself, perspiration, pizza breath, and the gym socks and towel that never quite dried yesterday. No matter what, he's got to do laundry today and get some sleep tonight. He had to move his car from the library parking lot earlier, when the police drove through, flashing blue lights at the parked cars and RVs, yelling into bullhorns that the lot was closed. Now he's only two blocks away from the house he grew up in.

He imagines his parents, sound asleep, with no idea of all the wild things creeping around outside in the dark. Coyotes slinking down the sidewalk, sniffing the air for dog food and outdoor cats. Possums waddling toward sidewalk-splattered avocados. Tree rats chasing each other across electrical wires. Two raccoons traversing the cinderblock walls like gloved and masked thieves. One scrawny, grey striped cat hiding beneath the Gormans' oleander bush.

Keith pees in an empty Gatorade bottle, opens the car door as silently as possible, and gets out. The blooms on the crepe myrtle trees up and down Summertime Lane catch the sun rising over Ensillado Mountain. He pours the urine out over the grass clippings in the Gormans' green yard waste container, then puts the empty Gatorade bottle in their blue recycling bin. Stretching his arms overhead, Keith hears his neck pop. He wishes he had an Advil.

The crepe myrtle flowers are beautiful—watermelon red, rose pink, deep lavender, fuchsia, and white—with a silver bark that glows in the sunrise. A small breeze picks up and the blossoms wave back and forth as if they're admiring each other. His dad would call him a pussy, but he loves these trees, the contrast of their crazy colors against the concrete sidewalks and driveways.

And then the Gormans' sprinklers go on and an icy jet of water shoots straight up his leg. "Fuck," he whispers as he jumps across the meridian, trying to avoid getting his feet wet too. He gets in the car, grabs the stinky towel from the backseat, and does what he can, but it looks like he's pissed himself. There's another pair of shorts in the trunk that also stink because he's worked out in them twice this week, but it's too hard to change in the car. He has a key to his parents' house, but they'll be up soon, making coffee, getting ready for work. He imagines his father's granite slab of a face, his mother's disapproving smirk. "Not so independent after all," she'd probably say. He checks his cell phone again: 5:43. He starts the car.

He's the first one through the door at the Seaview gym, holding his gym bag over his crotch so Cliff, the club manager at the front desk, can't see the wet spot.

"Your membership expires in July," Cliff says. "You want to go ahead and take care of that now?"

"That's two months away," Keith says. "I'll catch you next time." He changes his shorts, stows his gym bag in a locker, then goes out to the workout floor and does his weight routine twice. After he runs on the treadmill for forty-five minutes, he heads back to the locker room where he shits, showers, and shaves.

His chin in the bathroom mirror is the same as his dad's, square and solid. They used to have similar noses too, long with high bridges, but beer has pickled his dad's nose into something red and bulbous. Keith takes a blue button-down off a dry cleaner hanger. He always wears blue because his grandmother says it complements his eyes. He looks tired. He never gets enough sleep. Most people guess he's older than twenty-four.

The traffic on the freeway is heavy, but he still gets to the office early, takes his usual spot in the last row of the parking lot behind the bright blue trucks with "The Bug Guy" printed in bold yellow. He parks in the back because he doesn't like the idea of people looking at his towel and gym clothes spread out in the backseat to dry. The Accord is otherwise spotless, washed weekly at the drive-through car wash, no trash on the floor, the rest of his belongings packed neatly out of sight in the trunk.

The phone on his desk is already ringing. "It's a great day at the Bug Guy," he says as required in his job description. His father calls him a glorified receptionist because he answers the phone, schedules termite inspections, and listens to customers describe invasions of roaches, ants, and fleas and complain about inspectors being late. He'd make more money as an inspector, but he doesn't like chemicals, crawling in attics, or dealing face-to-face with weird people, going into their weird houses, looking at their weird shit. He's too big to crawl into attic spaces anyway. Five foot eleven and two hundred twenty-five pounds, according to the scale at the Seaview gym this morning.

He watches enough sports and news at the gym to make small talk with people at work. They seem to like him, but he keeps to himself because being too friendly would mean explaining his life in more detail. His coworkers have stopped inviting him to lunch and happy hour. "Keith's a health nut," they say. "Spends all his spare time at the gym." Once he can afford a training space of his own, he plans to convert them into clients.

At 5:00 p.m., he clocks out and heads to his usual laundromat with his duffel bag full of dirty clothes, but every single machine is taken. There's no place to sit and wait either. This place is never busy. He calls his grandmother and asks if she needs anything, hoping he can use the machine in the laundry room by her place.

"Pick me up some coffee filters and a box of chardonnay," she tells him on the phone. "You can stay for dinner too."

There's a line for the visitor pass lane at the Golden Years Retirement Community where Granny C lives. Catherine Nelson is her real name, but Keith's always called her Granny C, and she's always called him Sonny. She's the only one who isn't disappointed in him. He watches the guards as he waits to be waved in. Uniforms and gates still make him nervous.

"So handsome," Granny C says when she opens her front door. She's wearing her usual pastels, lavender today. She has a woman who comes to her apartment every Friday to wash and style her hair, and she always keeps her glasses clean and the batteries in her hearing aids charged.

Keith leaves his duffel bag on her front porch and kisses the top of her head. After he puts the wine in her fridge, he helps her switch from her walker to a wheelchair.

"Set that duffel bag in my lap," she says. "Let's go do some laundry."

They roll out of her apartment and down the sidewalk. Keith likes Golden Years' expansive lawns. They have an impressive collection of trees too—Southern Magnolias, Ginkgo Biloba, Mimosa, Jacaranda, and his favorite, Crepe Myrtles. "The hydrangeas are starting to bloom," he says, and Granny C smiles. She had a huge garden in her old house in Coyote Heights and taught him the names of all the plants and trees.

There's an OUT OF ORDER sign on the locked laundry room door.

"Shoot," Granny C says. "There's another laundry room across the greenbelt. Let's try that one." On the way they stop in front of a corner apartment with a display of twenty-five pink plastic flamingos arranged around a stand of jasmine and ginger.

"Remember that time we went to Hawaii?" she asks.

He remembers jumping over waves in bright sunshine, his dad holding tight to his hand. They bought shaved ice on the way back to the condo, green hills in the distance. "Any flavor you want," his dad had said. Keith's favorite was called Tiger's Blood: watermelon, strawberry, and coconut. "That was a long time ago," he says now.

The machines in the second laundry room are all in use.

"Sorry, Sonny," Granny C says. "But you could probably do laundry at your parents' house."

"Not a good idea."

"Don't be so stubborn."

"It was my idea to leave."

"I worry about you, sleeping in your car. There's so much crime."

"That room in Garden City will be available soon." He's on a waiting list and the room is actually just a sectioned off part of an unheated garage, but he'll have bathroom privileges and access to a washer and dryer.

"How about if I give you some money for a hotel in the meantime?" she says.

"You know my mother won't like that."

Back in her apartment, Keith cuts the stuffed bell peppers in the Meals on Wheels tray into two pieces and heats them in the microwave. When he pours her a glass of wine,

Granny C hands him a check for two hundred dollars. His mother will be angry when she finds out, and she will find out because she reviews Granny C's bank accounts religiously.

They eat in front of the television. Granny C pays for cable so she can watch James Garner in *The Rockford Files*. She admires how Garner never uses his gun unless he has to but isn't afraid to get into a fistfight. Rockford's fights are laughably fake, but Keith likes the show because she does. He wakes up when the credits roll. Granny C is snoring. He takes the check out of his pocket and admires her handwriting, then tears it in half and throws it in the garbage. On his way out he slips two twenties from her purse. He picks up his duffel bag of still-dirty clothes and goes back to his car.

Too bad he never got that blond woman's phone number, the one who'd subbed a cardio fit class a few Sundays ago at the Seaview gym. She was exactly his type. Blond and fit. Her class was organized and complete. She looked smart too. He'd noticed her wedding band and flashy diamond ring but followed her out to her car anyway. Despite the hour and a half cardio class she smelled fresh, like orange blossoms. Usually following women out to their cars doesn't go well for him, but he must have said something right because she mentioned a quiet place in the Gunner industrial complex where they could talk if he wanted to meet her there.

They parked next to a dumpster behind a closed auto paint shop and got in the backseat of her Chevy Suburban. The tinted windows were so dark, he could barely see her sitting next to him, untying her shoes. She pulled her leggings off and she wasn't wearing any underwear. When she straddled him, he couldn't believe it. It was over before he could really appreciate it—she came, he came, and then she climbed off him. She didn't want to talk either, never even gave him the chance to ask for her name or her number. He hasn't seen her at the Seaview gym since.

His best friend Wayne Connor's house is another option, but Wayne's wife Tina never seems glad to see him. When Keith asked if he could crash on their couch that first night out on his own, Wayne said they'd just remodeled.

Keith starts his car. He'll go back to the laundromat. They're open until midnight. Hopefully, the machines will be empty by now.

CHAPTER TWO
RAY MURDOCH

After Ray gets up to pee the second time, he goes back to his bedroom and cracks open the window, hoping to see the *LA Times* delivery truck come down Mountain Brook. The air is cool and damp, the start of another May Gray morning. At least the stink of rotten eggs from the offshore oil rigs has finally lessened. There's an open can of tuna on the patio table below. He'll have to talk to his mother again. Leaving food out for the Gormans' cat will only attract rats.

He'd had the craziest dream before his bladder woke him up. He was riding his bicycle across the country. The sun was on his back, there was blue sky above and Saguaro cactuses in the distance. Tucson, maybe? He was happy, which was how he knew it was a dream.

It might be too early for the newspaper. There are no lights on in the Nelsons' house behind him. They're probably sound asleep like gainfully employed people should be, unlike jobless old farts like him with only a Social Security check to look forward to each month. Bouncing from auto repair shops to construction sites and falling on and off the wagon was never a pathway to a pension or a home of his own. Or a cross-country trip on a bicycle.

That was a good dream though. Much better than his usual nightmares about helicopters and medics in Vietnam.

He liked how free he'd felt, out on the open road on his own. That old three-speed he bought in a garage sale to pedal around the neighborhood would never survive a trip like that. Neither would he. He can barely ride five miles without having to stop and pee or rest.

He should try to bump up his mileage, maybe ride down to the beach today. Except he has to take his mother to the podiatrist at nine-thirty and to her retina doctor after, and then he needs to go grocery shopping.

Headlights come up Mountain Brook. Maybe he'll actually get to read the paper with his breakfast this morning. Ray walks across the hall and opens the front bedroom shutters. This was his room when he was a kid. Now he has the master in the back and his mother sleeps down in the den because she can't manage the stairs anymore. A car passes his street, Hillside West, and turns right on Summertime Lane. It's the grey Honda the Nelson boy drives. That newspaper guy must have overslept again.

Ray glances up and down the street at his neighbors' driveways. It looks like a luxury car lot. Two matching BMWs next door. A tricked-out Lincoln Navigator parked beside a brand-new minivan across the street. That new couple halfway down the block has a black Mercedes, gleaming under the streetlight. Ray has counted five Teslas, three Airstream trailers, four Jeeps, and a Hummer on his bike rides around the neighborhood. Vehicles worth more than he ever made in a year. His neighbors are all about the show. They probably make fun of him for living with his mother and driving a sixteen-year-old Camry, but he doesn't care. He doesn't even know most of their names.

Ray closes the shutters. There are two sets of neighbors he likes: Neil and Stephanie Gorman over on Summertime Lane and Martha Kowalski and her son Josh three houses down. Martha loves to cook and always has leftovers to share. He never cared much for Martha's husband, Joe, who was some kind of pyromaniac, always fooling around with fireworks, but Joe seems to be out of the picture these days.

Ray knows the name of the gardener who takes care of most of the neighborhood lawns. Gregorio always stops by to admire his mother's roses. The real estate agent, Lisa Kensington, he knows only because she leaves an annoying newsletter with her name printed in large bold caps on his porch every week. And then there are the Nelsons behind him. Their son Keith appears to be living in his car these days. He's a full-grown man, much too large to be comfortable sleeping in a Honda.

Ray scratches his stomach under his T-shirt. He supposes the general lack of neighborliness might also have something to do with the Hillary flag his mother insisted on buying as soon as she saw the Trump flag next door. The election is over, but the flags are still flying. Ray doesn't remember any political signs when he was growing up. He never had any idea of how people voted or who they were for or against. Now everyone advertises exactly how they feel about everything when they'd all be better off not knowing. Ray remembers a line from a poem he had to memorize in grade school about good fences making good neighbors. He never really understood what it meant until now.

He doesn't understand why the Nelsons don't let Keith sleep inside their house. Keith's lucky to have a car, Ray supposes. More comfortable than sleeping on a bus bench or in a tent by the river like so many people are these days. Veterans, some of them, with a jones for drugs, alcohol, or both. He's had a spin on those merry-go-rounds. Maybe Keith has too.

One thing Ray's learned in his seventy-two years on the planet is he has no freaking idea what goes on in other people's heads. He hears the toilet flush downstairs, which means his mother's up. Might as well go start a pot of coffee. The newspaper should be here soon.

SANDCASTLE REALTY

LISA KENSINGTON

Prestige Haven Homes,
Where Your Home Is Your Castle

HAPPY MEMORIAL DAY

Once again Sandcastle Realty is providing Memorial Day flags to the entire Prestige Haven neighborhood. This beloved holiday is a chance to honor and remember our military service members who have died in the line of duty.

Memorial Day also marks the official start of summer. Time to get back in bikini shape! The Curves on Eckerd and Gunner has a special on memberships right now! Mention my name and get ten percent off your first workout!

Helpful Household Tips

" *To remove marks on wood furniture, cut a walnut in half, rub it into the scratch, rub the area with your fingers, and then buff it up with a cloth. Isn't that nuts?* **"**

In Case You Didn't Know

I'm Lisa Kensington, from Sandcastle Realty, and my territory (for almost 18 years!!!) is the Prestige Haven tract. Three miles inland from the Pacific Ocean, Prestige Haven offers the most affordably elegant classic beach homes in Wellington Beach. It's also where I live.

My husband Eric owns his own pest control business, and our two teenagers attend Wellington High School (go Wellies!).

I'm your forever real estate agent. I know the neighborhood. I'll get you the most money in the least amount of time.

PRESTIGE HAVEN IS A GREAT PLACE TO LIVE

Wellington Beach has always been an affordable Southern California beach town, perfect for raising a family. The Prestige Haven tract is a shining example of the Wellington coastal lifestyle. The neighborhood includes a mixture of one- and two-story plans with three to seven bedrooms ranging in size from twelve to thirty-eight hundred square feet.

Prices in the Prestige Haven tract have risen dramatically. A recent sale was $979,000! Call for a free estimate.

CHAPTER THREE
LISA KENSINGTON

Just before sunrise, Lisa picks up the stack of Sandcastle Realty newsletters and slings a backpack loaded with small American flags over her shoulder. She stops in front of the hallway mirror to examine her hair. The color isn't quite as red and glossy as it was two weeks ago when she paid the salon two hundred dollars. She loves the cut, a short bob with a center part and bangs, but her roots seem to have widened overnight to almost a quarter inch stripe. She's not ready to go grey yet—she's only forty-four.

There are also dark shadows under her eyes that no amount of concealer will hide. Last night, after she let Betsy, her mother-in-law, bait her into another ridiculous argument about whether or not Melania was trying to slap away Trump's hand when they landed in Tel Aviv (Betsy's convinced the video was altered, Lisa is sick of talking about it), she ate half a bag of caramel popcorn and lay awake with a stomachache most of the night.

She tells her husband she's leaving, receiving a muffled grunt in return. Eric's probably already clicking on his phone, buying something else they don't need from Amazon. Stress-eating and arguing with Betsy weren't the only things keeping her awake last night. Both kids will need to take their SATs soon and the tutoring sessions are pricey. Her teenagers do okay academically, but okay isn't enough in these competitive days of affirmative action, advanced placement classes, and the requirement to have a significant amount of volunteer work in addition to a four-point bazillion GPA. She'd like the kids to go somewhere more prestigious than the state university she and Eric attended, but they haven't saved nearly enough money.

Pulling an Angels cap over her grey roots, she heads out of their one-story house on Paradise Court—three bedrooms, one and half baths, the smallest model in the tract. As she places a flag in the yard of her next-door neighbor, John comes down his driveway in his robe and slippers and picks up the *Wall Street Journal*.

"Memorial Day already," she says, handing him a newsletter. "Can you believe it?"

John gives her a knowing smile, which usually means he has another rumor to share. "Have you heard the latest about the Riptide?"

"I heard it sold," she says. The Riptide apartment building sits on the northern edge of the Prestige Haven tract. People visiting the apartment dwellers are always parking in the neighborhood, as if they belong here.

"The Riptide tenants got sixty-day notices to vacate last February," John says.

"That place is pretty run down."

"They're planning to put in low-income housing."

She doesn't have time for John's nonsense this morning. "Where in the world did you hear that?"

"A woman from my church. She's moving out this weekend. They told her she's going to have to reapply if she wants to move back in. Thought you'd want to know." He leans over and pulls the flag out of the ground. "These are a lot flimsier this year. Are you using a different vendor?"

"Same as last year." If she allowed herself to dislike any of the neighbors, John would be at the top of the list. But neighbors represent future opportunities, and it doesn't matter if she likes them or not.

"Can't you do something about that kid pounding on his drums over on Hillside? We can't hear ourselves think with that racket."

I'm a real estate agent, she'd like to say, not the block warden. "Have you tried talking to him?" she says instead.

"I don't want to get involved. I figured you might know the parents."

"I'll speak to his mom. Have a nice day, John."

In a way, she is a kind of block warden, Lisa thinks as she heads out of the cul-de-sac. She definitely feels responsible for the neighborhood. Walking the tract is not only good exercise; it's the best way to keep her eye on things. Lawns suddenly gone untended. Dusty cars that never move. Newspapers yellowing in driveways. Trash cans left out on the street too long. All of that impacts property values.

A low-income housing project so close to the tract would be devasting, but John has always spread ridiculous stories. Last year he was convinced one of the houses over on Morningside was an Airbnb. Lisa already knew the owner had family visiting from the Netherlands. Two months ago, John told everyone the one-story next to Saint Benedict's had been turned into a sober living place because he saw three men sitting in the driveway smoking cigarettes. The men were actually newly appointed deacons, there to celebrate Palm Sunday, which Lisa knew because she doesn't assume anything, she asks questions. John's obviously wrong about the Riptide.

She sticks flags in each of the forty-six yards on Mountain Brook. The old man in the corner house with all the plumerias is too frail to live on his own much longer. He'll be ready to sell soon. She just sold a similar model for cash to a tech company that will probably rent it out and eventually flip it. Lisa would rather sell to a family just starting out. She loves making people's dreams come true, but six percent is six percent, regardless of who is buying.

She pulls twenty more flags from her backpack and turns on Hillside West. There are several homeowners on this street who haven't taken down their Hillary signs. Trump flags are still flying too, even though he's been in office for five months now. It's 2017. People need to move on. She's not a fan of Trump, but the economy might improve with a businessperson in charge. She puts a flag in Ray Murdoch's yard and admires his roses. Most yards are landscaped with the same pink ladies, boxwoods, night-blooming jasmine, creeping fig, and birds of paradise. It's slightly monotonous, but the consistency gives the neighborhood a uniform feel.

The yard in Martha Kowalski's two-story, three-bedroom further down Hillside is a different story. Martha is having her son Josh rip out all the grass in the front yard, which is a huge mistake since landscaping is the first chance to make a good impression. Most people have gardeners, but Martha might not be able to afford that anymore since her husband moved out. Martha might even be thinking about downsizing. Lisa makes a mental note to call and check in, then plants a flag in the dirt next to Martha's mailbox and moves on. She won't say anything to Martha about Josh's drumming. The boy needs an outlet. She can't imagine raising a teenager on her own. Martha works long hours at Wellington Community Hospital, which leaves Josh unsupervised most of the time.

A realtor's flexible schedule is a huge advantage for a mom. Lisa's been able to juggle clients and chauffeur her kids all over Citrus County to their practices, meets, and games since they were small. They'll be out of school for the summer soon. Seventeen-year-old Monique will spend every minute of her vacation playing water polo, building up her muscles, and doing nothing to improve her social life. Tyler, on the other hand, is sixteen and sure he's God's gift to women. He's signed up for a two-week wrestling camp but is otherwise free for the summer and already talking about all the upcoming parties. Lisa dreads the resulting phone calls from parents of sobbing daughters, sure that offering up their virginity to Tyler was a ticket to eternal love and commitment. Tyler thinks everything's a big joke and says not to worry, he's too young to settle down. Lisa worries that some pregnant girl might trap him into marriage.

No wonder she can't sleep.

When Monique got her driver's license, Lisa thought she'd have more time for herself, but then Betsy moved in. Lisa never leaves her mother-in-law home alone. She sees most of her clients in the evenings and on weekends. The kids help out when they can. Tyler even gave Betsy his bedroom and moved out to the workshop by the pool. In hindsight, this may have been a mistake. She suspects Tyler is smoking pot out there. Eric keeps promising to talk to him. She needs to remind him again.

Thank goodness there aren't any sober living places or Airbnbs in the Prestige Haven tract. It's a "homogenous neighborhood," she occasionally admits to the clients who look like her, laughing hesitantly about being politically correct, not wanting to offend anyone and lose the sale, because you can never tell these days what people will take offense to. That's why it's a huge mistake for people to put up political flags. It's so divisive. Like tends to follow like, after all. Everyone is more comfortable among their own kind. It's just human nature. There is some diversity in Prestige Haven, of course. One Jewish family marches virtuously through the tract on Saturdays to the synagogue next to the Goodyear Tire Store on Hefner Street. Two Indian women wearing saris push baby strollers through the neighborhood, but they speak English in a lovely musical tone. Lisa doesn't really mind those kinds of foreigners, especially when they have cute dogs.

There are also two interracial couples who seem nice enough, and a few Asians who keep to themselves and could possibly be caregivers for the "normal" residents. So far, no one's added any pagodas or elephants, unlike neighborhoods in nearby Fountain Springs, which are almost entirely Asian now; too many cars in the driveways, residents talking to each other in some foreign dialect. How's that supposed to make people feel? How can you not think they're talking about you? It's certainly not neighborly.

Lisa knows from online voting records that most people in Prestige Haven voted for Trump, although she and Eric most certainly did not. They are looking forward to electing a slightly less liberal governor and city council, and they're big fans of Carter Welch, the Wellington Beach city attorney who has filed several lawsuits against the State of California. They admire Welch's opposition to homeless shelters, sanctuary laws, and most especially low-income housing. California needs to stay out of Wellington's business.

Some of her neighbors are so fed up with California's politics that they talk about moving to Texas or Idaho. She and Eric have no plans to move anywhere. Sure, there are problems—too much traffic, too many homeless people— but if they left California, they'd never be able to afford to come back. California has always been home.

Lisa plants her last flag. The kids will be up by now, expecting breakfast. Eric always needs help figuring out which tie to wear. And Betsy will be awake soon. Lisa feels a headache start behind her eyes. Today, she vows, she won't let Betsy get to her.

CHAPTER FOUR

JEANNETTE LARSEN

Jeannette is still trying to get the crappy sound system to sync up with her phone when the members of the 9:45 a.m. Cardio Fit class at the South County gym start to file in and set up their steps and risers. She glances up at the banner hanging over the clock. *Don't just try. Do it.* She could teach the class without a microphone, but that would mean screaming for an hour, and the twenty dollars per class the gym pays her isn't worth losing her voice. She takes a deep breath and counts to ten, then reboots the system. So what if she's a minute or two late starting? It's not her fault the club bought the cheapest system available.

"This is my first time here," a woman says. "Is there anything special I need to know?"

Jeannette glances quickly over her shoulder at a young Latina with a pretty face and a soft round belly. "Start with one riser and two five-pound weights. You should be fine."

"I just had a baby." The woman crosses her hands over her belly. "I was wondering if the daycare here is any good. Do you have kids?" Jeannette shakes her head, turns back around, and reties her ponytail, pulling her blond hair back tight off her face. Giving parental advice is not in her job description.

The grey-haired woman who wears glasses laughs. "Jeannette doesn't talk much, but she gives us a decent workout."

The Botoxed redhead who always sets up in the front row says, "If you don't mind working out with a robot."

The grey-haired woman laughs again.

I can hear you, Jeannette almost tells them, but she really doesn't care what they say. They're right anyway, she is kind of a robot. She teaches the exact same class to the exact same music every Tuesday, Thursday, and Saturday morning.

"I use the daycare all the time," another woman says. "Just be prepared for your kids to get sick a lot."

"Builds up their immune systems," the grey-haired woman says.

Jeannette's phone finally connects with the sound system, and when she punches play, "Funkytown" blasts out of the speakers. "Eight-minute warmup," she yells. "Let's get started."

■ ■ ■

After class, the club manager, Cliff, stops Jeannette and motions her to follow him. Cliff manages three clubs in Citrus County. He is tall, Black, handsome, and most of the time seems to have a stick up his very firm ass. "We had another complaint," he says, not waiting until they get to the privacy of his office. "A member says you yelled at her."

Jeanette knows right away who it was, the Botoxed redhead. She'd told her twice to sit into her squats, not just bend over.

"It's the second complaint this month," Cliff says. "If you'd smile once in a while it would help. You're so serious. It scares people."

"Form is important. There's no point in exercising if you aren't going to do it right."

"Lighten up a little bit, okay? I don't want to have to let you go."

"Let me go? You can't even find me a sub when I need a day off."

"You know I have to treat all you girls the same." His eyes run up and down her body. "Even though you're my favorite. Come on. Let me see that smile."

She tastes her morning coffee in the back of her throat. It was a mistake to fuck him last month in his office. "I'll try," she says.

He gives her a slimy smile. "Don't just try," he says. "Do it."

She wants to scream as she hurries to the door. She breaks into a run as soon as she's out of the building. A Tesla backing out of a parking space nearly hits her and she has to leap out of the way. She raps her fist on the hood. "Watch where you're going!"

"Sorry," the driver mouths. "I didn't see you."

Shit. The grey-haired woman with the glasses. Jeannette forces a smile. "No problem. See you Saturday."

She should quit this job. The pay's lousy, the microphone is crap, the floor is dirty, and the mats reek. Her husband Bob is making good money now, thanks to his promotion, and they can easily afford the new house in Wellington Beach on his income. She likes having her own money though, and teaching aerobics keeps her in shape.

She lets her fingers hover over the Tinder app then puts her phone away and starts the car. She hadn't needed Tinder for that last guy. He'd followed her out of the Seaview gym, and she'd invited him to meet her over in the industrial park. Good looking guy too, firm jaw, and longish blond hair. He wore a blue tank top which showed off his sculpted torso and impressive biceps. His eyes said he'd lived through some tough times, but she wasn't interested in hearing about his life. She didn't want him to talk at all.

Afterwards, when he'd tried to ask her advice on starting his own personal training business, she'd shooed him out of the car. His feelings might have been hurt, but she didn't care. Her advice would have been to pick another dream. Personal trainers peaked years ago, and unless he had celebrity connections, he'd never make money on his own. The other choice is working for a chain like she does, which isn't likely for this guy because his body type's out of fashion. Even the man's gym clothes were out of style. No one wears tank tops anymore. His body was fine with her though. She likes big and strong. It's what attracted her to Bob.

■ ■ ■

Emmylou Harris is singing "Red Dirt Girl" on the satellite radio as Jeannette turns into her tract, driving a little too fast because she really has to pee. Her sports bra is damp and clings to her skin, and the waistband of her leggings is soaked. She slows as she turns down her street, wondering what there is in the house to make for dinner tonight.

One of the neighbors is outside, working in her front yard with her teenaged son. The boy holds a hoe; the woman leans against a shovel, a dejected expression on her face. There aren't many young families in this tract, but Bob says the neighborhood is starting to turn over. He thinks this will be good for their property values.

Jeannette recognizes something familiar in the defeated curve of the neighbor woman's spine. The boy, however, is full of energy—dancing around with the hoe, stabbing at dandelions. He needs a haircut. He says something and the woman halfway smiles and then looks sad again.

Jeannette licks her lips and tastes salt, suddenly furious at the woman for looking so unhappy when she has a living, breathing boy to spend time with, in a front yard soaked in sunlight. What she should do is slam on the brakes, pull over to the curb, get out and grab the boy by his arm, march him down the sidewalk, push him into the backseat of her Suburban, and speed off in the opposite direction. That woman has no business with a child. She can't even keep up with his haircuts.

Jeannette glances in the rearview mirror. She can't remember where she was going or where she's coming from. She doesn't recognize her own house until she passes it. She takes a quick look at the backseat, worried that the boy might be sitting there.

The backseat is empty, of course, and the boy and the woman are still working in their yard. Jeannette makes a U-turn and drives back to her driveway, punches the garage door opener, and allows herself a quick glance down the street. The woman and the boy don't look up. Emmylou Harris is still singing about red dirt. Jeannette pulls into the garage and closes the door.

■ ■ ■

After her shower, Jeannette sits naked on the upholstered vanity bench in her walk-in closet. Pink blouses arranged by shade and sleeve length hang above black slacks and pencil skirts lined up by fabric type. Her black dresses are on the opposite wall. Leopard skinned sandals and heels sit in separate cubby holes. White tennis skirts hang on their own rack, gym tops are folded and stacked by color on the shelves, leggings arranged by dominant shade, workout and tennis shoes at the ready.

The purses have their own section.

The first Coach bag her son, Zack, bought for her birthday with most of the money he earned working at Hot Topic is displayed on a shelf all its own. Zack had read somewhere the bags were made of leather and stitched together like baseball gloves. She loved the purse so much he bought them for Mother's Day and Christmas too. He would have approved of this closet, a museum piece of color coordination, her entire wardrobe artfully displayed.

The rest of her purses, all Coaches in tribute to Zack, are lined up in chronological order. They are her only extravagance and she's such a good customer; Coach is always sending her coupons. She's bought one every month since Zack's funeral. Bob never complains about what she spends.

The closet was originally a small bedroom next to the master suite, but the prior owners knocked out a wall and added shelving, double hangers, a tri-fold mirror, and a vanity and bench. It's the only reason she agreed to sign the papers to buy this place, but she still feels like a traitor, moving away from the house where Zack was born. She worries his ghost is haunting their old neighborhood, wondering why his parents have abandoned him.

She turns on the light of the magnifying mirror, although she's learned to take off and put on makeup without fully looking at herself. She hates what she sees in her deep brown eyes—a mother who should have done more, a wife who no longer wants her husband to touch her, a woman who has sex with strangers.

She's not careful with sunscreen. It won't be long before her doctor will suggest a dermatologist. She won't make the appointment. She doesn't get mammograms either. Let what will happen, happen. She stands and surveys her body in the full-length mirror. Her arms are strong, her stomach flat, her legs toned and tanned. She pulls on a short black dress. No underwear, she decides. Flat leopard skinned shoes and the pink flowered cross-body Coach bag that has just enough room for her phone, her keys, and a credit card.

She has a few hours before Bob will be home. She'll drive over to the Costco parking lot and check Tinder. She's been lucky this time of day when people might decide to cut out of work early and hook up with someone. Afterwards, she'll go inside Costco and pick up something for dinner. Their sushi is surprisingly good. Bob likes it anyway.

CHAPTER FIVE

JOSH KOWALSKI

"One, two, three, four." Every time Neil Gorman counts off the beat, Josh can't believe the man is almost eighty-six years old. Something magical happens when Neil sits down behind Josh's drum kit. His spine straightens. The pupils of his eyes brighten. His skin stretches tight over his cheek bones, and he looks decades younger.

The first time Neil knocked on his door, Josh assumed he was there to complain about the noise. He'd been banging on every available flat surface since his dad left; tapping his fingers on the kitchen table at breakfast, slapping his palms on his desk at school, smacking his hands on the tops of his thighs, keeping time with his right foot, switching it up with his left. Annoying everyone was his only objective. His mother finally suggested he set up his father's old drum kit in the garage. His dad was in a band for a while and then quit, just like he quits everything. All of his abandoned projects are stacked in the garage; books on how to win at blackjack, a metal detector, some paintball guns.

If Neil had been any other neighbor, Josh would have ignored him that day. He'd already googled Wellington's laws. Cops can't do much about noise until after 10:00 p.m. But when he saw Neil standing in the hot sun, his red adult tricycle pulled up on the sidewalk, he'd felt bad for the old man.

Turns out, Neil was a drummer too, for a rock band in the sixties called Electric Catfish. Josh read online later that their lead singer smashed his Corvette into the center divider of the 405 freeway the day after the band signed a record contract. The label dropped them and they broke up. Neil doesn't like to talk about it. "A cliché," he calls it.

Neil's the one who told him about Led Zeppelin. Josh found a grainy YouTube video of John Bonham playing the Moby Dick solo live with his bare hands, leaving blood prints on the drum skins. Now, Led Zeppelin is Josh's favorite band.

Neil's been coming over every afternoon since school let out for the summer. He's taught Josh single strokes, paradiddles, and double stroke rolls. This afternoon Neil shows him something called a bolero. When Josh switches places with Neil to try it out, he feels energy transfer from the sticks to his hands and straight through the drum skins.

"The bolero will make more sense," Neil says after Josh works through it a few times, "once you learn how to read music. You should join the high school band in the fall and learn another instrument. Piano's always good. Increases your options."

"I just want to play drums, Neil. The high school band is for losers, and I don't need to read music. That's what YouTube is for. Have you ever heard of a band called The Midnight Slinkers? They were my dad's favorite. They shoot fire when they play."

Neil shakes his head. "Sounds like a circus act. I don't know anything about YouTube either. We had record players when I started out. I can't count how many needles I wore out, playing tracks over and over again."

"What's a record player?" Josh grins. "Seriously, Neil. John Bonham was a genius."

"Charlie Watts is the genius," Neil says. "John Bonham is a maniac."

"You know John Bonham is dead, don't you?"

"Don't be ridiculous," Neil says. "Try the bolero again."

"Bonham died a long time ago," Josh says, but Neil is already counting down.

■ ■ ■

Later (five minutes? Two hours? Josh loses track of time when he's playing with Neil) he looks up, dripping with sweat and completely happy, and sees his mother in the driveway, home from work.

Neil lurches to his feet, stiff legged. "Can I help you?"

"It's just me, Neil. Martha?"

Neil nods. "I remember. Your boy here has real talent."

Josh grins. Neil's praise is rare.

"I made spaghetti for you and Stephanie last night," his mom says. "I'll go get the container."

"Stephanie loves your spaghetti," Neil says.

"How is she doing?" his mother asks. "Does she have to go far for her chemo?"

Neil's eyes widen and the color drains from his face. "I need to get home." He hurries out of the garage and climbs on his trike.

"Everything okay, Neil?" Josh asks.

"What about the spaghetti?" his mom says, but Neil is already halfway down the street.

"He's getting worse," she says as they watch the red trike turn at the corner. "He didn't even recognize me today."

"We were into the music," Josh says. "Neil forgets stuff sometimes, but he still rocks. Want to hear a joke he told me? How do you make a million dollars as a musician? Start with two million. Get it?"

"That's too true to be funny." She touches the circle of

freckles on his right cheek with her fingertips. A birthmark she calls his angel's kiss. "Don't start believing you can make a career out of this, honey."

■ ■ ■

After dinner, she holds up Neil's forgotten container of spaghetti. "Why don't you take this over to the Gormans? Make sure they're okay."

"Sure," he says. He likes the Gormans' house. They have an old upright piano in their living room, and they have really cool posters. There's one in the bathroom of Led Zeppelin at the Long Beach Arena back in 1972, before his mother was even born.

The lights are on at Neil's house, and he can hear the television. They're probably watching "Behind the Music," a show Josh teases Neil about but secretly likes. He knocks on the front door and waits. There's something rancid in the air; a skunk maybe, or the neighbor's trash cans. Whatever it is smells terrible. He rings the doorbell. No answer. Neil and Stephanie might already be asleep. As he turns to leave, the curtains open. Neil looks at him wide-eyed and quickly closes the drapes. After a minute, the door cracks open.

"Can I help you?" Neil asks.

"My mom wanted me to give you this." Josh holds up the spaghetti container. Neil mumbles something Josh doesn't catch. He leans past the old man and waves his hand at Stephanie, sitting in her recliner, wrapped in a purple afghan. Neil's recliner has a matching green one draped across the back. "Hey, Miss Stephanie. Jeez, Neil. It's cold in here."

"She likes it cool. She's sleeping."

"Is that Deep Purple?" Josh steps past Neil and walks toward the television set. The smell seems to have followed him inside. He checks the bottom of his shoes for dog shit and then hears a familiar minor chord. "Awesome! Is that 'Smoke on the Water'?" He glances over at Stephanie to see if she agrees. Her eyes are closed. Her skin is the same color as her purple afghan, her mouth open, her jaw slack.

His heartbeat quickens. "Neil?" he says. "She doesn't look right." He's never seen a dead person before and even though it feels disrespectful, he can't look away.

"She's just sleeping," Neil says. "Let's go outside so we don't wake her up."

"She's not sleeping, Neil. We should call someone." He's still staring at Stephanie when he feels soft fur slink between his bare calves. A jolt of terror jumps straight up his spine and every muscle in his body clenches. He looks down as Ringo, Stephanie's grey-striped cat, leaps up into her lap and licks her hand.

"Get off of her, you damn cat!" Neil flails his skinny arms up and down.

Ringo raises his head, blinks his yellow eyes, slides his pink tongue across his teeth, and lowers his head again. The blood rushes from Josh's heart down to his feet. Ringo isn't just licking Stephanie's hand; he's chewing on her palm. Josh's stomach lurches.

Neil grabs the TV remote and throws it at Ringo. He misses and the plastic case slams into the brick fireplace and shatters. The cat leaps gracefully off Stephanie's lap, down to the carpet, and then soars up the stairs, stopping at the landing to clean his claws with his teeth.

Josh can see definite bite marks up and down Stephanie's forearms. Her tendons are frayed. He thinks he might hurl. "How long has she been like . . . this?"

"She's tired," Neil says. "Let her rest. We should go outside and talk."

"No, Neil," Josh says. "I'm pretty sure she's dead." He's lightheaded. "We need to call someone." He reaches for his phone and remembers he left it charging at home. "Where's your phone? In the kitchen?"

"We don't need a phone." Neil hurries over and opens the front door. "We need to go outside so she can sleep."

Josh swallows hard. "We can't leave her here like this, Neil. It's not right." He blinks back tears. He's not going to cry. "We need to call 911."

"*We* don't need to do anything. *You* need to go home." Neil's eyes are frantic, darting from Stephanie to the open front door. "She'll be fine in the morning. I'll come by tomorrow afternoon, same time as usual."

Josh's feet feel cased in cement, like one of those nightmares where you can't move your legs. He should stay. He should leave. He wonders where the cat went as he finds himself moving toward the doorway.

"Good boy," Neil says. "Go on home. I'll see you tomorrow."

Josh is somehow outside now, still holding his skateboard and the spaghetti container.

"You don't need to talk to anyone about this," Neil says. "Like I said, we're fine." He spins around and goes inside, slams the door behind him, and turns off the porch light.

Josh hears the deadbolt click. The music from the television is muffled now. He wipes the tears from his face and flips his board down on the sidewalk. His mother will know what to do. The awful smell lessens once he's rolled down Neil's driveway. He breathes deeply, clearing the stench from his lungs.

He just saw a dead person. And right now, no one except him knows that she's dead.

LISA KENSINGTON

Prestige Haven Homes,
Where Your Home Is Your Castle

JUNE 16, 2017 | (800) WB4-EVER lisa.kensington@Sandcastlerealty.com

I LOVE MY JOB

Especially when I get emails like this one: "Lisa is amazing. From the moment we met, we knew we were working with the best in the business. Lisa is always available and full of sound advice. She's also willing to express her opinion, which we found refreshing and invaluable during our search for our dream home." Signed, Satisfied Customer

Making dreams come true is what I do. Call for a free estimate.

Helpful Household Tips

" *Fingerprints all over your stainless-steel appliances? Put a little baby oil on a clean, soft cloth, and run it over the surfaces. Those prints should lift right off.* "

In Case You Didn't Know

The first morning bells at our Prestige Haven neighborhood church, Saint Benedict's, ring at 8:15 Monday through Friday, chiming a hymn fifteen minutes before the 8:30 Mass. There are chimes five minutes before Mass, at Mass time, and every hour afterwards from 9 a.m. to 8 p.m. On Sundays, the first bell is at 9 a.m. and then bells chime before the 10:30, noon, 1:30, and 5 p.m. Masses. They aren't real bells of course. It's a recording. Personally, I find them comforting and an excellent way to keep track of time.

PRESTIGE HAVEN STREET SWEEPING

Prestige Haven is a gem of a neighborhood in the very special city of Wellington Beach, California. There are 609 houses with large yards and great curb appeal.

Speaking of curb appeal, here's a gentle reminder. Street sweeping occurs on the first and third Thursday of every month, which means all trash containers should be removed from the curb by the preceding Wednesday night.

Clean streets are an important ingredient in maintaining our property values. Bring in those containers!

CHAPTER SIX

JEANNETTE LARSEN

The Saint Benedict bells chime twice on Saturday afternoon as Jeannette follows Bob out of their front door to the Mercedes in the driveway. There's no one outside, except an older heavyset neighbor a few houses down, watering his rose bushes with a hose. The man waves, so she waves back. "Maybe we should stop and introduce ourselves."

"Maybe we should keep some distance," Bob says. "I doubt we have much in common anyway."

They drive out of the tract toward the ocean, and she stares out the window at the mile after mile of cinderblock walls covered with creeping fig.

"Don't you love this?" Bob asks when they turn left on the coast highway.

"It's pretty," she says, watching the Mexican fan palms sway and the waves crash against the pier. *Like a postcard*, she thinks, *from someone else's vacation.*

When Bob's phone rings he puts it on speaker mode. It's Amy, one of the auditors on his team. She says she has some questions about the St. Louis report changes.

"You shouldn't be working on your day off, hon," Bob says. "Go enjoy yourself. Do whatever it is twenty-year-olds do on the weekend."

Amy laughs, her voice a low purr.

Jeannette remembers the green, slinky slip dress Amy wore to the Christmas party last year. "If you need to work today," Jeannette says, "we don't have to go out to lunch."

"Is that Jeannette? I thought you were alone, Bob. Hi Jeannette. What are you guys up to today?"

"Just going out to lunch with my husband," she says.

"There are some new bars at Pacific Terrace that are pretty cool," Amy says.

"Do you want to join us?" Jeannette asks.

No, Bob mouths.

"Thank you," Amy says, "but my sister's having a co-ed baby shower at four o'clock."

"That sounds fun," Bob says.

"You've obviously never been to one," Amy says.

Jeannette can tell Bob doesn't know how to respond. Clearly, he hasn't told her about Zack.

"Take the rest of the day off," he says. "And come in late on Monday. You've been working your ass off." He hangs up. "I probably shouldn't have said ass."

"You really shouldn't call her hon either."

"I thought babe was the problem. I can't say hon either?"

"Amy is almost thirty, by the way. She told me that at the Christmas party."

"I don't know why she called me. That report's not even due for another week."

"Call her back if you want. She's cute."

"You know I'm not interested in Amy." He reaches for her hand. She lets him hold it until he pulls into the parking structure. Last night she didn't turn away when he'd wanted to make love. She'd thought he was satisfied when he rolled off her; but later, when he said, "It feels like you're so far away, babe," she'd pretended not to hear him. She felt guilty this morning and suggested they go out to lunch.

Bob parks the Mercedes and they get out and head down Main Street. Wellington is busy this afternoon; kids in bathing suits holding dripping ice cream cones, crowds spilling out of all the white stuccoed bars and restaurants. He takes her arm as they walk down the sidewalk. People nod at him and stand back. His size scares some people and makes others want to challenge him. He's a big man, six three, two twenty, clean cut, chivalrous, and protective. She likes feeling protected and having an arm to hold on to when she wears ridiculously high heels. Bob played football and wrestled in high school, and he's still in decent shape despite all his business trips, thanks to hotel gyms and a disciplined diet.

He's convinced Wellington Beach is safer than their old neighborhood, which is why they started driving down here to do their drinking and why he claimed he wanted to move here. They found a great house, four bedrooms, two baths. "A little out of our price range," Bob said after they signed the paperwork, "but a sound investment and a much-needed change."

She knows that's the real reason he wanted to move. Bob couldn't bear driving past that dark stain on the asphalt, while she couldn't stay away from it. The flowers and candles no longer stand guard next to the curb where Zack, wearing his usual black jeans and T-shirt, stepped in front of a car going the posted speed limit, but the stain is still visible. The young driver was on her way home from work. She was sober, unlike Zack.

Their first therapist warned that couples often split up after a child's death. "Won't happen to us," Bob insisted. Jeannette set up a profile on Tinder, just to see what could happen, just to try and feel something again. The second therapist said they needed to be patient with each other, that everyone grieves at their own pace. Jeannette upgraded to the Tinder Platinum plan. Bob never looks at the apps on her phone.

He stops now in front of a bathing suit shop window filled with tiny bikinis. "You'd look awesome in any of those. No one would ever believe you're forty-one. Pick one out. I'll buy it for you."

"I have plenty of bathing suits. Where do you want to eat?"

"Let's stop in Cyclone's first to see how the Angels are doing."

"Just one drink," she says. She follows Bob to the bar. "That's new." Jeannette points to a sign next to the bourbon shelf that reads: *Politically incorrect and proud of it. We support our flag, our troops, and One Nation Under God. If this offends you, LEAVE.* She'd like to leave, but Bob is already ordering a Stone IPA for himself and a Corona for her.

The bartender nods at the sign and grins. "We put it up after the inauguration. It's a brand-new world."

"That's one way to put it," Jeannette says. Next time, she'll insist they go somewhere else.

There's no place to sit, but they can see the screen. Albert Pujols homers to center field and Kole Calhoun scores, tying the game. A group of clean-cut men at the table behind them cheer.

Bob raises his glass. "The Machine comes through again," he says.

"Pujols is an old man," one of them says. "We need Trout back."

"You're right about that," Bob says.

"Why don't you guys sit down?" A dark-haired man at the table motions to two empty bar stools. "I'm Doug," he says, offering Bob his hand. His blue eyes are steady, his smile practiced and self-assured. He thinks he's better looking than he is, Jeannette decides.

Bob shakes Doug's hand and explains they've just moved to Wellington. Jeannette sits down and glances around the bar. Other than the waitresses in their tight shorts that look more like underwear, she's the only woman in here, and the men all seem to be trying to outshout each other over the television. Too much testosterone.

The men at the table must be military, Jeannette thinks at first, because they all have short hair and are extremely fit, but then she hears them talking about a boxing gym, asking Bob if he'd like to join. Bob tells them he travels too much. She wonders next if maybe Doug is their boss, the way they look at him before they speak, as if they're seeking his approval. When she catches bits of their conversation through the amped-up sportscaster's voice and hears them say something about monuments in Virginia, she decides they must work for an architect or a landscaper.

Finally, another woman, she thinks when a young Black couple wearing matching Black Lives Matter T-shirts come in the front door and head to the bar.

"Here we go," one of the young men at the table says. All the men rise, except Doug, who shakes his head. "Not today," he says. "Not the right time or place." The men sit down.

What the hell was that? Jeannette wonders.

Doug clicks his glass against Bob's. "Don't all lives matter?" he says.

Bob laughs nervously as he taps Doug's glass. When the men at the table raise their glasses in unison, Jeannette stands. "You promised me lunch, babe."

Bob finishes his beer and stands. "I did," he says.

"Before you go," Doug says, "here's my card. Let me know if you ever need anything. I'm pretty tight with the cops in WB. And Carter Welch. He's the city attorney."

Gag me, Jeannette thinks. *What a pretentious asshole.*

Bob glances at the card and hands it to her. "Hold on to this for me, babe." He pulls out his business card. "This is me."

Doug reads aloud. "United States Department of Agriculture Office of Inspector General. You're an auditor and an accountant?"

Bob smiles. "We show up and ruin your day."

"Impressive." Doug grins, obviously surprised.

This happens all the time. Bob graduated with honors from Cal State, earned a business degree, and passed the CPA exam the first time he took the test, but people are always surprised that a man of his size has a brain. It's reverse sexism.

"You're a straight arrow," Doug says. "I like that."

Bob drapes his arm around Jeannette's shoulder. "I promised my beautiful wife some lunch."

"She's gorgeous," Doug says. "Nice to meet you both."

"Those guys seemed off to me," Jeannette says as they head out the door. "Since when have you ever needed a friendly cop?"

Bob grins. "Never. But there's nothing wrong with getting to know people who are involved in their community. It can't hurt. So, what's your pleasure today? Burgers at Henry's or sushi at the Surf King?"

"Sushi," she says because she knows it's what he wants, and she really doesn't care. When he isn't looking, she drops Doug's business card into a trash can.

CHAPTER SEVEN

RAY MURDOCH

Late in the afternoon, when Ray goes in the kitchen to sort his mother's meds into her pill box, he catches her opening a can of tuna. "We've talked about this before. You have to stop leaving food outside. It attracts rats."

"I'm worried about Stephanie's cat," she says. "Neil's not going to remember to feed him."

"Neil's moved. I told you that, remember? His daughter said he's living in an Alzheimer's center now."

"What'd she say about Ringo?"

"I didn't ask. Maybe she took him to her house. Maybe a coyote ate him."

"We don't have coyotes."

"Yes, we do. I've seen them walking through the neighborhood when I'm out riding my bike."

"You'd probably like to stick me in a nursing home, just like poor old Neil."

"It's not a nursing home, it's a care center."

"Jill had a lot more patience than you do. Too bad she didn't stick around."

"Jill?" The muscles in the back of his neck constrict. Why is she bringing Jill up now? They've been divorced for more than twenty years. "I'm going to start a load of laundry and then go for a bike ride."

"You and your bike rides. You need to get a life. You're not getting any younger."

"There's something we can agree on."

"You don't get to make the rules around here either," she says. "It's still my house. Put the tuna out on the patio before you ride off into the sunset." She totters toward the den, cackling at her joke, then plops down and turns on CNN.

"You need to use the walker, Mom. You're going to fall." He sets the can outside. He'll throw it in the trash later when she's asleep. He strips the sheets from both beds and takes them out to the washing machine in the garage. He should have started the load earlier. He needs to manage his time better. The hands on the clock play tricks all day, ticking in numbingly slow motion through the drone of television soaps, talk shows, local news, and weather, and then spinning maniacally as the afternoon wears on. Every morning he thinks he has plenty of time to finish the crossword puzzle. Every night he ends up recycling the newspaper, puzzle unsolved.

When he closes the washer lid, he hears nails skitter behind the boxes of Christmas decorations stacked on the shelves. A rat, probably. He'll go to Home Depot tomorrow morning and talk to the guy in the garden department about setting a trap.

He rolls his bike out of the garage and rides down the street, passing the grey Honda Accord parked on the corner, the Nelson boy sitting in the front seat with his eyes closed. He could say something, but Keith isn't bothering anyone. He should have said something years ago when he'd first heard Jim Nelson screaming at the kid, but his mother convinced him it wasn't their business. She changed her mind when Keith and another boy climbed over the cinderblock wall into their backyard and broke into their house. Ray came out of the downstairs bathroom, zipping his fly, and caught the other boy opening up his mother's china hutch where she keeps her Hummel figurines.

Ray would have let it go. He'd done stupid things like that when he was a kid, but his mother insisted they tell Keith's parents. "There needs to be consequences for that kind of behavior," she'd said, so they'd walked around the corner after dinner, knocked on the Nelsons' door, and told Jim and Peggy what the boys had done. He still has a bad feeling about what might have happened after they left. Something in Peggy's cold eyes and Jim's clenched jaw, something about the way Keith trembled when his dad looked at him.

Ray passes Saint Benedict's and crosses Hefner Street into Church Park. He heads toward the eucalyptus trees in the back, parks his bike, and sits down at a picnic table. Church Park isn't much, bordered by busy streets and sidewalks slimed with bird crap, but sometimes he can almost tune out the traffic noise and pretend he's somewhere else. He takes a deep breath. The eucalyptus smell reminds him of the menthol cigarettes he'd finally managed to quit smoking years after his discharge.

A white pelican circles the island in the small lake the city stocks with fish. Last month Ray and an old man with a fishing pole counted thirty-five pelicans circling the island, scooping up fish as if they'd been informed of the city's refill schedule. "The city council needs to do something about that island," the old man said. "There's thousands of possums over there, living in the bushes." The old man's voice became more insistent. "They swim across the water at night, little baby possums clinging to their backs, and then they creep into the neighborhood. They're out there right now, watching us with their beady little eyes. The city needs to do something." Ray walked away from the man. The idea of thousands of possum eyes watching him still creeps him out.

He rolls his head in a semi-circle and tries to clear his thoughts. Weird, his mother bringing up Jill like that, out of the blue. He's managed not to think about Jill for a while now. He'd thought they were fine the way they were and when he realized they weren't fine; he'd suggested they adopt. Jill said if she couldn't have her own, she didn't want any. And then she said she didn't want him either. It was a long time ago and not worth thinking about right now.

The sun sinks toward the power lines and snowy egrets congregate on the low branches of the trees by the water. Peaceful, he thinks, until he hears a helicopter in the distance. He watches it circle around and turn toward Ensillado Mountain. He takes ten more deep breaths and heads home.

He and his mother eat bowls of Martha Kowalski's spaghetti and watch the six o'clock news. Michelle Tuzee has the lead story about Trump withdrawing from the Paris Agreement. Marc Brown does a piece on what the word "covfefe" really means.

"You do crossword puzzles," his mother says. "Is 'covfefe' even a word?"

"Nope."

His mother snorts. "Trump's turned the White House into a circus."

"He's even worse than I expected."

"When did you say Stephanie's funeral is?" she asks.

"Saturday morning. Are you sure you're up to going? It'll mean a lot of walking."

"Stephanie was a good friend to me. Of course, I'm going."

"Neil probably won't even recognize me." Ray used to run into Neil playing at clubs years ago, back when he was drinking and carousing. Seeing Neil now, with Alzheimer's, will be miserable.

"If you don't want to go," his mother says, "I'll get someone else to take me."

"I never said I didn't want to go." Ray gets up and takes the bowls in the kitchen, loads the dishwasher, wipes down the counter, and remembers he's forgotten to put the sheets in the dryer. When he turns on the light in the garage, he hears the rustling noise again and sees a possum scurry behind the shelves.

He gets the broom. The possum is wedged between the shelf and the wall, but he can see its tail, almost a foot long, pink, and hairless. He'll have to move all the boxes of Christmas decorations to get back there. He stacks them on the floor, feeling his heartbeat accelerate. He doesn't have time for this. Why the hell is his mother keeping all this junk? She never decorates anymore. No one ever comes over, and there aren't any grandchildren, as she keeps reminding him. He should put it all out with the trash. In his rush, he's careless and doesn't notice one of the lids isn't closed all the way until he puts a heavier box on top of it. The entire stack crashes over. Glass shatters and tinsel, plastic evergreen, boxes of lights, and the quilted snowman Jill made years ago spill out on the garage floor. He remembers Jill working on that snowman for hours while he watched football. She was probably already unhappy with him then, but she never said anything. How was he supposed to know how she felt?

The possum darts out from behind the shelves and heads toward the dryer. Ray blocks its path with his broom. The insides of its nose and ears are also pink. "Get the hell out of here." He slaps the broom down hard. The possum hisses and runs behind the dryer. Outsmarted by a damn rodent, Ray thinks, suddenly furious. He gets the machete from where it hangs over the toolbox and takes it out of its leather case. It had been useful in Vietnam, for clearing a place to sleep at night, so he'd brought it home as a souvenir. It's been useful lately to cut the creeping fig off the cinderblock wall in the backyard.

He yanks the dryer away from the wall. The possum hisses again, flashing primeval teeth. He stabs the back of its body with the machete, severing the tail and then once more, cutting a deep gash in the right hind leg. It squeals and stares up at him, quivering, with black, unblinking eyes. He slaps hard at the crown of the possum's head with the flat edge of the knife until it finally flops over on its side and is silent.

A flood of light angles across the garage floor. His mother stands in the open door, her mouth in an O-shape as if she doesn't recognize him. "Stay in the house," he says, holding the machete behind his back. Something drips off the blade and runs down his heel.

Her lips tighten. "I heard something break."

"There was a possum trying to get in the house. I took care of it."

"I hope you didn't kill it. Possums are a protected species."

"Don't come out here."

"You'd better put those boxes back where they belong. I can't have anything nice with you living here."

Once she closes the door, he wipes off the machete blade with a wad of paper towels and slides it back in its leather case. His hand trembles as he hangs the knife back on the wall. What an old fool he is. He gets a shovel and scrapes the possum off the floor. It's smaller than he'd thought. A baby, really. He drops the body in a black trash bag and ties the ends twice. It might be risky to put it out with the trash if his mom's right about possums being protected. He remembers seeing a trash can in Church Park and gets on his bicycle.

The night's warm and his body makes a slight breeze as he rides through the quiet streets, the black plastic bag in the basket, his heart beating wild. He smells jasmine, onion, garlic, and charcoaled meat, hears a woman singing from an open upstairs window. A child laughs. There are lights on in the houses, but the blinds are all tightly drawn.

Ray parks his bike next to the trash can and picks up the plastic bag with one hand, using the other to open the lid. The bag shifts suddenly and a long pink claw stabs through the plastic.

"Holy crap!" Ray drops the bag. The possum blasts through the plastic and hisses at him, angry and very much alive, and then hobbles off toward the dark water lapping against the deep brush on the island.

It takes Ray a minute to realize he's not breathing and then he starts laughing. Should have just left the damn thing alone. He jumps on his bike and pedals quickly out of the park.

"That cop show you like is starting," his mother says when he comes inside through the garage, his heart still pounding.

"I need to wash my hands first and then put the sheets in the dryer."

"What did you do with it?" she asks when he sits down.

"Turns out it was playing possum. It'll be limping for a while, and it doesn't have a tail anymore, but it's not dead."

His mother throws back her head and belly laughs. "I bet that scared the shit out of you."

"Serves me right. I don't know why I got so angry."

"You were frustrated," she says.

"That's no excuse."

"You want some ice cream? Or are you still on a diet?"

"I'll get it."

"Sit." She pushes up out of her chair. "I can manage to dish up two bowls of ice cream."

"I'll take you to Stephanie's funeral. But you have to use the walker."

"People will think I'm an old woman."

"You are an old woman who needs to use a walker. That's the deal. Otherwise, I'm not going."

"Fine." She stops behind him and rests her hand on his shoulder, lingering long enough for him to feel her pulse. "Chocolate or vanilla?"

"Both," he says.

"I knew you were going to say that." She squeezes his shoulder and goes into the kitchen.

CHAPTER EIGHT

KEITH NELSON

"It's a great day at the Bug Guy," Keith says, emphasizing the word great this time. This morning, desperate to think about something other than what time it is and how many more hours before he can clock out and go find someplace to sleep, he's been experimenting with different inflections.

"What's so great about it?" the woman on the phone says. "I've been waiting all day for the inspector."

Keith checks the clock even though he already knows it's not eleven yet. He's exhausted. The cops came through the library lot early last night, so he drove over to Home Depot and tried to sleep there for a while until a security guard tapped on his window and told him to move along.

"You're scheduled for inspection between nine and noon," he tells the woman on the phone.

"I have better things to do than just sit here and wait."

"Let me check with dispatch." He looks up and sees Grace, the boss's secretary, walking toward his desk.

"Your mother's in the office," Grace says.

"I'll be right there," he says, not sure he's heard right. Why wouldn't his mother call instead of just showing up? He gets the woman off the phone as quickly as he can and hurries to the front of the warehouse where his mother stands near Grace's desk. She's come from her office, judging from her business suit and heels.

"Son." She takes in his dress slacks, shirt, and tie. "You look like you're doing all right."

"I am."

"Then I really don't understand why you're taking money from your grandmother."

Keith glances over at Grace, who is staring hard at her desk blotter. "Let's go outside and talk."

His mother follows him out onto the sidewalk. "Your grandmother fell in the bathroom last night," she says. "What were you were thinking, buying her wine?"

"Is she okay?"

"She ripped most of the skin off her arm so no, she's not okay. She's not supposed to drink with that new medication. We're hiring a live-in caregiver."

"I didn't know about the medication. I could move in with her. I could quit this job and take care of her."

"And take even more advantage? I know about the check, Keith."

"I tore it up. I never cashed it."

"You haven't cashed it yet. We've talked about this already. You are not to ask her for money."

"She offered."

"She obviously can't live there on her own unsupervised. I need your Golden Years pass. From now on, you'll have to call the caregiver first, before you just barge in."

"I'm not barging in. I go there to visit. She's my grandmother. I need to see her."

Her eyes soften for a moment, and he thinks she might change her mind, but then she holds out her hand. "You'll have to get permission first."

He takes the pass out of his wallet.

"You're not still sleeping in your car, are you?"

He can't stomach another one of her disappointed looks. "I'm renting a place." She doesn't need to know that he's still on the waiting list or that the place is in a portioned-off garage.

"Good." She puts the pass in her purse. "I'll let you get back to work."

"I didn't cash that check," he says but she's already walking away from him. He stands outside until his heart rate slows.

■ ■ ■

Keith watches a Little League game from the deep shade of a tree near the athletic field next to the library. The field and the library are surrounded by Wellington Beach Central Park, which covers a full city block and has walking trails around a green lake choked with algae bloom and two scummy public restrooms. The library is air-conditioned and has decent Wi-Fi, ancient computers, almost comfortable couches, and a not-quite-as-scummy public restroom. Thanks to recent budget cuts, the library closes at 5:00 p.m. now instead of 9:00.

Keith takes a long drag from a cold Budweiser. He doesn't usually drink beer because it's fattening and reminds him too much of his father, but he needs alcohol if he's going to sleep tonight. When he'd stopped at the Golden Years' security gate after work, the guard told him he wasn't on his list and to call his grandmother. Keith tried to explain that Granny C doesn't always hear her phone ring, but the old man turned his back on him and shuffled back to the guard house. Keith pulled over and called Granny C's number. A stranger answered and told him he "wasn't allowed."

"Give me that phone," he heard Granny C say in the background. "Don't worry," she told Keith. "I can get you another pass. I'll get what's-her-name here to give me a ride to the office. We'll figure this out."

He should have just taken that check since his mother thinks he did anyway. He finishes the beer in one swallow and crumples the can. The tweakers over by the public restroom eyeball his Budweisers, the parents in the grandstands stare at the tweakers, and one of the mothers glances over at him and frowns.

Keith stretches his arms overhead. The trees in Wellington Central Park are mostly eucalyptus, with an occasional pine and scrub oak, and a few ornamental cherries no longer in bloom. The blue ceanothus is flourishing in the heat. He opens another beer. The kid on deck strikes out and one of the fathers starts screaming. The muscles in the back of Keith's neck tighten. His dad was the same way.

It's been almost two months since he's seen his father. That night Keith had worked out in the garage after his eight-hour shift at the Bug Guy and was treating himself to a small bowl of ice cream. He was tired and planned to go to bed early, after he'd watched more of that lesbo series on Showtime. But then his dad asked, "What the hell is a Confederate Flag sticker doing on my beer fridge? I don't want that racist shit in my house."

"Wayne put it there as a joke," Keith said, although he doubted it was a joke since Wayne has a small swastika tattooed on his wrist where you can't see it under his watchband. Ever since Wayne joined that fight club gym he's really gotten into politics. "Wayne says the Confederate Flag is part of history."

His mother looked up from unloading the dishwasher. "I thought we agreed you'd stay away from Wayne Connor."

His dad snorted. "Since when is that moron a history expert?"

"Don't call him that." He and Wayne have been tight since grade school. Wayne was a small kid with a stepmother who didn't like him and a big mouth that got him into fights he could never win. "Wayne's my friend."

"Then you're a moron too." His dad's voice was sarcastic

and mean and his breath reeked of garlic and yeast. "Let me refresh your memory, son, since you've obviously forgotten. That friend is the one who convinced you it was okay to stroll into the Athlete's Foot and walk out with whatever you wanted." His dad moved even closer. Keith could count every broken vein in his nose. "Moron number one carried out twelve boxes of brand-new Nikes because moron number two was sure that mall stores never call security. Cost me a fortune."

Keith set the spoon carefully in his empty bowl of ice cream and stood, scraping the chair legs against the tiled kitchen floor. "Why do you keep bringing that up?" He saw his dad's chin quiver, his lips tremble, and realized, *he's afraid of me*. It made him feel powerful and sick to his stomach at the same time. "I'm paying you back."

His dad stepped away from him. "How? You spend every cent you make on steroids and vitamins. Twenty-four years old with the mind of a second grader. A second grader who stabbed a girl in the eye with a pencil."

"That was an accident," Keith said.

"That was just the beginning," his dad said, turning away from him, walking toward the television in the den. "You were just getting started. And now I'm stuck supporting you for the rest of my life."

"Not anymore. I'm out of here." It was an unexpected decision, but the words felt good coming out of his mouth.

His dad sat down on the couch in the den. "Where the hell would you go?"

"I'll get my own place."

"Keith," his mother said. "You don't need to do this tonight."

"Let him go," his dad said. "If that's what he wants." He turned on the television set.

When Keith came downstairs with armfuls of his clothes, his mother handed him a duffel bag. "There's some money in the side pocket," she whispered. "This will blow over in a few days."

"I'm done," he said.

It's weird, he thinks now as he sips his beer, how she knew exactly where that duffel bag was and had the money ready for him, as if she'd expected him to need it.

A redheaded kid hits the ball hard and solid. Keith watches it sail over the fence. He loved coaching Little League when he was in high school, except for the parents who constantly insisted their kid needed to start, needed to pitch, needed extra batting practice. He needed them to get out of his face, which he demonstrated one night by spreading his arms a little too vigorously, sending one father flying six feet across the field with a broken nose. The man filed charges, the league fired him, and Keith spent the rest of that summer and part of tenth grade at a correctional camp in the Sequoia Forest.

The redheaded kid rounds the bases and all the parents cheer. A woman flops down on the grass next to Keith. He's seen her before—rotten teeth and oily yellow hair. Her skin is gray and mottled. "Can I have a beer?" she asks. "I'll make it worth your while." She smells like piss and has a dumb look on her face. It's insulting, her thinking he'd want someone like her. That girl in second grade had just peed her pants too and she got too close to him when he was trying to concentrate. "Get away from me," he says.

The tweakers stand and roll their bikes across the grass toward him. He could easily knock their heads together, teach them to show some respect, but there are too many witnesses right now and he's not like that anymore. He picks up the beer and leaves the empties behind.

He drives around for a while until it's almost dark, up and down the Wellington streets, a concrete maze of cinderblock walls covered with creeping fig. He takes Patton across to Eckerd, cruises down the hill past the horse trail houses. A blond girl is up ahead in the bicycle lane, white top off one shoulder, long legs in shorts, nineteen, maybe twenty. No helmet, flip flops, riding carelessly as if nothing bad could ever happen to her.

Someone should tell her to wear real shoes when she's riding a bike. She shouldn't ride alone at night either. Her bike doesn't even have a light. He passes her and pulls over where the streetlamp has burned out. He'll scare some sense into her.

She doesn't see him until he steps out of the shadow.

"You need lights on that bike."

"What the fuck, dude?" she says. "Get out of my way."

When she swerves to avoid him, she loses her balance, and he grabs her shoulders to keep her from falling. Her skin is soft under his grip, the kind that shows bruises, and even though she's wearing some rank perfume that smells like decayed incense, he immediately has an erection. She jerks away from him. "Asshole! What's wrong with you?"

"You shouldn't ride alone at night."

She laughs, too stupid to realize she should be afraid. He twists the handlebars just enough so that her bike tips over, scrapes between her thighs, and drops to the ground. She yelps as she trips over it, ripping the strap of her flip-flop from the sole.

That's enough, he decides. He makes himself turn around and go back to his car. He watches her in his rearview mirror as he pulls away from the curb. She's trying to fix her shoe and doesn't look up to read his license plate. Stupid girl. He cranks up the volume on the radio.

How do you own disorder?

The bass vibrates from the steering wheel up into his arms and adrenaline comes alive in his heart. Whoever wrote this song understands what it means to be alone.

The feeling of connection lasts until the song ends. He pulls into his parents' tract and parks away from the streetlights. He'll put a towel over his lap and jerk off. There's one beer left for afterwards. It's warm, but it might help him sleep.

CHAPTER NINE
JOSH KOWALSKI

Before Stephanie's funeral starts, Josh follows his mom to the front of the church. "You don't have to look in her casket if you don't want to," she says, "but we do need to say hello to Neil."

Josh actually does want to look in the casket, which is probably messed up and wrong. He's never been to a funeral though and he's not sure what he's supposed to look at. There aren't many people in the church. Ray Murdoch and his mother are the only other neighbors he recognizes. Stephanie's casket is white and lined with blue satin. She's wearing a long-sleeved blue blouse with lacy cuffs that cover her hands. She looks a lot better than she did the last time he saw her, almost normal really, better than normal, which is weird.

Neil sits next to his daughter, Joni, in the front pew. He stands when he sees Josh and hugs him. Josh feels the calluses on Neil's fingers through the back of his dress shirt.

"I'm sorry you were the one who found her," Joni tells Josh when Neil finally lets him go. "But I really appreciate what you did."

"I really didn't do anything," Josh says.

Joni lowers her voice. "We've decided not to mention the particulars of what happened. No one needs to know about the cat or how long my mother was there before Josh found her. What's the point, right? I hope you both understand."

"Of course," his mom says. She turns to Neil. "Are you getting settled into the new place?"

Neil is staring at Josh. "I screwed up, didn't I?" he says. "Missed your lesson today."

Josh stuffs his hands in his pockets, realizing for the first time that Neil might be missing lessons from now on.

"He likes the care center just fine, don't you, Dad?" Joni says.

"Can you have visitors?" his mom says.

"Absolutely," Joni says. "You'd like that, wouldn't you, Dad?"

"I'm sorry," Neil says, still staring at Josh.

"We'll come see you real soon Neil," his mom says.

■ ■ ■

For the rest of the week, his mom treats him as if he has chicken pox or something, doesn't say anything when he leaves his room a mess, doesn't complain that he hasn't made any headway on the front yard project. She even agrees to let him go to the Midnight Slinkers concert at the Orion Club. "Your dad always liked that band." She doesn't laugh at him either when he spikes his hair up into an almost Mohawk. He nods when she asks if twenty dollars is enough for a ticket. The concert is already sold out, but he's not telling her that. He's not going to need a ticket anyway because he has a plan.

■ ■ ■

"I hope that's Jack Daniels," the Orion Club bouncer says in front of the backstage door when Josh pulls his dad's old flask from the front pocket of his cargo shorts. Jack Daniels might have been a smarter way to impress the bouncer, Josh thinks, but it's too late now. The man watches as Josh takes a shot of lighter fluid. He's nervous. He's only practiced this a few times after watching a YouTube video of the Midnight Slinkers doing the same thing, which is why his dad liked them.

His dad loves fire, and Josh is the same. The power of it, the mystery. How fire makes its own rules. How the colors and the shapes are indescribable because they keep changing. Josh knows the danger too. His dad made him stick his finger in a flame when he was three, so he'd know what it felt like. His mother was furious.

The bouncer is still watching. Josh purses his lips and flicks the strike wheel on an old Zippo lighter that also belonged to his dad. As he spews out an arc of liquid, a drop of lighter fluid splashes down on his thumb and catches the flame. "Fuck!" He drops the lighter.

The bouncer laughs. "That musta hurt."

From the way the man crosses his arms over his chest, Josh knows he's not going to let him backstage, even after he says he's been a Slinkers fan since their first album. "You weren't even born then," the bouncer says. "Get out of here."

Josh walks toward the club entrance. So much for the plan. He'd envisioned the Slinkers inviting him on stage once they saw him shooting flames. They'd let him shoot a few more and then maybe ask him to take over for the drummer for a song or two. The idea seems completely stupid now. He has a good three hours to kill before his mother will be back to pick him up.

A familiar voice behind him says, "Hey Josh." Tyler, his older sister Monique, and two wrestlers from Wellington High School surround him, smelling like weed.

"Cool Mohawk," Monique says.

"Thanks." Josh stands up straighter, hoping his spikes give him another inch or two. "You guys like the Midnight Slinkers?" he says.

"I've never heard of them." Monique says. "We're only here because Brittany's brother's band is the opening act."

Josh pretends he knows this already and Monique says she wants to meet Brittany down in the pit, and then they're gone. Josh stares after them, watching Monique's dark hair swing back and forth across her shoulders. Everyone goes inside the club. Josh sits down on the curb, wishing he'd brought a hoodie. He flicks the lighter on and off to warm his hands. His dad always said that fire only needs oxygen, fuel, and heat to burn forever.

Which is bullshit, Josh knows now, because nothing is forever.

■ ■ ■

When he hears the band start the chorus of "We Used to be Pretty," he figures it's the encore. He stands and shakes out his legs. People stream out of the club, raving about how awesome the Slinkers sounded. He hears complaints as well, about the opening act. "A drum machine?" someone says. "Totally lame."

Brittany's brother's band was the opening act, Josh remembers. Maybe they could use a drummer. Finding out would mean talking to Brittany though, and Brittany is proud of being a first-class bitch. She calls it her job.

He gets his lighter fluid ready and despite his burned thumb and cold fingers, his flames work perfectly, and he attracts a good-sized crowd. Just after he pours the last shot of lighter fluid in his mouth, he sees his mother get out of her Prius and march across the parking lot straight toward him. He sparks up the Zippo anyway, holds it out an arm's length, and spews the liquid up and over the flame. The blaze shoots out in an eighty-degree angle, and everyone cheers.

His mother pushes her way through the crowd. A few people laugh, but they all get out of her way. She grabs him by the arm. "Don't you know how dangerous that is?" she asks as she marches him toward her car. "I never should have let you come to this concert."

He glances over his shoulder. Tyler, Monique, and the other kids from school are gone.

■ ■ ■

"This kind of behavior isn't like you, Josh," his mother says later, home in their kitchen. "Do you need to talk to a therapist? I know that what happened to Stephanie was a horrible experience."

"I thought we weren't supposed to talk about what happened to Stephanie."

"You can always talk to me. And I can get you some help if you need it."

"Neil's never going to get out of that place, is he?"

"He can't live on his own, honey. At least he's somewhere safe."

"It's not fair."

"I know. It's not." She traces the circle of freckles on his right cheek with one fingertip. "You know that your dad leaving had nothing to do with you, right?"

"I know." The burned place on his thumb stings like hell. It'll be hard to hold drumsticks tomorrow. "Don't worry about me. I'm not shooting flames anymore."

"You could have been seriously hurt, honey. Give me the lighter."

He pulls the black enamel Zippo from his pocket and hands it to her.

She turns it over and studies the green dragon. "This is pretty."

"It's not worth anything." Josh has three more just like it hidden away in an old backpack upstairs. "Dad took all the valuable ones."

"I have to be able to trust you, Josh. We're supposed to be a team." She combs his hair off his face with her fingers. The Mohawk has collapsed. "You need a haircut," she says.

■ ■ ■

Josh wakes up with a boner the next morning. As soon as he hears his mom leave for work, he jerks off to the picture of the woman in the red bikini top that he keeps hidden under his mattress. It's an escort ad from an old *Wellington Herald*. The woman has long thick hair and huge boobs, which he likes, and a blank expression on her face he finds disturbing and tries not to think about. Afterwards he pulls the sheets off his bed and takes them downstairs to the washer.

He eats four untoasted Pop Tarts and washes them down with half a carton of orange juice. He can still taste lighter fluid in the back of his throat. There's a note on the counter from his mother reminding him to work on the front yard. She's decided grass is too expensive to water, feed, and cut and wants to put in drought tolerant plants. It's thankless work, ripping out clumps of crabgrass and some kind of spiky thistle. He hasn't made much progress.

He puts a Band-Aid over the burn on his hand, pulls on gloves, and goes outside. It's a typical June Gloom morning, the sky slate metal, the neighborhood silent except for the church bells at Saint Benedict's, ringing out 9:00 a.m. Empty sidewalks and concrete driveways outline tiny plots of lawns up and down the street. The houses are all different shades of beige. This is the most boring place in the world.

■ ■ ■

After his four-hour box-boy shift at Albertsons is finally over, Josh rolls his skateboard out of the parking lot, crosses the street, and flies into his tract, sailing his board past the guy in the grey Accord sitting behind the wheel with his eyes closed. Josh has seen the car a few times parked on different streets. Uber driver, he figures, waiting for a customer. When he passes Tyler's house, the garage door is wide open as usual. No matter what time it is, day or night, rain or shine, the Kensington family always leaves all their doors wide open. It drives Josh's mother crazy, worrying about some animal or thief getting in.

His neighbor Ray is out in front of his house, watering his roses. "Tell your mom thanks for the spaghetti," Ray says as Josh rolls by. "It was delicious as usual."

"I will." Josh increases his speed. Ray's okay but he talks too much, and Josh is in a hurry. The blister on his hand popped halfway through his shift and he needs a new Band-Aid. Then he'll skate over to the school and try to find Brittany, ask about her brother's band. She and Monique should still be at water polo practice.

The pool at the school is empty, but he spots Monique and Brittany sitting with some other girls in the stands above the football field watching the varsity team practice. Josh climbs up the bleachers and sits down behind the girls, who ignore him as usual, except for Monique, who turns and gives him a quick smile. The girl with the pierced nose lights a joint with a yellow Bic lighter and passes it to Brittany. They keep the joint low and their eyes on the football coach. Brittany sets the lighter down on the bench next to her. Josh taps drum rolls with his fingertips on the skateboard in his lap. He's almost worked up enough nerve to ask Brittany about her brother's band when she turns around and blows smoke in his face.

"Are you having some kind of spastic attack?"

"What?"

Her eyes are round and blue, and she has a zit on her chin. "Stop the tapping, Pyro Boy. It's annoying."

Pyro Boy is a step up from Cart Boy, which is what Brittany usually calls him. She must have seen his flames last night. "I was practicing."

"Practicing what?" Brittany says. "Being a moron?"

"I'm a drummer," he says. All the girls laugh, except Monique.

"I've heard him play," she says. "He's actually pretty good."

Josh's heart rises as Monique lifts her hair off her shoulders with both hands, flips it up, and lets it fall. It cascades down her back in satiny ribbons which hold the sunlight. All the girls have long hair, but none of them have hair like Monique's. "I was wondering if your brother's band might need a drummer," he says, and his voice cracks an octave. The girls laugh, even Monique this time, which sucks. He clears his throat. "What kind of music do they play, anyway?"

Brittany shrugs. "David calls it rockabilly. They're the Nashville Kings. They have videos on their YouTube channel. They like setting things on fire too. You'd fit right in. But don't you already have that Cart Boy job at Albertsons?"

The girl with the pierced nose looks over her shoulder. "I didn't realize grocery stores hired children. How did you ever learn how to play drums anyway?"

"Neil Gorman is teaching me," Josh says. "He was in a band in the sixties. Electric Catfish? They were famous."

"I never heard of them," Brittany says.

"His wife just died," Josh says, surprising himself. His voice sounds loud and weird.

The girls look at each other.

"That was random," Brittany says. "What does that have to do with anything?"

"Shut up, Brittany," Monique says. "How sad for Mr. Gorman."

"I'm the one who found her." He shouldn't have said that.

He promised not to, but when they all turn around and look at him, their eyes are different, like they're actually interested.

"Seriously?" Brittany says. "You found a dead woman?"

He feels a buzz of energy that he likes except for the metallic taste it leaves in his mouth, and the way his temples start to throb. "She'd been dead for a couple of days too. Her cat started eating her."

"Gross!" the girl with the pierced nose says. "That's seriously messed up."

"Wow," Monique says. "Did Mr. Gorman just not realize she was dead?"

"Don't tell anyone about this," Josh says, slightly nauseous now. "I wasn't supposed to say anything."

"I don't believe you anyway," Brittany says.

"Why would he make up something like that?" Monique says.

"To get attention," Brittany says.

"I'm telling the truth," Josh says.

"Whatever," Brittany says as a player on the field breaks away from the pack and races toward the goal posts. The girls turn away from Josh and rise to watch, no longer interested in him or his story. The coach blows a whistle. Josh leans forward and cups his fingers around the yellow Bic lighter. His dad showed him how to take off the cap and adjust the slider so the flame shoots straight up six inches next time it's lit. Eyebrows and lashes and hair hiss up and stink like sulfur when they burn. He's not like his dad though. He leans forward and hands the lighter to the girl with the pierced nose. "You dropped this."

"No, I didn't," she says, but he's halfway down the bleachers heading for home.

■ ■ ■

His dad calls that night. "I'm proud of you, son. You did a standup thing for old Neil. You should feel good about that."

He feels like a huge phony. "When are you coming home?"

His dad exhales and doesn't answer for a few seconds too long. "I got on with a solar company," he finally says. "In Yucca Valley. It's good for me. I'm outside all day."

"Where's Yucca Valley?"

"Near Joshua Tree. We went camping out there once. Remember all the stars?"

"Maybe I'll come out there and visit you," Josh says. "I like looking at stars."

"We'll see."

Josh knows what that means.

"It's complicated," his dad says. "I have some things to figure out."

Things to figure out means figuring out how not to drink. That's what all the arguments were about before his dad left, although his parents pretended it was something else because pretending is what adults do. His dad pretended he had a job until his mother figured out he'd been sitting in a bar, waiting for it to be time to come home. His mother pretends she doesn't care his dad left although Josh can hear her crying sometimes at night, when it's late and she thinks he's asleep.

Even Neil pretended that Stephanie wasn't dead. Josh never expected Neil to pretend anything because Neil always says exactly what's on his mind. Put on gloves when you do yard work. Protect your hands. Learn to read music. Get a piano. Join the school band. And practice more. That's what Neil says the most, that he thinks Josh has real talent, but it won't do him a bit of good unless he practices.

So that's what Josh does. He practices.

SANDCASTLE REALTY

LISA KENSINGTON

Prestige Haven Homes,
Where Your Home Is Your Castle

JUNE 23, 2017 | (800) WB4-EVER lisa.kensington@Sandcastlerealty.com

WHAT PRICE WOULD YOU SELL FOR?

Are you dreaming of new surroundings? I'm Lisa Kensington and I can make those dreams come true.

Whether you're looking to upgrade, downsize, move out of state, or stay right here in Wellington Beach, give me a call. I can provide a complimentary property estimate, stage your house to its best advantage, find a qualified buyer, and ensure a smooth transaction.

Helpful Household Tips

"Drop a couple of cinnamon sticks into your vacuum bag and the sticks will provide light odor protection via their natural scent and antimicrobial quality."

In Case You Didn't Know

Wellington Beach is a canine-friendly town. Our Dog Beach is consistently rated the best in Citrus County. The Dog Lover's Association of Wellington maintains Dog Beach. Their mission is to protect and preserve access to the beach for well-behaved canine companions and their responsible owners. The Association receives no public financing or government handouts and relies completely on private donations. That's the Wellie Way.

WHAT MAKES WELLINGTON WONDERFUL

Two words: our beach! We have nine miles of wide-open surf, sand, and sun. We have an iconic pier and an annual surfing contest. Musicians have been singing the praises of Wellington surfer girls since the 1960s.

Owning a Prestige Haven home allows a sense of belonging to a community and gives you the freedom to create your own version of paradise.

Surf's up!!!

CHAPTER TEN
LISA KENSINGTON

Lisa folds laundry in the kitchen and glances out the sliding glass door at her mother-in-law, Betsy, sitting by the pool in her wheelchair, sipping something out of a coffee cup she didn't have last time Lisa checked. She looks down at the floor and frowns. The drips of water mean Betsy has pulled the bottle of vodka out of the freezer again. Impressive for a woman in a chair, but it's not even noon yet. She should go out there and take the cup away, except it's easier to pretend she doesn't know about the vodka. A tipsy Betsy doesn't argue as much as a sober Betsy does, which might allow Lisa a few hours of peace.

Betsy had an accident last night, which meant an extra load of laundry this morning. These days the washer and dryer run all the time. Thank goodness Eric put in solar panels when they did the remodel, although they were expensive. All of it cost more than they'd planned—the updated kitchen and bathrooms, and the brand-new roof required to install those solar panels. That, plus the private water polo club for Monique, the wrestling team for Tyler, the leased white Mercedes she needs to impress her clients. The leased bottle-green Volkswagen Bug for the newly licensed Monique so she can chauffeur herself and her brother to practices and meets all over Citrus County.

The Tesla Eric insisted they buy, since they'd installed all those solar panels.

Lisa blames Eric's hippie parents for his compulsive consumerism. His sister Susan is even worse. They both feel like they missed out on a real childhood, growing up on a commune with parents who were anti-war, anti-establishment, and anti-saving for the future.

She met Eric in a business law class after she let her working-class parents convince her that majoring in Creative Writing would be a waste of time and money. Tall, dark-haired, and full of contradictions, Eric believed in saving the planet but was on a management track at the Bug Guy. "The company has great benefits," Eric explained. He was by no means handsome—his large nose was crooked because he broke it when he was ten, and his parents didn't believe in doctors. His teeth were crooked too because his parents also didn't believe in orthodontists. He had a corny sense of humor, but his face was kind, the sex was thrilling, and he made her laugh. He still does. She married him, got her real estate license, and went to work at Sandcastle Realty. She's been there ever since.

When Eric's dad died, Betsy could have moved in with Susan. She owns a two-story brick Colonial in Alexandria, Virginia with three extra bedrooms. Susan has a mid-level administrative job with the Social Security Administration. She never married and has no kids. But Eric decided Virginia was too cold in the winter and too hot in the summer. Betsy's been with them for almost a year now, which everyone seems to think is just fine. Eric goes off to work each day and doesn't give Betsy another thought until he comes home for dinner. Susan takes exotic vacations whenever she wants and doesn't even send her mother a postcard. The kids aren't much help either. Everyone in the family is convinced Lisa's role in life is to serve them.

She really should take more time for herself and stop acting like her family's doormat. This morning she decides not to put away the towels after she folds them. The kids can sort out their own clothes. She'll hang Eric's shirts up when she takes them out of the dryer, but she's not ironing them. Instead of going out to the pool and taking the vodka away from Betsy, she sits down at the counter and turns on her laptop.

The newsletters are her one creative outlet. She likes finding helpful household hints and researching the history of Wellington Beach. Last night she watched something on public television about the red cars back in the 1900s that might be perfect for the history portion of the newsletter.

When she hears a splash, she thinks, *ducks*, because she's shooed a mallard pair out of the backyard twice this week. Eric insists on leaving out bird seed. He loves baby ducklings, but they make a mess in the pool. A few minutes go by (Five? Twenty? Forty-five? Later on, Lisa isn't sure.) Google reveals a ton of information about the red cars. They were part of a privately owned mass transit system that connected Wellington Beach with Los Angeles and served as a catalyst for real estate development. It's fascinating, but it's way too much information for a short column.

Frustrated, she stands, stretches, and glances out the patio sliding door. Betsy is floating face down in the water, her arms and legs at wide crucified angles, her nightgown trailing up over her balding pink scalp, the wheelchair tipped forward into the pool.

It doesn't seem real.

Which is probably why her memory is a little fuzzy from this point on. She races outside and jumps in, but Betsy is incredibly heavy, and Lisa has zero upper body strength, so she has to leave her mother-in-law in the shallow end of the pool. She runs back inside and calls 911 and then stands in her driveway, soaking wet, waving her arms frantically when the emergency vehicles pull into the cul-de-sac. The paramedics haul Betsy out of the water and perform mouth to mouth resuscitation.

I should have done that, Lisa thinks as she watches them, but she's never learned CPR. She can barely swim. She spends too much money coloring her hair to stick her head in chlorinated water. She tries to explain to the police officers who arrive next that she'd been folding towels when she heard the splash and thought it was the ducks.

"They're nesting. My husband insists on leaving seed out for them."

The younger police officer suggests she sit down. "You might be in shock. Was your mother-in-law confined to the wheelchair?"

"She can walk a little," Lisa says. She glances outside where the paramedics are pulling a white sheet over Betsy's body. She needs to call Eric. Through the front window she sees two men in dark suits get out of a Dodge Charger and have a lengthy conversation with the paramedics and the police officers. Her next-door neighbor, John, waddles down his driveway to put his two cents in. "The second one this month," she hears John say, proving that he's a complete idiot. Betsy drowning in the pool isn't anything at all like poor old Stephanie Gorman, left dead in her recliner for three days because her husband was too demented to do anything about it. Everyone's been gossiping about Stephanie's awful cat.

Focus, she tells herself as the two men come inside and show her their badges. They're detectives, she realizes, confused. Do the police think this wasn't an accident? She tells them about the ducks. The detective with an off-putting mustache never changes his expression. The other detective raises his bushy eyebrows and says, "What kind of ducks?"

"Mallard, I think." Lisa wants to be accurate, but surely it doesn't matter. Did she tell the police officers something different? Did they even ask about the breed of ducks? Why can't she remember? She's never like this. The detective with the eyebrows points to the cell phone in her hand. "Did you want to call someone?"

"Am I only allowed one phone call?" She's kind of joking, but neither man smiles. They walk out to the pool, and she calls Eric's office. Grace answers the phone with the same stupid expression Eric makes his all employees say. "It's a great day at the Bug Guy."

"I need Eric," Lisa says. Out on the patio, the mustached detective picks up Betsy's coffee cup and sniffs the contents. A police officer takes photos of the vodka in the kitchen freezer. Are they supposed to have a search warrant? It doesn't seem like the right time to ask.

She's standing in the garage with the detectives when Eric gets out of his car, pale faced and red-eyed. As he throws his arms around her, she notices the grey in his dark hair and wonders when that happened.

The mustached detective says he's sorry. "We just have a few more questions. Your next-door neighbor mentioned your garage door is always open?"

Eric blows his nose hard, making a honking sound that causes two of the officers standing in the street to look up. "We like to keep things open. This house can feel a little claustrophobic with five of us living here."

The detective turns to Lisa. "When the accident occurred, the door was open just like this?"

Lisa surveys the garage. Tidy, unlike most of the houses around them. Plenty of room for two cars to park, also unlike the other garages around them. Most people have too much stuff. She's planning on writing an article about hoarding in a future newsletter. The kitchen door is wide open, as is the side door to the pool. "Sure," she says. "Just like this."

"Someone's always here," Eric says. "We close the doors when we're gone, of course."

The mustached detective looks at Lisa. "You don't work outside the home?"

His voice is so dismissive. "I'm a real estate agent," she says.

"Plus, she takes care of my mother," Eric says.

The detectives look at each other and then at Eric. They all look at her.

"I'm sorry," she says.

"It was an accident, honey." Eric turns to the detectives. "Why did you ask about the open doors?"

"It's unusual," the mustached detective says. "Most people keep things locked up tight. Especially when they have a swimming pool."

"The gate is locked," Eric says.

"But your house is wide open," the other detective says. "You don't want some kid wandering into your backyard who doesn't know how to swim."

"You're right," Eric says.

"Have you noticed any suspicious-looking people in the neighborhood lately?"

"No," Lisa says. "I mean there's FedEx, Amazon, gardeners. People visiting those apartments. You don't actually believe someone broke in and pushed Betsy in the pool? I was sitting in the kitchen. I would have heard something." She did hear something. And she ignored it. "At least we don't have a starving cat like that old woman on Summertime Lane." Why in the world did she say that?

Eric looks alarmed. "That doesn't make any sense, hon."

The detectives exchange glances. "The coroner will be here soon," the mustached one says. "Sorry for your loss."

"Maybe that wasn't appropriate," Lisa says after the detectives leave. "To mention the Gormans' cat, I mean. Those rumors probably aren't even true."

"You're in shock," Eric says. "We both are. Where are the kids?"

"Monique's picking up Tyler from camp. They should be home soon."

"I don't want them to see Betsy like this." He exhales. He looks exhausted. "I'm going to call that new Hyatt and make a reservation for tonight. Can you call Monique and tell her to meet us there? And then I'd better call Susan. She'll want to come out."

■ ■ ■

Lisa stands next to the mini-fridge/coffee-station in their King Premier suite, both arms wrapped around as much of her daughter's muscular shoulders as she can reach. "I'm so sorry," she says. Monique hasn't sobbed in her arms since she was seven. At seventeen, she's a full head taller than both her parents.

"I should have been nicer to Betsy." Monique burrows her face into the space between Lisa's shoulder and neck.

We never even gave Betsy a nickname, Lisa thinks. Not Granny or Nanny or Mee-maw. Betsy was just Betsy. Monique's hair is thick and glossy and smells like vanilla bean and lavender, amazing considering all the time she spends in a chlorinated pool, and also a completely shallow thing to be noticing right now. Lisa glances over at Tyler, sprawled on the couch. He has a dazed expression, and his eyes are red. Eric is stretched out across the bed in the other room and hasn't stopped crying since he got off the phone with Susan.

Eric blows his nose. "We can go home if you guys want. This place isn't as nice as it looked online."

"We've paid for the room," Lisa says. "We might as well stay. You kids help me unfold the sofa bed."

Tyler pulls out a mattress, which at least is already made up with what look like clean sheets. Lisa smooths the blankets and finds extra pillows. "They have HBO," Tyler tells Monique. "We can watch *Game of Thrones* if you want."

Monique is still crying. "Cool," she manages.

Normally Lisa would not approve of them watching all the sex and violence on *Game of Thrones*, but tonight she's grateful they aren't arguing about sharing the sleeper sofa. "I'm going to take a quick shower." She pulls out clean sweats and a T-shirt from the bag she'd thrown together before they left the house. In the bathroom, she strips and turns on the shower, lets the water run as hot as she can stand it, and gets in. The knots in her neck start to loosen. She should be crying. She hasn't yet. Sometimes accidents are meant to happen.

She reminds herself to never say that out loud.

When she comes out of the bathroom, she tries to ignore the naked breasts on the television screen. "Don't stay up too late," she tells the kids. "Love you guys." They look up at her and nod. *They blame me,* she thinks, *and they are right. This was my fault.* She goes into the dark bedroom. Eric is finally asleep. She lies down next to him, wishing she'd brought a book to read. Another completely shallow thing to be thinking about right now.

The hotel bed is hard, the sheets are scratchy on her skin, and she can hear the toilet whistling. Susan's probably already made airline reservations and packed her suitcases for California. Susan will have a million questions and she will also blame Lisa for everything.

Go to sleep, she tells herself. Tomorrow is another day.

CHAPTER ELEVEN
JOSH KOWALSKI

Josh leans up against the wall in Noah's living room and watches a boy and girl wrestle against each other on the couch. The boy's hands are underneath the girl's shirt and there's an inch of pink skin just above the top of her jeans. Noah's party is exactly what he expected. Football players hang around the keg on the patio. Tyler and his friends stand under a willow tree in the backyard, passing a joint. He used to be invisible around these kids but tonight, everyone except the couple on the couch is watching him. He's suddenly famous, either for being the guy who found a cat eating a dead woman or for being the guy who made up a story about finding a cat eating a dead woman.

He brought fireworks to shoot off later, hoping the kids would talk about that instead of Stephanie Gorman. His dad left behind a stash of rockets, cherry bombs, M-80s, and mortars. Fireworks are a year-round thing for Joe Kowalski, not just for the Fourth of July, although that's when he makes the biggest show.

The Nashville Kings are playing in Noah's backyard tonight, which is the only reason Josh is here. Brittany's older brother David is out there now, running an extension cord across the grass. His hair is in a greasy pompadour and he's wearing a starched bowling shirt tucked into a creased pair of jeans. There's another older guy dressed the same, sitting next to the keg. Josh takes a deep breath and goes outside. "Make way for Corpse Boy," one of Tyler's friends says as he passes them. Josh clenches his hands. Ignore them, he tells himself. The extension cord snaked on the grass has a kink in it, so he shakes it loose.

David turns around. "Thanks, man."

"I'm Josh." He nods at the drum machine. "Looks like you need a drummer."

David laughs. "Yeah, although the machine doesn't bitch as much as that last drummer did. You play?"

He swallows hard and wills his voice to deepen. "I do."

David looks at him again. "Oh, yeah. You're the fire-breather, right? My sister said you have serious skills."

"She did?" His voice changes octaves, and he doesn't trust it enough to explain he's not breathing fire anymore. At least David didn't call him Corpse Boy. Old pieces of carpet cover the grass as a makeshift stage. An open guitar case for a beautiful red Gibson sits on one carpet and a standup bass lies across another. The bass is a weird charred brown color, and Josh walks closer to examine it. He can see it's been scorched severely more than once. "What happened?"

"Pretty cool, right?" David says. "Most nights Richie, over there sucking down beers, lights it up twice during each set."

"It still plays?"

"Damn right, it plays. Richie's not flaming anything tonight though. Noah's parents aren't into it." David grins. "They didn't say anything about you though. Did you bring your fluid?"

"I don't really do that anymore."

David raises an eyebrow. "Why not?"

"It's not my thing now. I brought some fireworks though."

"Excellent. Maybe you can shoot them off during a couple of our songs."

Josh looks around him. The backyard is small and full of people, and there are too many trees for the rockets and the M-80 he has in his backpack. "Maybe afterwards. Cool guitar."

"Cost me five grand, but it's worth every penny."

"If you want, I could go home and get part of my drum kit."

"You need to audition first. Maybe you could come by the house sometime."

"That'd be cool. How about tomorrow?"

David grins. "Eager, huh? I like that." He pulls out a bright pink business card. "We have a strict dress code. No skater boy clothes. You'll need to check out this store. And you really need to think about shooting flames again. You and Richie could trade off. It'd be cool."

The store's name, Hep Cats, is printed in bold black letters on the card. Josh puts it in his pocket and returns to his post on the living room wall where the couple is still grinding it out on the couch. He looks down at his cargo shorts and T-shirt. He didn't know these were skater boy clothes.

The front door swings open and Brittany comes in with that girl with the pierced nose and the tall, skinny one who wears glasses. They're all wearing short, ruffled skirts, and high heels. They brush past him, smelling like too many different kinds of dead flowers, and head straight to the punch bowl where Noah is filling red plastic cups. "Ladies," Noah says, handing each girl a drink. "An old family recipe. Take everything out of your parents' bar, pour it in a bowl, add a gallon of Fruit Juicy Red Hawaiian Punch, and stir."

Brittany takes inventory of the room and spots Josh. The girls follow her over to where he's standing. "Hey, Corpse Boy," Brittany says. "Monique's not here yet?"

"Don't call me that." She said not here *yet*, he thinks, which means Monique might be later.

"So, tell us all about what it was like finding that dead woman." Brittany pops a wad of gum in his face. "I mean, seriously? That old man was living with her corpse for what, a week?"

"His name is Neil. And it was only two days." His mother took him to the care center last week. Josh brought along two small hand drums, and he and Neil played together just like old times until a nurse interrupted and said it was time for lunch. Neil got so angry he couldn't speak, and then he started crying. Josh isn't sure if he'll go back. He misses Neil a lot, sometimes even more than he misses his dad which he should feel guilty about, but he can't handle seeing Neil cry. "I thought you didn't believe me," Josh tells Brittany.

"I don't. But you get points for creativity."

"It is kind of bizarre," the pierced nose girl says. "All these old women dying and shit. I mean, like, Tyler's grandmother drowned? It's like an epidemic or something."

"This summer has a weird vibe." Brittany glances outside. "Maybe you should drum for my brother's band, Corpse Boy. They can't suck any more than they already do."

"What do you mean, they suck?" Josh asks.

The girl with glasses says, "Let's mingle. There must be someone worth talking to here tonight."

The three girls turn as one and go outside to the patio. The couple on the couch sits up. The girl's eyes widen when they register on him. "You're that guy!" she says. The boy leans forward, squints at Josh, and farts.

"Gross," the girl says, fanning her hands. The boy pulls her back down on the couch.

Josh waves away the smell as Monique walks through the front door. Her hair shines. She's wearing shorts and a T-shirt, like a normal person. Two wrestlers from Tyler's team rise from their chairs and follow her, as if she's the one they've been waiting for.

"Hey, Corpse Boy," the taller one of them says. "Did you bring your cat?"

"Don't be rude," Monique says.

"What's that on your face?" the shorter guy asks Josh. "Some kind of tattoo?"

"Or a sign of the devil?" the taller guy says.

"It's a birthmark," Josh says.

"That figures." The taller guy looks at Monique. "You want punch?"

"I'm not drinking that crap," Monique says. "I'll meet you guys outside."

"Brittany's looking for you," Josh says, just to have something to say.

"She probably wants a ride home too. I'm sick of being the only one with a car. So how do you like being famous?"

He studies the carpet. "Most people don't believe me."

"It'll blow over," she says. "Something else will happen and people will talk about that instead."

"I'm sorry about your grandmother."

"Thanks." She stares straight ahead. In this low light, her eyes have gold flecks in the iris. "Betsy was old and everything, but it was still a big shock. And my mom's already given away most of her stuff. It's like she was never there."

Feedback screeches from whatever it is David is plugging in outside. Monique covers her ears. "I'd better go make sure those two idiots don't drink too much. I don't want them puking in my car later."

Josh waits a minute so it doesn't look like he's following her and then goes outside. Richie holds the bass in one hand and a red cup in the other. David takes his guitar out of the case and plugs it in. "Ready?" David says. Richie sets his cup on the ground. Josh wonders why David doesn't tune up first, but Richie is already leaning over and starting the drum machine. They begin what sounds like "Blue Suede

Shoes." The bass is off beat and David's guitar chords are clumsy. They're loud though, and although they don't get any better, the kids bob their heads in unison. Josh takes the card David gave him out of his pocket.

"David works there." Tyler stands next to him now, smelling of beer and weed, his glassy eyes at half-mast. "He should stick to selling clothes and quit trying to play that Gibson."

"How did he get that gig at the Orion Club?" Josh says. "They opened for the Midnight Slinkers."

"His dad paid for him to play."

"You can do that?"

"You can do anything if you have money. Did you bring something to blow up tonight?"

"Let's wait until the band stops. And then go out front."

"Good plan," Tyler says. He heads back over to the keg.

The Nashville Kings finish and unplug their equipment. Post Malone's "Congratulations" jarringly floods through the speakers and some people start dancing. Josh gets his skateboard and backpack and meets Tyler in the front yard.

Tyler holds up a blue plastic paint bucket. "This'll blow up, won't it?"

"It'll do something," Josh says. "Where'd you find it?"

"On the side of the house when I went to take a leak."

"You pissed on the side of Noah's house?"

"Everyone does it." Tyler grins. "Leslie just gave me a blow job back there."

Josh is not about to ask if the blow job was before or after the pissing. He wonders if one of the girls standing on Noah's front porch is Leslie.

"Give me some sparklers," Tyler says.

Josh pulls a box out of his backpack. Tyler hands one to each girl and lights them. The girls squeal like ten-year-olds as the sparks start flying.

"Tyler's so nice," one of them says.

He could have told them the sparklers were from me, Josh thinks, as he and Tyler walk out into the street. He pulls the M-80 out of his backpack, sets it down, then puts the plastic paint bucket over it, leaving the fuse exposed.

"I want to light it," Tyler says.

"This one's got a short fuse. You need to be careful. You're kind of buzzed."

"I'm fine," Tyler says.

"Go ahead then. Blow your fingers off." Josh grabs his board and slings his pack over his shoulder. Tyler lights the fuse and hustles backwards. The M-80 explodes, the bucket flies a good ten feet straight up in the air and bursts apart in tiny blue plastic pieces. The girls on the front porch scream and car alarms go off up and down the street. Tyler whoops and the girls rush down the sidewalk and circle around him. "You scared me," one girl says.

Josh jumps on his skateboard. "I'm out of here," he says, but no one's listening. He was going to light the rockets next. The girls would have liked them, but it would have been a waste because somehow Tyler would have made it about him.

■ ■ ■

In the morning, when Josh shows his mom the website of David's store, he's slightly shocked when she says she can barely afford his school clothes and she's most certainly not paying for costumes. He was sure she was still in her post-dead-Stephanie mood and would do anything he asked. "This is important to me," he says, although he isn't sure it is anymore.

"Last month you wanted to be a fire eater. Today you want to be in a rockabilly band. Tomorrow you'll want something else. You're just like your father. You need to finish the front yard like we agreed."

"I should go live with Dad then. Since I'm just like him."

Her eyes flash and she starts to say something and then tightens her lips. He goes outside and takes the hoe from the garage and starts whacking away at the front yard dandelions. "I'm not like him," he tells himself. "I'm not like him at all."

There are just as many weeds now as when he'd started. The roots are deep and stubborn. He raises the hoe up over his head and smashes the ground. That band was stupid. David sounded terrible, Richie was drunk, the train beat was boring. He's not ever going to get any better without Neil helping him.

"Josh," his mother says from the front porch. "Your hand's bleeding. Sit down. I'll be right back."

He crouches on the edge of the planter watching blood drip from the blister on his thumb into the dirt.

She comes back with the first aid kit. "I'm sorry about what I said. You're not like your father. Although you do look like him. Give me the hoe. You need to keep that bandage clean." She starts on the weeds closest to the street. "This is harder than I thought," she says after a while. She sets the hoe down and draws patterns in the dirt with the toe of her sneaker. "We'll put river rock here. Sages back against the house, maybe some lavender. A big Aloe Vera in the middle. Aloe Vera's good to have around for burns."

"I'm not shooting flames anymore." He pulls the hair back off his forehead.

"You should try some pomade. It would keep the hair out of your eyes. Plus, it's very rockabilly."

"I thought you were against that idea."

"I'm against spending money on clothes you can't wear anywhere else. Besides, if David really wants you to be in his band, your clothes shouldn't matter. I remember the Blasters drummer wore a white T-shirt and a pair of Levi's."

"The Blasters aren't rockabilly. And I don't have any Levi's."

"I'm willing to buy you a new pair. And you have plenty of white T-shirts. You'll need new shoes for school anyway. What kind does this band wear?"

David had cowboy boots. Richie wore wingtips. Neither appeals.

"Black Converse would be cool. Jack Purcells, maybe?"

"I'm not spending $150 on shoes, Josh."

"Fine. I'll buy them on my own then. I have money."

"We agreed you'd save for college."

He has no intention of going to college, but this isn't the right time to tell her. He combs the hair off his face again.

"I'm pretty sure there's a half a jar of Suavecito," she says, "in the medicine chest in my bathroom."

That bathroom used to be *theirs*, not hers. She might have already given up on his dad coming back, but that doesn't mean he has to.

SANDCASTLE REALTY

LISA KENSINGTON

Prestige Haven Homes,
Where Your Home Is Your Castle

JUNE 30, 2017 | (800) WB4-EVER lisa.kensington@Sandcastlerealty.com

FOURTH OF JULY

The 2017 Wellington Beach Fourth of July Parade begins at 10 a.m. and lasts about two hours. The theme this year is "One United America."

There's a 5K race and a pancake breakfast before the parade. Stick around all day. There's a fireworks show on the pier after dark.

Rumor is the Grand Marshall this year is a local resident and famous mixed martial artist. But you didn't hear that from me!

Helpful Household Tips

> **❝** *Microfiber towels weigh nearly nothing compared to fluffy beach towels, and sand doesn't stick to them. They wash up and dry superfast too.* **❞**

In Case You Didn't Know

The Wellington Beach Parade has been held for over one hundred years and is the largest Fourth of July Parade west of the Continental Divide.

The parade includes marching bands, vintage woodies, classic cars, horses, city council members, state representatives, celebrities, military vehicles, veterans, Boy Scouts, Girl Scouts, clowns, dancers, cheerleaders, and much more. It's even televised on local stations.

WELLINGTON FIREWORKS STANDS OPEN JULY 1

It is legal to use safe and sane fireworks in the City of Wellington Beach on the 4th of July from noon to 10 p.m.

You can buy fireworks in the Albertson's parking lot and support the Wellington High School wrestling squad as well as the girls water polo team, two athletic groups that are near and dear to my heart. Go Wellies!

CHAPTER TWELVE
LISA KENSINGTON

"I don't really blame Ringo," Joni Gorman tells Lisa. "My dad just forgot to feed him. But how honest do we have to be with potential buyers about what really happened?"

"Dying at home isn't all that uncommon in this neighborhood," Lisa says as she stacks the listing paperwork on the Gormans' old dining room table. "California law requires disclosing any death on a property that occurred within the last three years. We'll say that your mother died of a heart attack and leave it at that."

"I just hate the idea of neighbors gossiping about my parents."

"Not much we can do about gossip except ignore it." Lisa is sure the neighbors are all gossiping about Betsy's death too and blaming her. She hands Joni a pen. "Sign next to the little yellow arrow tabs." She can already tell this listing is going to be a challenge. Joni has made it clear she doesn't want to spend any money on repairs, and the house needs a lot of work—new carpet, new paint, and a new roof. Joni is also expecting a quick and lucrative sale.

"Thank you for trusting me with your home," Lisa says when the signatures are complete. She stands. "The listing should be online by the end of the day."

Joni walks her outside. "I'm really sorry about your mother-in-law, Lisa. I didn't know Betsy, but that must have been terrible."

"Thank you. It was."

She wonders if the neighbors are watching her and Joni through their windows, judging if the amount of grief on their faces is sufficient for two women with dead female relatives. She still wonders why the police made such a big deal about them leaving their garage door open—as if someone could have broken into the backyard, tossed Betsy in the pool, and held her underwater until she stopped struggling. She would have heard something. And who would do such a thing?

She hears Saint Benedict's bells ring eleven times as she heads down the Gormans' sidewalk toward home. Maybe Betsy decided to kill herself out of spite. Maybe she was angry at something Lisa said and intentionally rolled her wheelchair up and over the pool coping and into the water. She wasn't a strong woman, but she was definitely stubborn, always determined to have her own way. Lisa can't even remember the last conversation she had with her mother-in-law. Most likely it was about breakfast. They were out of grape jelly that morning.

Caught up in her thoughts, Lisa almost doesn't notice the man sitting with his eyes closed behind the wheel of an older grey Honda Accord parked on Mountain Brook. Probably waiting for someone in the Riptide apartments, she thinks as she passes him, although those people don't usually park all the way down here. Random strangers visiting those apartments and parking in her neighborhood has always been a pet peeve. She spins around, marches back to the Honda, and taps on the window.

The man jerks awake, looks up at her, and blinks.

"You need to move along," she says. "This is private property." His face hardens. He's older than she'd originally thought, and his muscular torso and huge biceps give her a moment's pause, but he immediately starts the car and drives away. Satisfied, she heads toward home. If you see something, say something, and so many people don't. She could write about that in her next newsletter.

The phone is ringing when she walks in the door. Susan. Again.

"I was thinking I'd stay in a hotel when I come out for the service," she says.

"Why?" Lisa asks, although she's actually relieved. "You've always stayed with us."

"I really don't think I can stand being near your swimming pool," Susan says. "Doesn't it bother you?"

"Of course, it bothers me." None of them have used the pool since the accident. Tyler's been going to the beach with his friends, Monique spends her days in the pool at school, and Eric has been too busy buying funeral urns.

"I have hotel points," Susan says. "I'll just stay at the Ritz-Carlton."

Of course, Susan has Ritz-Carlton hotel points, and of course she needs to rub it in.

She used to like her sister-in-law. Susan hosted her bridal shower, didn't complain about not being a bridesmaid, and gave them a generous wedding gift. For their first anniversary she'd had an impressive bottle of champagne delivered. But then Lisa started noticing how Susan always has to mention the exotic trips she was planning, the new pairs of boots she'd just ordered, some award she'd received at work. Susan's a terrible influence on Eric too. They're constantly trying to outspend each other, and now they've planned an expensive ocean burial for Betsy next month. Lisa glances at the blue ceramic urn embossed with butterflies sitting on the living room bookshelf, one of the three that Eric has ordered.

"Have you and Eric decided on a date yet?" she asks. "I need to think about what we're all going to wear."

"August twenty-first," Susan says. "I can't take off work until then. I was wondering about Mom's jewelry. Eric says you've already given a lot of her things away?"

"I donated some of her things to the women's Assistance League. I can't imagine Betsy's clothes would fit you. And I don't remember her ever wearing any jewelry except those silver hoop earrings and her wedding band. I saved them for you."

"She also had a set of pearls. Earrings, a ring, and two necklaces. They belonged to her grandmother."

"I never saw them. I never even heard about any pearls, and I didn't find a jewelry box either."

Susan laughs. "Mom thought jewelry boxes were bourgeois. She kept the pearls rolled up in a tie-dyed bandana."

"I never saw that either." Lisa has a sudden sinking feeling as she remembers stuffing something tie-dyed into one of the giveaway bags. Only Betsy would wrap antique pearls up in a bandana.

"Could you look again?" Susan's voice catches. "I don't have anything left of hers."

I took care of your mother, Lisa wants to say. Which was your job. And if you'd come out sooner or said something earlier, I would have waited to get rid of everything.

"Fine," she says instead. "I'll look again."

"I know Betsy was a difficult woman," Susan says. "I really appreciate all you've done for her."

She's baiting me, Lisa decides. She means that if someone else had been here, Betsy would still be alive.

She finally gets Susan off the phone and opens up her newsletter template on her laptop. She'll start with the problem of strangers visiting the Riptide apartments and parking in her neighborhood. She remembers hearing that the Riptide building was sold, so she searches online for the new name, wanting to be accurate.

She sits back in shock when she finds it. The city of Wellington Beach bought the Riptide building last year in a joint venture with a South County corporation, using government funding from Citrus County and the California Department of Housing and Community Development. How did she not know this? The building will still be called the Riptide, but the plans are to demolish the structure and rebuild a four-story complex with one hundred twenty units. Twenty-five percent of those units will be reserved for low-income residents.

John next door was right, for once; the current residents are going to have to qualify to move back in. She should have been paying more attention to this. It has to be stopped. What kind of people will this project attract—gardeners? Kitchen helpers? House cleaners? They'll never fit into the Wellington Beach lifestyle.

Reading further, Lisa is outraged. There are only one hundred eighty parking spaces planned. Those people will have to park their trucks and crappy used cars in her neighborhood. It's not fair for the homeowners to be invaded like this. More people need to know about this awful plan, not just the ones who read her newsletter. She'll write an essay and maybe get the *Wellington Herald* to print it.

To bump up the tension, she tweaks her confrontation with the man in the Honda slightly and alters his appearance. She shaves his head, makes him six-foot-three, puts him in an old blue Chevy truck, and gives him full sleeves of tattoos on both arms and around his neck. She has him argue with her and admits he'd scared her a little, but she'd summoned the energy to stand up to him because as a realtor she's representing her community even if the city council won't.

She summarizes the plans for the Riptide and makes a compelling argument that people need to be their own advocates or risk being taken advantage of by those who haven't planned well enough yet still expect to have the same lifestyles as those who worked hard and saved their money. She writes about parking, property values, and the inevitable increase in crime, then closes with a call to action. "We need to stop that housing project at the Riptide. Call the city council members now and tell them how you feel."

She sits back, satisfied. This feels like the start of something bigger.

■ ■ ■

"Your grandmother's service is set for August twenty-first," Lisa says when Monique comes home from water polo practice. "We need to think about what we're going to wear."

"Can we talk about this later?" Monique says. "I'm going over to Brittany's house."

Monique suddenly has someplace to be every single moment of the day. When she is home, she's in her room, either on her phone or the computer, which she immediately snaps closed when Lisa is in the vicinity. She's incredibly moody too, which means there's a boy to blame. Lisa is worried. Monique is a sensitive girl. Unreciprocated love can be so cruel. Whoever he is, better not hurt her.

"We're just going out on a boat, Mom. What's the big deal?"

"It's a yacht and your father is spending a fortune. We all need to look nice."

"Fine. I'll wear that black dress with the ruffled skirt I wore to the award ceremony."

"That dress is a little tight in the arms, isn't it?"

"I have muscles. The dress is fine."

"That dress makes your arms look huge, honey."

"Wow. Way to give a girl confidence."

"I'm just being honest. We should have bought a larger size and had it altered to fit you." Monique's body has always been difficult to fit, much less flatter. "You don't have to wear a dress if you don't want to. Slacks and a loose-sleeved blouse would be fine."

"I'm not wearing long pants in August."

"Let's make an appointment with a stylist at Nordstrom then. You're going to need new clothes for school anyway."

"No one gets dressed up for school, Mother. Everyone wears shorts in the summer and sweats in the winter. I'm all set."

"You're going to be a junior. There will be dances and proms and more award ceremonies." Good Lord, she thinks, imagining Monique's shoulders in a strapless dress. She'll look like a linebacker. A flat chested linebacker. "You know I'm proud of you, honey." She is proud. Monique swims like a dolphin and her lung capacity is impressive, but her overlong arms and powerful shoulders do nothing for her femininity. "You're a beautiful girl. Your hair is amazing. Your skin is lovely. Your eyes are too."

"It's my body that you have a problem with."

"That's not true." Lisa's face flushes. It's uncanny how often Monique can read her mind. "But we really should start thinking about breast enhancement."

Monique groans.

"I know you don't like talking about this," Lisa says. "And we can't schedule the surgery until you're eighteen, but we need to get on the surgeon's calendar now. I want you to go to the same doctor in Pelican Bay who did mine. And in the meantime, we need to get you fitted for better underwear. It's all about proportion, dear. Your shape just needs a slight adjustment."

"I'm fine with my shape. My shape is what wins matches. Big boobs would slow me down."

"There's more to life than water polo matches, honey. You don't want to scare the boys away."

"If they're afraid of me, I'm not interested."

"Oh, really? Is there someone you are interested in?"

"No," Monique says. "There isn't."

Which means yes, of course there is someone. Her intuition is confirmed when Monique glances over at her wedding photograph, framed in crystal and carefully placed on the middle shelf of the china hutch under a small spotlight.

"That was the best day of my life," Lisa says.

"That's your dream, not mine. And you don't even look like that anymore."

Which is true but still stings. "You're right. I starved myself for months to fit into that dress. I had a makeup artist and a hairdresser. My parents went all out."

"Was it worth it?"

"Of course, it was worth it. I remember the expression on your father's face. He couldn't believe it was me."

"Why couldn't you just be yourself?"

"I wanted to be better than myself. All women have a few tricks up their sleeves."

"It's false advertising. It seems dishonest, to me anyway."

Monique has a habit of seeing the world in black and white. She has a lot to learn, but she's young. "It's part of being a woman."

"I don't agree."

"You'll understand when you're older. I felt like a princess coming down the aisle on your grandfather's arm, your father waiting with his groomsmen, nervous and happy, my seven bridesmaids lined up at the altar. None of them as beautiful as me, of course."

"Did you seriously pick women uglier than you to be your bridesmaids?"

"No! They were all beautiful, but they understood it was my day." Did they really though? She remembers an argument with one bridesmaid who insisted on altering her dress to show more leg. What was her name? Actually, she can't remember any of their names right now.

"Have I met these women?" Monique asks, reading her mind again. "I don't remember them."

"We lost touch. It happens once you get married. My family is the most important thing to me now. I guess I don't have any real girlfriends anymore."

"That's sad, Mom. Maybe it's because of your job. I mean, you spend a lot of time with people when they're selling their houses, and then you just move on to the next customer."

"You make it sound as if I'm using people. That's how this business works."

"I wasn't criticizing you."

"It sure sounded that way. It's harder to have friends when you're older. Do you actually think you're going to be friends with Brittany forever?"

Monique pulls her lower lip under her front teeth before she speaks, which means she is considering what to say next. Lisa's watched her do this since she learned to put sentences together. Sometimes she recognizes her thoughtful, sweet child under all the teenage prickliness.

"Brittany can be kind of shallow, but she's always there for me."

"That's important."

"If it makes you feel better, Brittany has her wedding planned out in infinite detail, down to the color of nail polish and type of manicure."

Lisa laughs. "Good for Brittany."

"I know a big wedding was important to you, but it's not what I want."

"Don't give up on yourself so easily."

Monique's laugh is bitter. "You're not listening to me."

Lisa hesitates, and then says, "You can decide about the surgery when you turn eighteen."

"I've already decided."

"I'm going to schedule an appointment anyway. And you're not wearing shorts to your grandmother's funeral."

"I bet Tyler is."

"Let it go, Monique. You need to learn to pick your battles."

After Monique leaves for Brittany's house, Lisa takes the wedding photo out of the hutch and wipes off the dust. She wore amethyst earrings that day. Pretty, but pearls would have matched her dress perfectly. Betsy should have offered. Betsy really should have left her jewelry to Monique, her only granddaughter. She wonders how valuable those pearls were. Hopefully, the Assistance League still has them. Maybe she can buy them back.

CHAPTER THIRTEEN
JEANNETTE LARSEN

"Pretty swanky," Jeannette says after the guard at the Peninsula gate checks their names off his list and waves them in. "Except for the oil derricks across the street."

"This must be Doug's place," Bob says as he pulls in front of a fake Mediterranean two-story, with a red tile roof, a three-car garage, and no front yard.

Jeannette checks her lipstick. "Isn't it weird that he invited us for dinner? Is he selling something?"

"Not that I know of," Bob says. "This is a chance for us to make some new friends."

"I wasn't impressed with him at all."

"We've only met him once." He follows her up the sidewalk. "You look gorgeous tonight. As always. Those are my favorite shoes."

They used to call these four-inch pink heels her fuck me shoes, but they don't joke about sex anymore. They don't talk about why Bob hasn't reached for her in bed lately either. He pretends to be sleeping, but she's caught him lying awake, staring at the ceiling. She should make the first move, but the idea exhausts her. It was easier to agree to come with him to this dinner party.

She smells oil and salt as she takes in the American flags snapping in the breeze in front of every house up and down the street. "I haven't seen this many flags since 911."

"The Fourth's always been a big deal in Wellington," he says.

A squadron of white pelicans flies in formation overhead. She counts seven, then twelve. Bob rings the doorbell, which chimes out the chorus to "Dixie."

"Jesus," Jeannette says. "I guess we should be glad they're not flying the Confederate flag."

"Hush," Bob says as a tiny blond woman opens the door.

"You must be Bob," she says in a very perky voice. "I'm Carla, Doug's wife. Welcome, welcome."

"Thanks for inviting us. This is my wife, Jeannette."

"We're out on the patio. Everyone's looking forward to meeting you guys."

"She sounds like a chipmunk," Jeannette says under her breath as they follow Carla through the house. "Why are they looking forward to meeting us? Are you sure this isn't a cult?"

"Babe," Bob whispers. "Be nice."

Outside, Carla hands Jeannette a margarita. Bob asks for a light beer. There are two other couples besides Doug and Carla. The men stand next to an elaborate outdoor kitchen watching Doug grill a full rack of ribs. Their wives sit in front of a stone fireplace. The sunset flames the sky in deep oranges and purples, the pool water refracts the colors. She and Bob join the men by the barbecue.

"I hear you guys just moved to Wellington," the man introduced as Frank Palmer says, narrowing pale grey eyes under wire-rimmed glasses.

"We're happy to be here," Bob says.

"What tract are you in?" Frank asks.

"Prestige Haven," Bob says. "We're on Hillside West."

The other man, Greg Oppenheimer, nods. "Near Saint Benedict's. I'm familiar with that area." Greg is deeply tanned and has longish blond hair. Jeannette recognizes his face from somewhere.

"Your neighborhood has had some excitement recently," Greg says.

"Seems pretty quiet to us," Bob says.

"Greg's in real estate," Frank says. "He's got the scoop on everyone."

"My territory is Wellington Marina," Greg says. "But I know all the neighborhoods. An old woman died on Summertime Lane a month ago. Rumor has it that the husband didn't report it for a couple of days. They say the cat got to her."

"Dear God," Jeannette says. "That's awful."

Greg takes a sip of his beer. "And a couple weeks ago, a woman drowned in her backyard pool on Paradise Court. She fell out of her wheelchair and into the water. It was all over the news. I'm surprised you didn't see it."

So much for Bob's theory that Wellington is a safer place to live, Jeannette thinks.

"Well," Bob says. "Accidents happen I guess."

"Those houses were built back in 1964," Greg says. "They were never meant for seniors."

"Speaking of accidents," Frank says, "doesn't our mayor live in that neighborhood?"

"He's on Mountain Brook," Greg says. In the setting sun, Greg's skin is almost the color of a copper penny. "Dumpy little one story. Hasn't done a thing to it since he moved in."

"You don't sound like a fan," Bob says.

Frank sniffs hard and pushes his glasses up his nose. His thin face has the pinched look of a ferret. "The mayor's a Democrat," he says. "I'm not a fan either. He's a big proponent of affordable housing. I'm sure you've heard about that low-income project in your neighborhood."

"No," Bob says. "I haven't."

"I'm in the city planning department," Frank says. "They're

tearing down those apartments near you and putting in a four-story building."

"It'll ruin your property values," Doug says. "And increase the crime rate."

"Anything we can do to stop it?" Bob asks.

"The developer's met all the requirements so far," Frank says. "It might be a done deal."

"We need people with enough balls to stand up to the State of California," Doug says. "This can't happen again. You might be able to help us, Bob. You understand government regulations, right? And how to get around them?"

So that's why Doug invited us, Jeannette thinks. *He thinks he can talk Bob into helping him. What a creep.*

Bob laughs. "Don't you remember calling me a straight arrow? I *enforce* regulations. And I'm a federal auditor, not State of California."

"It's got to be similar," Doug says.

"Real estate laws are a whole different ball game," Bob says.

"Where'd you guys live before?" Frank asks.

"Angel City," Bob says.

"So, you were inlanders," Frank says.

"They're locals now," Doug says.

"Did you live up in the hills?" Frank asks.

"Not exactly." Bob puts his arm around Jeannette's waist. "We've always wanted to live in Wellington," he says. "Haven't we, babe?"

Why so vague? Jeannette wonders. Is he worried they might think our former neighborhood was too working-class? It's the truth. Why's he trying to impress these people?

"I wouldn't live anywhere but Wellington." Greg rakes his fingers through his hair again.

"Here's to paradise," Doug says, raising his glass.

Carla brings out a pitcher of margaritas and the other two women join them next to the grill. Tom Petty's voice rises over the guitars, singing the praises of American girls. The sound system is excellent.

"This is one of my favorite songs," Jeannette says.

The woman standing next to Frank leans over and clinks her glass against Jeannette's. "I love Tom Petty," she says, in a deeper voice than Jeannette expected.

She smiles, glad to find something in common. "We have tickets to see the Heartbreakers in September."

"Tom Petty's a junkie," Frank says.

"Well, I still like his music," the woman says. "I'm Barbara, Frank's wife."

"Here's to American girls," Greg says, tapping his beer bottle on the margarita glass of the woman with dimples and large breasts standing next to him. "This is my wife, Krystal."

Doug raises his bourbon, his expression serious. "Here's to Wellington. And to making sure our paradise doesn't change."

"It's not just the low-income housing the mayor's trying to cram down our throats," Carla says. "It's all the homeless people too. Some guy who works out at our gym is living in his car."

"The dude's there all the time too," Doug says. "Charging his crappy old phone next to the elliptical machine. You guys have probably seen him. Blue tank top? Huge arms?"

"I've seen him," the dimpled wife says. "He looks like he belongs on Venice Beach. One of those Arnold Schwarzenegger types."

Jeannette coughs and sets her empty margarita glass down.

"You okay, babe?" Bob asks.

"Nothing wrong with Arnold," Barbara says. "Best governor since Ronald Reagan."

"You mean *governator*," Carla chirps, and everyone laughs.

"Is this the gym you were talking about at Cyclone's?" Bob asks.

"No, that's a different place," Doug says. "I'm talking about Citrus County Fitness. The one at Seaview Village."

"Don't you teach there sometimes, babe?" Bob asks.

"Not lately." Her face feels hot, and she coughs again. "I need some water."

"Come with me, ladies," Carla says. "I'll make another batch of margaritas."

"So, what's this other club you were talking about?" Bob asks.

"It's a fight club," Doug says. "The guys do a little boxing, a little MMA."

"You mean like in that Brad Pitt movie?"

"Not exactly," Doug says. "It's more of a community service club."

Bob laughs. "I get it. Rule number one is never talk about fight club, right?"

Jeannette expects the men to laugh, but they don't. As she follows Carla inside, the other two wives trail behind her and she can't help but think of sharks chasing blood. There's something overly intense in these women's expressions, their form-fitting dresses, their blood-colored nails, the sound of their stiletto heels clicking on the stone pavers.

Carla's kitchen is straight out of one of those HGTV shows she's been watching lately, trying to figure out what to do in their new house. "Sparkling or still?" Carla squeaks.

"Still, please." Jeannette takes a sip of water then reaches across the counter for her purse. It's the deep rose leather one tonight, riveted with silver studs.

"That's a cute bag," the dimpled wife of the surfer-looking man says. Krystal, Jeannette remembers. "It's Coach, right? My aunt used to have one of those. I didn't know they were still a thing."

Jeannette pulls out her mirrored lipstick case and almost tells them about Zack buying her Coach bags when Barbara proclaims in her authoritative voice that the Coach company has gone downhill lately. "Their purses are made in China now," Barbara says. "The quality's totally gone. I'm a Louis Vuitton girl myself."

"I love Tod's," Krystal says.

"Chanel all the way." Carla raises both hands as if to testify, her voice like chalk screech.

Jeannette snaps her lipstick case closed and wonders if anyone's ever told Carla how irritating she sounds. How rude of Barbara to dismiss her treasured Coach bag as inferior. How arrogant of all of them to not disagree.

"Are you a personal trainer?" Barbara asks.

"I am," Jeannette says.

"Well, that explains your amazing body," Barbara says. "I'm a probate attorney."

"And she never lets us forget it," Krystal says. "Me and Carla are stay-at-home moms."

Barbara asks if there are any exercises she can do "to postpone the underarm wings."

"Light weights and lots of reps," Jeannette says, putting her lipstick back in her purse.

"What about exercises for the glutes?" Carla says. "Suddenly my ass is flat as a board."

"Squats," Jeannette says. "Plus, tons of cardio."

"My mother always said there's a certain point in life where a woman can have a nice ass or a nice face, but never both," Krystal says.

"That was before Botox," Barbara says. "What kind of fitness classes do you teach, Jeannette?"

"Cardio fit, Zumba, Water Aerobics. I coach tennis too, in South County."

"I'd love to play tennis again," Krystal says, "but between my volunteer work, the memoir, and homeschooling three kids, I just don't have time."

"You're writing a memoir?" Jeannette asks, hoping to avoid the inevitable next question.

"Oh, Krystal's led a fabulous life," Carla says. "She grew up in South Africa and married a surfing legend. But if you really want to know what busy is like, try raising five kids."

"Well," Barbara says, "you also have a nanny."

"You did too," Carla says, "when your kids were in grade school."

"Do you and Bob have kids?" Krystal asks.

Usually, Jeannette says 'no' whenever anyone asks this question because it's the easiest answer. Telling the truth makes people uncomfortable and always, always changes everything. But tonight, she decides that these smug women with their fake smiles and pretentious lives need to feel uncomfortable. "We had a son." Her heart rises in her chest. Her voice sounds surprisingly sure and strong, but she keeps her eyes focused on the dark grain in the planked floor. "Zack died in an accident a little over a year ago."

"Oh, my goodness!" Carla puts a tiny, freckled hand on Jeannette's arm. "That's dreadful."

"I'm so sorry." Krystal's blue eyes are moist. She wraps her arms around Jeannette and then Barbara's arms are around all of them.

Jeannette holds her body completely still and waits as long as she can stand it before she says, "I need some air."

"We're smothering her," Barbara says, and they all step back. "How old was he, if you don't mind me asking. And we don't have to talk about it if you'd prefer not to."

"Nineteen. Almost twenty."

"I can't even imagine," Krystal says. "I need a Kleenex."

Carla passes around a box of tissues, and they all dab their eyes. Jeannette takes a tissue too although her eyes are bone dry.

"You sure you're okay?" Carla asks. "We're all good listeners."

"Thank you. I appreciate that." They stare at her expectantly. "Your margaritas are delicious. What kind of tequila do you use?"

"Cuervo's fine with me," Carla says. "But Doug's a tequila snob. He insists we use this artisanal mescal from Oaxaca." Carla pulls another bottle from the bar and shows off the label, then opens the freezer, fills the blender with ice, and squeezes limes. Barbara proclaims that Oaxaca was beautiful the last time they went, "before it got so violent with all that cartel stuff."

Krystal asks what they think about the Seaview gym because she's wondering if they should find another place to work out. "I've been trying to talk Greg into joining something a little more exclusive. We're thinking about the Pelican Bay Club."

"I bet that fight club gym would be fun," Carla says as she fills their glasses. "But Doug's completely against the idea of me joining. He claims it's for men only. Pretty chauvinistic if you ask me."

"We need to leave that business to the men," Barbara says, the voice of authority.

"I agree," Krystal says. "I'm not crazy about Greg going there to be honest. Some of those guys seem like thugs to me. The Seaview gym is convenient, but if they let homeless people hang around, I'm not interested in being a member there either. What do you think, Jeannette? Didn't Bob say that you teach there?"

"Not very often," Jeannette says, "and I've never noticed any homeless people." She could tell these women she'd fucked the blue tank top man in the backseat of her Suburban a few Sundays ago, make it clear it had been all her idea, that it wasn't the first time she'd had sex with a stranger, and it wouldn't be her last. That would rock them backwards in their stilettos. They would think she's a terrible person and they would be right, and they would feel sorry for Bob, which they should. She had no idea the guy in the blue tank top was living in his car—if that's even true. She doesn't want to talk about him though. She'll never see him again. Her rule is one and done.

They're no longer discussing him anyway. They seem to have also forgotten about her dead son and are now raving about some new chef at the Ritz-Carlton, arguing about where he worked last, talking over each other. They may not know what else to say to her since she's made it clear she doesn't want to talk about Zack.

She decides she'll get quietly and completely drunk, something she used to be really good at and hasn't done in a long time. She sips margaritas until dinner, when she switches to red wine. She offers no controversial opinions, although she finds much to disagree with, she flirts with each of the husbands just enough to be friendly, although she finds none of them remotely attractive. She pretends to be interested in every conversation no matter how trivial, smiling at the right moment until it feels like her lips are stuck to her teeth. But apparently, she's not even good at getting drunk anymore because when she and Bob finally say goodnight and walk out to their car, she feels sober.

"That was fun," Bob says as he opens the passenger door for her. "Aren't you glad we came? These are two-million-dollar homes, babe. Doug's done well for himself. And that was Greg Oppenheimer from those surf movies. These are great connections for us to make."

"They're arrogant," she says. "All they care about is their property values."

"I don't like the idea of that low-income housing project either."

"People who work in Wellington need to live somewhere they can afford."

"They can live out in Riverside," Bob says.

"And spend their lives on the freeway? Jesus, Bob. Listen to yourself."

"We lived where we could afford to live, we saved money, and then we moved here."

"Doug seems sleazy to me. That remark about helping him get around regulations was completely out of line. They're trying to use you."

"He was kidding, babe. The wives seem nice."

"I don't have anything in common with those women. They're obviously all Republicans."

"So what? I was a Republican when you met me."

"We voted for Bernie." They'd walked precincts with Zack, knocked on doors, put up campaign signs.

"Bernie lost." Bob starts the car and pulls away from the curb. "So did Hillary. The world's changed, babe. We need to change too."

"I told them about Zack."

He slams his foot on the brake. She jerks forward and braces her hands on the dashboard.

"What did you tell them?" he asks.

"That he's dead."

"Are you crying?" He touches her hand.

"No, I'm not crying." She pulls away from him. Maybe she is a little drunk. "They asked if I had children. What was I supposed to do? Lie and say no?"

"You are crying." His eyes flood with tears. "This is huge, babe. This could be the breakthrough we talked about in therapy."

"Therapy was a complete waste of money." She reaches in her bag for Kleenex and hands one to him.

He wipes his eyes. "You've never told anyone about Zack. You haven't said his name to me in months. I'm proud of you, Jeannette. I'm just sorry I wasn't there with you."

"Proud of me for what? Telling some random women who I'll never see again that I have a dead kid?"

"Did you say it like that?"

"How would you prefer I say it?"

"You really don't want to see them again?"

"No." She blows her nose. "I do not."

"You'll change your mind." He turns right toward the gate. "They asked me to join their service club."

Jeannette groans. "I knew this was a setup. How much is that going to cost us?"

"We can afford to contribute. I want to be part of something, babe; make some real friends. They do educational programs for young men in the community. Mentoring. That sort of thing. I thought you'd like that."

"Why, because we're *beach people* now? You expect me to forget about Zack. You already have."

"That's not fair." His jaw tightens, his big shoulders stiffen. "And you know it's not true."

He's right—what she said isn't fair or true and she should apologize right now, but she knows whatever she says won't sound like an apology. It's only a ten-minute drive back to their neighborhood, but it seems longer in the stony silence. "You're obviously angry," she says when they're finally home. "Why don't you just say whatever it is you're thinking?"

"We're both tired. I'm going to turn in." He heads down the hallway.

Not even a kiss good night, although she doesn't blame him. She takes her heels off and goes into the living room. The pieces they brought from their old place in Angel City look shabby and worn in comparison with Carla and Doug's stylish furniture. She picks up the photo on the shelf of her, Bob, and Zack tailgating at an Angels game, holding red cups of beer. She traces Zack's upper lip with her fingertip. He was just starting to change from boy to man before he got hit by that car.

Bob thinks she blames him for letting Zack drink, but he's wrong. She never agreed with his theory that since kids will drink anyway, they might as well drink at home, but she didn't stop Zack either. She turns the photo face down. Tomorrow she's teaching classes all over Citrus County. She will have to rush back and forth and eat her lunch on the freeway. The traffic coming home afterwards will be a nightmare. She should go to bed.

After Zack's funeral, she'd dreamed about him every night and felt him watching over her during the day, but she hasn't dreamed once since they moved into this house. She imagines him now, prowling around their old place, wondering why there are strangers living inside. She turns out the lights and carries her heels and her purse down the hall to the bedroom. Bob should be asleep by now or at least pretending to be.

CHAPTER FOURTEEN
KEITH NELSON

On Tuesday, the Fourth of July, Keith gets to the gym early. The parking lot is full of runners with race bibs for the 5K over on Main Street. The gym is busy too. Keith walks on the treadmill as he watches Fox and Friends on the TV screen. North Korea just launched a missile toward Japan. The world gets more messed up every day, but there's nothing he can do about it except keep his head down and try and take care of himself. He knows the routine that works for him. Put time in on the weight bench. Get plenty of cardio. Watch the sugar and carbs, beef up on protein. Drink lots of water. It took him awhile to figure this out.

After he jammed the pencil in that girl's eye in second grade, a psychiatrist prescribed pills that turned him into a slug. He put on weight and got in fights when kids teased him. He didn't know how to defend himself, so his dad took him off the pills and taught him a few moves. He got into more fights, defending Wayne mostly. He got expelled. He was ten.

His dad signed him up for wrestling after his release from the court-mandated farm, a scared-straight facility out in Blythe. "Give you some discipline," his dad said. Wrestling introduced him to a weight routine. He bulked up. He was twelve. His dad almost seemed proud of him.

After the first stupid robbery with Wayne, the routine made his time at the fire camp almost bearable and prepared him for the insane amount of energy required to clear brush in front of eighty-foot flames, beside men who were actual criminals and guards who were certifiably insane. He was eighteen.

By then, his dad was angry at him all the time. His mother was disappointed. Granny C wrote him letters, sent him books to read, took his phone calls. Her faith in him, plus his routine, carried him through his second time at fire camp after the even stupider robbery and a short stint in state prison after he hit one of the guards in the head with a shovel. The routine also kept his probation officer happy after his release. He was twenty-one.

And now he's twenty-four, his dad is still angry, his mother's even more disappointed, and he owes them a fortune in attorney fees and court charges. He'll be broke the rest of his life unless he finds a better paying job.

When he unplugs his cell phone from where it's charging on the floor next to him, an older woman with dyed hair and a know-it-all expression gives him the stink eye. "Why don't you charge your phone at home?"

"Because I'm not at home right now."

Her laugh is rude. "You're living in that Honda, aren't you?"

"That's none of your business."

The woman's voice gets louder. "I've lived in Wellington for twenty-five years, so it is my business."

"I'm a member," Keith says, his voice louder too. "I pay my dues."

Cliff, the club manager, races over and asks if everything's okay. "I'm fine," Keith says. "She's the one with the problem." He expects Cliff to defend him. They've always been friendly, sharing training tips and vitamin strategies. But now he realizes Cliff isn't talking to him, he's looking at the woman.

"You need to be more careful checking membership cards," she says. "This isn't a homeless shelter."

"How about a bottle of water?" Cliff says. "Nice and cold, from the fridge in my office." The woman mutters something under her breath and walks away.

"I'd like a bottle of water," Keith says.

"That's not the first complaint about you," Cliff says. "You need to keep a lower profile."

"I have a right to be here, same as anyone else."

"Your membership expires this month."

"No problem," Keith says. "I'll bring my credit card next time."

"I'll be waiting." Cliff turns and walks away.

Keith finishes his weight cycle and stretches out in a lounge chair outside by the pool. Today, Denise, a cute Asian girl with creamy skin, is teaching the Aqua Fit class to the grey hairs. Keith smiles at her, but she ignores him. After an hour, the seniors start their cool down stretches and then get out of the pool. It takes them awhile to put away their water weights and gather their towels. The class is more of a social hour than a real workout, but Keith likes how all the old people are friends. Once they're gone, he takes off his tank top, jumps in, does a few laps, and then goes in the locker room to shower.

After he's dressed and brushing his teeth, a middle-aged man stands behind him at the mirror, watching. Most of these guys act like the gym belongs to them. Keith guesses this one's a retired businessman, judging from the grey-flecked hair, rounded gut, and Surf Dog Brewery T-Shirt. Armani aftershave, like his dad wears.

"You're friends with Wayne Connor, aren't you?" the man asks. "The Wayne who drives the red F-150 with the big tires?"

Keith spits in the sink and rinses his toothbrush. "Who wants to know?"

"I'm Brian," the man says, offering his hand.

Brian's nails are manicured, and his hands look soft. Keith's never liked handshakes. Too many germs. He walks over to his locker and puts his toothbrush away in his shaving kit.

"Wayne's a good dude." Brian chuckles. "A little nuts though. I can't believe he took a dump right in front of the *Herald's* office after they wrote that editorial against the march."

Keith hasn't heard this, but he's not surprised. Wayne did the same thing in front of a girl's locker in high school when she wouldn't go out with him. Keith was sure no girl would want anything to do with Wayne after that. Instead, the truly psychotic girls were wild for him.

"What march?" he asks.

"You haven't heard?" Brian says. "It's 'Take Back America' Day."

"Trump won, didn't he? What's there to take back?"

Brian reaches into a bag on the floor and pulls out a stack of Make America Great Again hats, still in their plastic bags. "You hang out with Wayne at Cyclone's downtown, right?"

"Sometimes."

Brian holds out a hat. "If you wear this there next Sunday, it'll get you a free beer."

Keith thinks Trump's a blowhard with weird hair, if he thinks about him at all, but his dad hates the new president and he'd go ballistic if he saw Keith wearing this hat. "How much do you want for it?"

"It's yours," Brian says. "Try it on."

Free is free and if this guy knows Wayne, he's probably legit. Keith removes the plastic wrapping and widens the strap, then puts the hat on and adjusts the brim.

"It suits you," Brian says. "You look like a different man."

Keith agrees. Red's a good color for him, makes his eyes

bluer, and the hat frames his face so his jaw looks square. He feels different.

"You heading over to the pancake breakfast later?" Brian asks.

"I don't like pancakes. Too many carbs."

"You going to the parade?"

"I don't like parades either."

"Do you ever train with Wayne at the fight club gym?" Brian says.

Wayne keeps asking him to join, but the fight club gym doesn't have a shower. They have too many rules anyway. He'd have to cut his hair. "You ask a lot of questions," Keith says.

Brian shrugs. "Cyclone's. Sunday, July 16th. Be there around two."

Keith nods. He's not making any promises although he's always looking for something to do on Sundays. When he walks out of the locker room wearing the red hat, he likes how people react. Denise is talking with a woman from the Aqua Fit class. They both make a face, but most people nod in approval, which is different. It's like they've decided he might belong here after all.

He gets in his car and drives to the laundromat, which is empty except for a woman folding towels who frowns at his hat and a young guy washing mechanic uniforms who gives him a thumbs up. Keith buys a Gatorade at the liquor store next door and splurges on the latest Flex magazine. He likes the smell of bleach and fabric softener and watching his clothes toss in the dryer. When they're dry, he matches his socks, folds his T-shirts into flat squares, rolls his gym shorts so they don't take up as much room, hangs his dress pants, waits for his towels to finish drying, and loads his car.

If it weren't a holiday, he'd head over to his parents' house next. He always parks around the corner and double checks that their cars are gone before he goes inside the house. He makes a point of never being in their neighborhood when they're home and awake. He keeps expecting them to change the locks, but his mother props up whatever mail he gets on the table by the front door, so she obviously knows he comes by. He never stays long, never takes more than they'll notice is missing.

They obviously don't miss him.

They'll be home today for the holiday though, so he steers clear of their neighborhood and heads into the tract on the other side of Hefner Street instead. He parks under a tulip tree in front of a house with an empty driveway. Across the street, a gardener Keith recognizes pushes a mower up into the back of a wood slatted truck, toward a young boy standing in the truck bed. Gregorio has saved Keith from getting a ticket on street sweeping days more than once, and he knows everything about trees. "They communicate with each other," Gregorio told him once. "Underground, through their root systems. It's how they feed their saplings. They take care of each other, like family."

Not like my family, Keith thought. Gregorio was right, though, Keith used the library's Wi-Fi to look it up. He rolls down his window now. "You're working on the holiday?"

"Playing catch up," Gregorio says. "My helper was out sick this week. Got my son with me today. That's Gabriel." The young boy waves.

Keith waves back. "I like those trees you put in over on Evening Song."

Gregorio smiles. "The melaleucas. They're from Australia. They're beautiful, aren't they? Australian plants do really well here. I wish I could do more landscaping instead of just mow, blow, and go. Speaking of which, we'd better keep moving, Gabriel. Good to see you, Keith. Take it easy."

Yesterday's *Citrus County Register* is yellowing in the empty driveway. Keith gets out and stretches, then leans down and picks up the newspaper. A gray squirrel comes headfirst down the trunk of a tulip tree and charges out to the center of the lawn, chattering and snapping his bushy tail up and down. "What's your problem, dude?" Keith says. "No one cares about yesterday's news." The squirrel races to the side block wall and disappears.

He can pretend no one has seen him except the squirrel, but he knows better. Someone is always watching, and it's never safe to assume no one is home. When he was younger and didn't know any better, he'd followed Wayne over the cinderblock wall behind his parents' house, jumped down into Vickie Murdoch's backyard, and walked into her house through the open sliding glass door. Vickie's son busted them and told his parents. His mother said he'd humiliated them once again. His dad was happy for a reason to give Keith another beat down.

Just another day at the Nelsons.

He opens the newspaper looking for movie ads. *The Fate of the Furious* is playing at the AMC. There's a big color spread for Tuxedo Wine on the next page. He refolds the paper and puts it back in the driveway. He's not allowed in Tuxedo Wine anymore. He and Wayne had no idea the bottles they'd stuck down the front of their shorts were so expensive. They were only stocking up for a camping trip in the Sierras. Keith had no idea Wayne would drop everything, run out of the store, and leave him behind to explain.

He got locked up and Wayne went on the Sierra trip without him. That pissed him off, but later when he got out, Wayne came around to see him when no one else did. He and Wayne haven't been camping for a long time. Now that Wayne's married to Tina, she makes him rent an RV. He can afford it. The Citrus County Sanitation Department pays him enough and the benefits are good. Wayne's promised to get him on next time they're hiring.

His phone rings just before he starts the car.

"I've got some good news," Granny C says. "Fay got you a pass. You can visit me whenever you want."

Fay is the new caregiver. "How did you talk her into doing that? Isn't she going to tell my parents?"

"She's sworn to secrecy, Sonny. Come by tomorrow and pick it up. This afternoon I'm going to your parents' house. Your dad's cooking ribs. I'll bring some home for you. Some of your mother's potato salad too."

His mouth waters. He misses his dad's barbecue, his mother's cooking. "Thank you. I'll see you tomorrow then."

The movie's probably already started, but he doesn't care. He'll catch the ending and then watch it again.

CHAPTER FIFTEEN
RAY MURDOCH

Ray adjusts the brim of a combat green Vietnam Vet cap in the downstairs hallway mirror. He and Louie Garcia have been going to the Fourth of July flag raising ceremony in Dolphin Beach for a few years now. It's a way to pass the time on a way too noisy day. Dolphin Beach doesn't allow fireworks, unlike Wellington, which is a freaking battle zone weeks before the Fourth.

He and Louie never attended veterans ceremonies when they were first discharged. People called them baby killers and worse, so they put away their uniforms and stopped admitting they'd served. They were drinking buddies for years until they got into a dumb argument about something neither one of them can remember. They went their separate ways, reconnected in AA, and joined the Dolphin Beach Veterans group as a way to make amends. It was Louie's idea, and Ray was happy to tag along. He wouldn't be here if it weren't for Louie dragging his ass to the helicopter after he got shot in Loc Ninh.

He goes into the kitchen to tell his mother goodbye. "I'll be home early."

"Just in time for the shit show," she says. "Why don't you and Louie go to the movies tonight? That's when the fireworks will be worse."

"I don't like driving at night when there are fireworks going off all over the place. It's too distracting."

"Gets the dogs all riled up too. I'll be glad when this holiday is over."

He looks at his watch. He'd promised Louie he'd meet him there by six forty-five. "I should probably go."

"You look nice, son. I'm proud of you."

He blinks, not sure he's heard her right. "Thanks, Mom. You feel okay?"

"I'm not planning on dying today if that's what you mean. Tell Louie hello for me."

That was unexpected, he thinks as he drives up the coast highway toward Dolphin Beach, his mother, saying she's proud of him. He hopes she's okay. She's ninety-six and although her diabetes and blood pressure are mostly under control, she obviously won't last forever.

He and Louie park their cars on Ocean Avenue and walk down to the Dolphin Pier where a small crowd of veterans and civilians has already gathered. The flag goes up at 7:00 a.m. sharp, a Boy Scout plays "To the Colors" on a bugle, some congressperson Ray's never heard of thanks them for their service, and then he and Louie go out to breakfast at Denny's.

"I probably should have ordered oatmeal instead," Ray says after the waitress takes their menus.

"Live a little," Louie says. "It's a holiday. You can go back on the diet tomorrow."

"Kind of a small turnout today. Not as many of us Nam vets alive anymore. And the younger vets probably have better things to do on the Fourth of July."

"They get more respect than we ever did. Hopefully, that'll change with Trump."

Ray shakes his head. He knows Louie's pulling his chain. "Trump doesn't give a shit about veterans. He was a draft dodger."

"So what?" Louie says. "Obama wasn't in the military either. Neither was Clinton."

Ray pours cream in his coffee. "I guess it's just dumb fucks like us who get drafted."

"Nobody gets drafted anymore either." Louie puts three teaspoons of sugar in his coffee. "You give any more thought to joining that writing group I told you about?"

Louie's writing poetry these days with a group that meets at some coffee shop in Buena Loma. He keeps pestering Ray to come with him. "It's great therapy," Louie says like he does every time he brings it up. "It's good to get the feelings out and down on the page."

Ray thinks feelings are better left inside and unsaid. "I don't know jack shit about poetry, and I doubt you do either."

Louie laughs. "I'm not saying I'm a poet, not like the other people in the group. There's this young chick who's flat out incredible. I wish I could write like she does."

"How old is she?"

"I don't know. Old enough to drive. She comes by herself in one of those new VW bugs. A green one. I don't remember VWs ever being that color."

"I hope you aren't flirting with her. Women these days don't have much of a sense of humor about that stuff. They don't like to be called chicks either. You've heard about Me Too, haven't you?"

"Oh, give me a break. She's just a kid. And I like the stuff she writes. You should come with me."

"I'm not interested in hearing some teenager moan about her feelings."

Louie's lips tighten. "It's not like that. I wish you'd be a little more open minded."

"That's pretty rich coming from a Republican."

"See? That right there is not an open-minded statement. We got to do something to keep our minds sharp."

"I do the crossword puzzle every day. That keeps my brain alive."

Louie chuckles. "That and trying to figure out what to do with possums that aren't exactly dead."

"I never should have told you about that. I just got frustrated."

Louie raises his coffee cup. "I hear you, buddy. I get that way too."

The waitress brings his Grand Slam and Louie's pancakes. Ray keeps his head down so he doesn't have to watch his friend eat. Louie doesn't have many teeth left and watching him gum pancakes isn't at all appetizing. Louie's a good man though, even if he is a Republican. It's not his fault the VA has terrible dental insurance. Louie even grabs the bill when the waitress brings it.

"You don't have to do that," Ray says.

Louie takes a big gulp of coffee and grins. Thankfully, the pancakes are no longer clinging to his teeth. "You've been fronting me for months. The movie's my treat today too. I finally got paid." Louie has an upholstery business that's struggled for years, but he's hooked up with an antique store that's kept him busy redoing chairs for some tech guy who's refurbishing a Victorian house up in the hills. "Used to be Victorian furniture was dirt cheap," Louie says. "Now it's what they call trendy."

"Trendy, huh," Ray says. "Everything comes back in style. Even Volkswagen bugs. We'll all be wearing bell bottoms again before you know it."

Louie laughs and takes the check up to the register. They drive their cars over to the AMC for the two-movies-for-the-price-of-one veterans deal. They sit next to the aisle because each of them will have to get up a few times. After *Wonder Woman* finishes, they move to the theatre next door and wait for *Fate of the Furious* to start.

"That last movie was pretty good," Ray says.

Louie snorts. "You slept through most of it. You want some popcorn?"

"We just had breakfast. How can you be hungry?"

"I got a hollow leg, I guess. I'll be right back."

Ray glances around the nearly empty theatre. There's one family sitting behind them with three small children and a man sitting closer to the screen wearing a red baseball cap. *Interesting*, Ray thinks, *a guy sitting alone on a holiday. Maybe he's a vet too.*

Louie comes down the aisle whistling and stops to clown around with the kids. The guy in the hat turns around. It's one of those Trump caps and Ray realizes with a start that the man wearing it is Keith Nelson. Ray lifts his hand, but Keith turns back around before he sees him. He wouldn't have guessed Keith would be a Trumpster. The movie starts as Louie sits down. He'll go say hello after the film.

■ ■ ■

Louie nudges him awake. "You missed the best part," he says. Ray stretches and stands. The theatre is empty. The sun is bright when they go outside. "Guess I'll head on back to the trailer park," Louie says. "Watch the Twilight Zone marathon until I fall asleep. Think about the writers' group. We meet at Coffee and Words next Wednesday afternoon."

"I'll think about it."

"No, you won't."

Ray laughs, and they shake hands and go their separate directions.

When he turns into his track the neighbor kid, Josh, is riding his skateboard down the middle of the street. He wishes the boy would at least wear a helmet. Josh glances over his shoulder and lifts his chin at Ray, then rolls his board up on the sidewalk. Ray waves as he passes him and watches in his rearview mirror as Josh turns into Paradise Court and up Lisa Kensington's driveway where a bottle-green VW bug is parked. The poet girl Louie mentioned drives one of those. He hopes Louie isn't making a fool of himself with that group. People don't always appreciate Louie's sense of humor.

Ray pulls his car into his garage and gets out, flinching as a string of firecrackers pops off in the distance. Better go inside before it gets worse, he tells himself. And then there's a huge explosion that sounds like it's right underneath his feet. "Motherfucker," he yells, leaping forward. All the neighborhood dogs howl. He tells himself to breathe and think about something else. Louie writing poetry. Those hash browns from breakfast.

When the second explosion goes off, Ray gets angry and decides to go have a little conversation with whoever these suckers are. They could at least wait until after the sun goes down. He marches down his street and around the corner. Summertime Lane is quiet though, and he feels foolish. What was he going to do anyway? Charge up to some little kids and scream at them? He hears a helicopter. Police or news, he can't tell from here. He turns around to go home and sees Joni Gorman getting out of a white Acura further down the street.

She visors her hand over her eyes. "Is that you, Ray?"

Neil Gorman named his daughter after Joni Mitchell, but other than the blond hair and blue eyes, there's no resemblance to the folk singer at all. Neil's Joni has always seemed hellbent on being the complete opposite of her rock and roll parents. She got a degree in business and a management job at a credit union. Neil used to laugh about how she'd saved every penny anyone had ever given her. "She sure didn't get that from us," Neil said.

Ray thinks he should at least go say hello. He barely got to talk to Joni or Neil at Stephanie's funeral. The helicopter circles over Eckerd Street. WBPD. Hopefully here to shut down these damn fireworks.

"Good to see you, Ray," Joni says when he gets closer.

"How's your dad doing?" Ray asks.

"He's okay. Not very happy with where he's living right now, I'm afraid. I found a better place, but it's really expensive. . . ."

Joni's lips are moving, but the helicopter overhead, chopping up the air, drowns out whatever she's saying. Ray looks up at the blades circling above him. There's nothing but white noise for a second. Joni's face comes back into focus.

"You all right, Ray? You're a little pale."

"I didn't hear what you said before." For a minute there, he was right back in Nam.

"Want to come inside for a minute?" she asks. "Get away from all this noise? I could use your opinion on a few things anyway."

There's obviously still something wrong with his ears. No one's asked his opinion in a long time. "Sure," he says. He watches the helicopter circle back toward Eckerd Street as Joni struggles with the key. Catching his breath, he surveys Neil's yard. If the grass had more water and some fertilizer, it would green up. The roof looks old though, original wood shingles, and the house needs paint. The helicopter moves on.

Up closer, Joni's a good-looking, take-charge kind of woman in her fitted white jeans and crisp denim shirt. He guesses she's fifty-something; too young for him, not that he's interested. Her fingernails and toes are painted blood red and she's wearing too much makeup for his taste, but he admires the effort.

Ray hasn't been inside the Gormans' house in a while. The upright piano sits in the same corner. There are two ratty recliners in front of an old television, and the carpet is a faded navy blue with yellow stains in every corner. From Stephanie's cat, he assumes.

"What ever happened to Ringo?"

"He's my cat now," Joni says. "And just like my dad, he's not happy with where he's living either."

"So how can I help you?" Ray hopes she isn't going to ask him to move anything. He should have mentioned his bad back earlier.

"You've lived in this neighborhood a long time. I need a reality check. The realtor wants me to make all kinds of changes. She's insisting we need a new carpet."

"It is kind of an unusual color." Ray sniffs. Definitely eau de cat. "You should probably ask someone else though. I'm no expert. You're selling the house?"

Joni nods. "Whoever buys this place is going to change everything anyway, right?"

"Like I said, I'm no expert." Ray studies the posters on the walls. All the bands Neil opened up for at clubs all over the country. "Quite a bit of music history here." He stops in front of a John Prine poster. He remembers going to this show at the Grizzly Bear. Jill held his hand when Prine played "Sam Stone."

"You should take some of those posters home," Joni says. "I'm sure my dad would love for you to have them."

Ray almost laughs, imagining his mother's reaction. "We don't have room. You could sell them on eBay. Probably get ten bucks a pop for them anyway."

Joni's eyes dart around the room, calculating potential profits. "That's a great idea."

"I'd give you ten bucks for this one." He pulls his wallet out of his pants pocket and takes out a ten.

"Did you want the frame too?" Joni says. "I'm sure that's worth another ten dollars."

He has another ten in his wallet but Christ, what a cheapskate.

"The realtor expects me to paint too," Joni says. "She says we need a clean slate so buyers can imagine themselves living here."

"Sounds like good advice." He's still holding the ten-dollar bill.

Joni frowns, making tiny little wrinkle marks in between her eyebrows. "I guess I could have an estate sale." She points to the recliner with the purple afghan. "My mom died in that chair. How much do you think I could get for it?"

"No idea." Ray tries not to visualize Stephanie sitting there with Ringo chewing on her hand. The cat piss smell is overwhelming, and he feels his Grand Slam breakfast come up in the back of his throat. "I should get going."

Joni follows him out to the front porch. "I've heard these houses are selling for nearly a million dollars these days."

"That should be enough for a nice place for your dad."

The little wrinkles appear again in Joni's forehead. "Not if he lives much longer. Dementia care facilities are outrageously expensive. Besides, this is supposed to be my inheritance."

Not just cheap, cold hearted too. "What realtor are you using?"

"Lisa Kensington at Sandcastle. You know her?"

He almost smiles. That annoying newsletter woman. "She seems pretty sharp."

"She's charging me six percent, so she'd better be sharp."

Lisa and Joni might deserve each other, two bean counters, focused on the bottom line. Poetic justice, Louie might say. Ray puts the ten-dollar bill back in his pocket. That poster will only remind him of things he's worked too hard to forget. There's another explosion. Sounded like it came from Paradise Court. He hopes Josh isn't over there blowing up his fingers with the Kensington kids. "I'd better get home, Joni. Happy Fourth."

He walks around the corner and eyeballs his mother's house, trying to imagine it with a buyer's eyes. The roof's okay. The grass is green. The house could use some paint though. What sounds like endless rounds of mortar pops off behind him and he hurries inside.

SANDCASTLE REALTY

LISA KENSINGTON

Prestige Haven Homes,
Where Your Home Is Your Castle

JULY 7, 2017 | (800) WB4-EVER lisa.kensington@Sandcastlerealty.com

QUESTIONS TO CONSIDER REGARDING THE RIPTIDE

Should government agencies function as land-lords? Should the state mandate how much housing we need in Wellington Beach? Where will those people park? What is the impact on fire, police, sewage, schools, and CRIME? We've all worked hard and saved money to afford our homes. This housing project is un-fair and unwise.

Helpful Household Tips

> ❝ *Keep cockroaches out of your home by closing gaps around windows and doors with weatherstripping and sealing up cracks with caulk.* ❞

In Case You Didn't Know

The Wellington City Council has pur-chased the Riptide apartment building on Eckerd Street and plans to tear it down and build a high rise for low-income people, financing the project with government funds.

High-rise as in four stories, tower-ing above the single-family homes in the Prestige Haven tract, allowing private backyards to be on full display. Why didn't the city council request input from the residents before making this decision? We want answers.

WELLINGTON BEACH IS SPECIAL

Wellington is a shining example of life the way it used to be in California. Cruising down Coast Highway in a convertible, spending the day on the beach in the surf, sun, and sand. Watching the sunset from the pier. Living free and easy. There's no reason for all of this to change.

Low-income housing belongs in some other city, definitely not Welling-ton. Please attend next Monday's City Council meeting and let them know how you feel. 6 p.m. sharp.

CHAPTER SIXTEEN

LISA KENSINGTON

Lisa puts together a green chile enchilada casserole for dinner as she listens to Eric try to convince Tyler to go with him to see John Fogerty at the Citrus County Fair next week. "Front row seats," Eric says. "My dad took me to see Creedence when I was your age."

"Never heard of him," Tyler says.

"You've never heard of John Fogerty?" Eric's voice gets more nasal when he's agitated. "I've obviously failed you as a father. John Fogerty is a rock god."

"Rock isn't even your generation, Dad. You're not a boomer."

"Well, what kind of music should I be listening to? What do you like, son?"

"Stuff you've never heard of."

"Try me."

"Kendrick Lamar. Chance the Rapper. Lil Wayne."

"I never heard of any of them."

"My point exactly."

Poor Eric, Lisa thinks as she hears a car horn beep. Tyler comes through the kitchen. "I'm out of here, Mom. Party at Leslie's tonight after the beach bonfire."

"Be nice to your dad," she says.

He grins. "I'm nice."

"When do we get to meet Leslie?"

"We'll see." Tyler kisses the top of her head and is gone.

When Eric joins her in the kitchen Lisa holds out her arms. "I'll go see John Fogerty with you," she says as she pulls him close.

Eric kisses her neck. "I wish Tyler and I had more in common."

"He's just going through a stage." She should ask Eric if he's talked to Tyler about the pot smoking, but he looks too crushed right now. She turns back to her casserole. "So how was your day?" she asks, although she never really listens when he talks about work. She hates bugs and hearing about all the chemicals his employees use to kill the bugs. She thinks about her essay instead. She'll take one more look after dinner and send it off to the *Wellington Herald*.

"I might hire a few more ex-cons," Eric is saying.

"I didn't know you hired ex-cons." She sets the oven temperature dial to three seventy-five. "Is that a good idea?"

"It's a state program." Eric takes a beer out of the fridge. "The Bug Guy gets a tax credit. Like I was saying, this guy Keith? He's a great employee. You might know his parents. The Nelsons? Over on Beverly Court?"

Eric reaches for a slice of cheese and Lisa swats his hand away. "Don't spoil your dinner. I don't like the idea of an ex-con living in our neighborhood."

"Keith's served his time. No harm in giving him a second chance. He's a super nice guy."

"You think everyone is super nice." Lisa opens the oven door. "Have I met him before?"

"You'd remember him if you had. He looks like the strong man from the circus."

"What does that mean?" She slides the casserole in the oven.

"Big arms. Gigantic." Eric sips his beer. "He could give Schwarzenegger a run for his money."

"Does he drive a grey Honda? Because I might have seen him parked on Mountain Brook, sound asleep. Don't you want a glass for your beer?"

"Bottle's fine. Why was he asleep in his car?"

"I have no idea. He left as soon as I tapped on his window."

Mid-swallow, Eric spits out his beer. "You tapped on his window?"

"I knew he didn't belong there, and I told him so."

"You need to be careful, honey." He reaches for a paper towel.

"I thought you said he was a good guy."

"Maybe it wasn't Keith! You can't go around challenging people, especially when you're alone. This is a crazy world."

"Don't be silly. It was broad daylight. Whoever he was, he left right away. The signs posted on Mountain Brook are very clear. Parking is only for the people who live here. It's going to be worse if that housing project is approved. There's nowhere near enough parking planned. Those people will be leaving their cars in front of our house. I'm writing an essay about it."

Eric wipes his mouth, obviously trying not to laugh. Lisa feels her blood pressure rise. "What's so funny about me writing an essay?"

"Those people are never going to park in front of our house, hon. Our cul-de-sac is too far away from that building."

"Don't change the subject."

"I'm proud of you, honey. I love your little bulletins."

"They're newsletters, and you've never read one of them." Lisa glances at the oven. She forgot to set the timer and can't remember how long the casserole has been in there—fifteen seconds or fifteen minutes? "I want a beer."

"That was the last one. I'll go check the garage fridge. Where's Monique tonight?"

"Dinner at Brittany's house. Again."

"Before I forget, Susan called me today. She wondered if you've had a chance to look for Mom's pearls."

"I'm sick of hearing about those pearls. Betsy probably lost them a long time ago."

Eric raises both hands. "Don't shoot the messenger." He goes out in the garage.

When she'd stopped by the Assistance League yesterday, there were no pearls in the jewelry case. "They're very popular with young brides these days," the volunteer said. "All the rage." Which means Monique will probably want pearls whenever she gets married.

Lisa sighs. Something else to feel guilty about. She glances at her wedding photo in the hutch. Monique was right, she doesn't look like that person in the photograph anymore. She shouldn't have a beer. She needs to go on a diet. Why does she make such fattening meals? Eric doesn't need extra calories either. No one appreciates her efforts. The kids don't confide in her anymore. Monique's mooning over some boy who probably doesn't even know she exists, and Tyler is out breaking poor Leslie's heart, whoever she is.

"You're in luck." Eric holds up a six pack of IPAs. "I didn't mean to insult you, honey. I'd love to see your essay. And I'll have a talk with Keith tomorrow."

"One beer. That's it. I'm starting a diet tomorrow."

"Why?" he asks. "I like you exactly the way you are. You don't need to diet."

She smiles in spite of herself. Sometimes Eric knows the right thing to say.

CHAPTER SEVENTEEN

KEITH NELSON

The red hat is lucky, Keith decides. Fay the caregiver agrees to let him visit Granny C while she goes grocery shopping. He gets green lights all the way to the freeway on his way to work, doesn't have to wait for any of the weight machines at the gym, or argue with any cops about parking his car in the library lot. Even the customers at work are less obnoxious. He knows better than to wear the hat in the office though. Eric seems like a liberal type.

This morning, as he parks in the Bug Guy's lot, Grace is waiting for him. "Another day, another donut," she says, holding up a pink bakery box. "You can have first choice. As long as you don't take the maple bar. That's Eric's favorite."

"I try to stay away from sweets."

"You're so disciplined," Grace says. "I could stand to be a little stricter."

Keith nods. Grace could stand to be a lot stricter. She's not a bad looking woman though, and she owns her own condo. She might even let him park in her driveway at night if he asked, but then he'd have to explain his situation. He's not that desperate yet.

"Eric's on a diet too," she says. "He keeps telling me to stop bringing in donuts, but he always eats them."

"Carbs are addictive," Keith says, although he knows no response is actually required. Grace will continue talking whether he says anything or not, popping from one random subject to another.

"Eric's mother's funeral is going to be on a boat," Grace says. "She's been cremated. I'm thinking I might do that too. What do you think about cremation?" As usual, she doesn't give him a chance to answer. "Are you Catholic? I was raised Catholic. I think they're okay with cremation now. I've been to funerals where there's an urn instead of a casket, but it's awkward." Grace launches into a detailed description of all the different urns Eric has ordered ("from Amazon? Can you believe that?"), the boat Eric rented and how much it cost ("not that Eric told me," Grace adds, "but I googled it.") She says Eric's sister Susan is coming out for the ceremony and they're going to the Flying Fish Oyster Bar on Pelican Island for lunch afterwards. "Susan isn't even staying with them this time," Grace adds, "although she normally does. And please don't repeat any of this."

Keith nods.

"Susan doesn't want to stay anywhere near the pool where her mother died. It breaks my heart, thinking about Eric's poor kids having to look at the swimming pool every day where their granny drowned. If I were Eric, I'd move. Although, and please don't tell anyone I said this, they spent way too much money remodeling that house. You would not believe how many hours he was on the phone talking to his contractor. Although I really shouldn't have said that, so please don't tell anyone I did."

"Okay."

"Just between you and me, I actually think Eric is addicted to spending money. He gets every catalog you can think of here at the office, probably so his wife doesn't know. Sharper Image, Brookstone, Land's End. Some I've never even heard of. And every time I go in his office, he's got Amazon up on his computer screen and two or three credit cards out on his desk. He usually says he's buying something for his kids, but I really think most of what he orders is for himself."

It must be nice to be Eric with money to burn. "How old are his kids?" Keith asks.

"His son is a sophomore and his daughter's a junior," Grace says. "That's why I feel so bad for them. I can't imagine going through a tragedy at that age. High school was the best time of my life. I'm sure that was true for you as well."

Keith isn't sure what he'd call the best time of his life, but it certainly wasn't high school. "I changed schools a lot. We'd better clock in."

■ ■ ■

It's barely a half-hour later when Keith looks up from his desk at Grace heading straight toward him. "Eric wants to see you in his office."

"About what?" Eric's never called him in the office before.

Grace smiles, which is a good sign, he decides. Grace doesn't look worried, and she always knows everything that's going on, so she would know if he's in trouble. He thinks about recent customer calls as he walks to the office, trying to remember if anyone has been particularly angry or more upset than usual. When he knocks on Eric's open door, Eric says "Sit down," without looking up, which is probably not a good sign.

Keith takes a deep breath. The thing to do is not get defensive. He glances around the room. A half-eaten maple bar sits on a napkin near Eric's phone. There's a Sharper Image catalog open next to the computer and, just like Grace said, two credit cards by his coffee cup. The family photo on the shelf behind Eric is framed in a nice wood, cherry maybe.

The wife looks familiar for some reason. At least neither kid inherited Eric's giant crooked nose. The son looks like a typical jock, but something in the daughter's eyes makes Keith think she's smart. It would be smart of him to say something, instead of just sitting here. "Nice-looking family."

Eric glances up from the folder on his desk. "What?"

The folder has Keith's name on it. It's his personnel folder. Is he getting fired? "In the photo," Keith says. "Your kids look like athletes."

"Wrestling and water polo. My wife says she saw you parked in our neighborhood on Wednesday. You want to tell me what that's about?"

Shit, Keith thinks. *Eric lives in my parents' neighborhood?* "Wednesday's my day off."

"I know when your day off is."

Keith swallows and glances back at the woman's face in the photo. Glossy hair, know it all expression. She's the woman who told him not to park on Summertime Lane. "My parents live on Beverly Court. I didn't know you lived in their tract."

"We've lived on Paradise Court for almost twenty years." Eric taps the folder. "You don't live on Beverly Court with your parents anymore?"

"No sir. I'm in Garden City now." He will be, eventually.

"You need to put in a change of address then. Update your file."

The man's nose is so misshapen it's almost like a kid's cartoon drawing. How can he breathe out of that thing? "My mail goes to my parents. The mailbox where I live is a big mess."

"So, you were picking up your mail when my wife saw you?"

"I really don't remember seeing your wife, sir. I have to wait for my mother sometimes. She changed her work schedule and I keep missing her."

"You don't have a key?"

"No, sir. They're in process of getting me a new one."

"Why don't you park in front of your parents' house?"

"Their neighbors have a lot of cars. You know how it is in a cul-de-sac. My dad doesn't like me parking in the driveway. Accord's dripping a little oil."

"You need to get that fixed. You need to watch where you park too. My wife's a stickler for rules. You might get your car towed."

"Not if I'm sitting in it."

Eric looks confused. "Was that supposed to be a joke?"

"No, sir. I always stay in my car."

"You just sit there? And do what?"

"I like the trees."

"You like what?"

This is how he gets himself in trouble, not thinking before he speaks, saying the first thing that pops into his head. "The crepe myrtles," he says. "They're my favorite. They need to be cut back every year, but if you cut them back too far, they don't bloom." Eric looks lost. "My grandmother knows a lot about plants. I've picked up names of trees and stuff from her."

"You spend your day off sitting in your car, looking at trees?"

"Oh no, not the whole day. Just while I'm waiting for my mother." There's no way Eric believes any of this. "Please tell your wife I'm sorry. I didn't mean to bother her."

"Sounds like you've got a lot of mess in your life, Keith. Oil leaks, your mother tells you to come by when she's not home, you don't have a key, and you can't get your mail where you live. Meanwhile, you're staring at trees and pissing off my wife. You need to straighten yourself out."

"I'll do that, sir." He stands. Is he fired or not?

"We took a chance hiring you. Don't make me regret it."

"I won't, sir."

Eric finally smiles. "You can call me Eric."

"Yes, sir. Eric." It sounds like he still has a job, for now anyway.

"I have a question for you," Eric says.

"Fire away," Keith says and realizes he shouldn't have used the word fire. "Ask me anything."

"You probably heard about my mother's accident."

"Yes, sir. Sorry for your loss."

"It was on a Wednesday."

"Okay," he says, not liking where this is going.

"You ever see anything unusual when you're sitting out there on Wednesday? Any strange people walking around my neighborhood?"

"No, sir. I don't always park in your neighborhood."

"You like the trees in other neighborhoods too?"

Why did he tell Eric about the trees? Stupid, stupid, stupid. "The tulip trees over by Saint Benedict are cool. Hummingbirds love them."

"Hummingbirds?" Eric looks at him as if he isn't speaking English. "I don't follow. Do you have any friends who live in those apartment buildings? Maybe someone you knew from when you were, you know, locked up?"

Because of course all ex-cons keep in contact with each other. "No. Why do you ask?"

"The police wanted to know if we'd seen any suspicious people in the neighborhood."

Like me, you mean. "Wasn't it an accident? What happened to your mother, I mean?"

"Yeah, it probably was. It was a big shock, losing her like that. Just trying to put the pieces together."

"I'm sorry for your loss," Keith says again. He's not sorry. He'd like to tell Eric to go fuck himself.

"Thanks," Eric says. He picks up the Sharper Image catalog. "I'm thinking about installing a security system.

There are some awesome smartphone apps available now. Wide-angle lenses, night vision, live video."

Was that a warning?

"So, tell me a little bit about yourself, Keith." Eric glances at the folder on his desk. "You were a firefighter, weren't you? For the Department of Forestry? Is that why you like trees so much?"

"I went to Conservation Camp twice." He loved trees before he went to camp. Camp was where he learned to respect them.

"I like that program," Eric says. "Seems like a good opportunity to do some meaningful work. Give back."

Both judges said the same thing when they sentenced him. Keith liked the work though. He'd felt respected. "It was brutal."

"That explains why you're in such good shape. What else do I need to know about you, Keith? Any hobbies? What kind of music do like?"

"Music?"

"My son is really into rap. Is that what you like too?"

What the fuck? Whatever I say will be the wrong answer anyway. "No, sir. I like metal. Metallica. Queens of the Stone Age."

Eric grins. "I love rock and roll. I don't understand rap at all."

"Okay." Eric looks at him expectantly. *Does he want to know my favorite color too?* "I should go back to work," Keith says.

"You should probably find someplace else to park. My wife's kind of a rulemonger."

"I will, sir."

"You can call me Eric. After all, you're part of our Bug Guy family now."

What a hypocrite, pretending this place is a family.

134

He calls Granny C on his lunch break and tries to tell her what happened. "It's none of his business what I do on my day off or where I park."

"Honey," she says. "You can't blame people for not wanting you to park in front of their houses. He's your boss and you're lucky to have that job. Did you need something else? Fay is taking me to get a pedicure and then I'm taking her to lunch."

He needs someone to agree with him. It used to be her, but now she has Fay.

"No," he says. "You go have fun."

CHAPTER EIGHTEEN
JOSH KOWALSKI

Josh leans into the train of shopping carts, pushing his one hundred twenty-five pounds forward, trying to get enough momentum so the carts will make it over the speed bump. He watches a black Suburban turn into the Albertsons shopping center. The woman driving is on her phone, but she sees him and slows down. He recognizes her—the blond with the big boobs who lives further down his street. He banks the carts to the left and they line themselves up in the corral in front of the store.

Success! he thinks, until he glances over his shoulder. There are already five abandoned carts in the lot. He could retrieve them now or go back in the store and leave them for the other box boy, Adam. The black Suburban parks near CVS. Josh waits for the woman to get out. Today she's wearing a pink top and pink leggings with a swirled pattern. Josh likes the way the swirls move on her ass as she walks away from him.

Inside the store, the lead checker, Darlene, who is technically his boss even though everyone in the store acts like they're his boss, waves him over to register six, where a blue-haired woman stands, clinging to a shopping cart. Darlene hands him a large carton of original Quaker Oats. "Can you exchange this for instant?"

"I'm so sorry," the blue-haired woman says. "I got the wrong kind. I can't cook oatmeal on my stove top. My daughter only lets me use the microwave. She worries too much if you ask me, but . . ."

Darlene cuts her off. "Aisle twelve, Josh, near the end cap. Hurry back. And if you see Adam, tell him to get his butt back up here. I've already paged him twice."

"I'll look for him," Josh says. Adam is easily distracted, especially when he doesn't take his Adderall. A customer will ask him where the instant pudding mix is and he'll disappear down an aisle, gone so long the customer gives up and decides to get ice cream instead. Josh heads down aisle twelve as Mrs. Kensington turns the corner and pushes her cart straight toward him.

"Hi there, Josh," she says. "Do you know where the frozen meatballs are?"

"No, sorry. I usually work outside. But I can go ask." He grabs a container of instant Quaker Oats. "I need to take this to Darlene. She has a customer waiting."

Mrs. Kensington frowns. "They should give you some kind of orientation. I mean, I'm sure you get lots of questions. I'm not complaining. It just doesn't seem fair to you, is all I'm saying."

"It's all right. Darlene knows where everything is. I'll be right back." He starts up the aisle toward the registers when Mrs. Kensington says, "Wait a sec, Josh. Do you know Monique's boyfriend? She won't tell me a thing."

Josh stops so quickly his knees lock. The store aisles narrow and feel even more claustrophobic than before. Of course, Monique has a boyfriend. Normal kids are out living their lives, not wasting their summer working in some stupid store. "Monique hardly ever talks to me."

"Oh, I'm sure that's not true. You kids have known each other since grade school. You were at my house yesterday. It sounded like she was making plans for today. Who is he?"

"I don't know." *Probably one of the varsity wrestlers,* he thinks, *or a football player.* "I need to get back up front or Darlene will be mad."

Yesterday when he stopped by to visit Tyler, he'd walked by the open door of Monique's bedroom. She and Brittany were writing the words Love Trumps Hate on a purple poster board. "What's that for?" he'd asked. "Nothing to see here, Cart Boy," Brittany said as she slammed the door in his face. Josh read online later about a 'Take Back America' protest going on at the pier today at three o'clock and figured that's what the sign was for.

"I wish Monique wasn't so secretive about everything," Mrs. Kensington is saying. "But I'm sure I don't have to tell you about teenage girls and their secrets, Josh. You must have a string of sweethearts as good-looking and hardworking as you are."

"Not really," he says, moving out of the way of a shopping cart pushed by an older man in a Dodgers cap. "I'll go ask about the meatballs."

"Aisle six," the man in the Dodgers cap says. "By the ice cream. Which doesn't make any sense at all." He glares at Josh as if this is his fault.

"By the ice cream?" Mrs. Kensington says. "I never would have guessed." She wheels her shopping cart around and heads off in the opposite direction.

"Where are you hiding the Cream of Wheat?" Dodgers Cap asks.

Josh has been asked this question before and knows exactly where the Cream of Wheat is, which earns him a small smile from the old man. He hurries back to Darlene's register with the oatmeal.

The customer beams. "You found it!"

"Can you help her load her car?" Darlene says.

They walk at a glacier's pace out to the parking lot. "I left my walker in the trunk," the woman says. "I hope you don't mind putting the groceries in the backseat." She watches him load her bags and then says she has something for him.

"You really don't need to give me anything." Josh says as he glances around the parking lot, planning on which carts to retrieve first, but mostly trying to figure out what kind of guy Monique would like. She never seems impressed with anyone.

It takes the woman forever to get her wallet out of her purse. Her spotted hands shake as she hands him two crumpled dollar bills. "Thanks for finding the right kind of oatmeal. My daughter will be happy." She gets in the car, slams the door, and backs up without even looking in her rearview mirror. Thankfully, no other cars are coming down the aisle. He'll be lucky if he doesn't get run over this summer by some old person.

For the rest of his shift, Josh wonders who Monique is meeting and finally decides he'll just go downtown when he gets off work and find out. He has a story figured out to tell his mom by the time he gets home, but he hesitates when he finds her in the backyard, curled up on the lounge chair reading a book. He hates to bother her on her day off, but it's almost two-thirty now and if he doesn't leave soon, the protest might be over before he gets there.

As he slides the screen door open, a mourning dove flies straight out of the basket hanging under the eave, nearly sideswiping his face.

His mom laughs. "They're trying to make a nest in my string of pearls."

The dove sits on the cable wire and stares down at him. "That's not a good place for a nest," Josh says.

"They're not always smart about picking a place to raise a family. How was work?"

"Could you drop me off at the library? I'm meeting some friends. I can get a ride home."

She looks surprised. "The library? Really?"

"We're going to compare notes on the reading list for fall. I want to make a good start in September."

She smiles as she gets up. "I like this idea, Josh. Let me put some shoes on and we can go." When he grabs his skateboard, she frowns. "Why do you need that?"

"We might skate around the library parking lot afterwards."

"Which friends are these?"

"Monique and Brittany. Some other kids too."

She looks confused. "They're older than you are."

He shrugs. "They're Junior Ambassadors." When she raises her eyebrows, he goes on. "It's some program to help kids get ahead." This part is true, although Monique and Brittany are only ambassadors for the freshmen girls joining their water polo team.

"I've always liked Monique," his mom says. "But I thought you were more friends with Tyler."

"Tyler's not much of a reader."

"Those girls ride skateboards?" He hadn't expected this question but then she says, "Good for them. Girls are so athletic these days. I never was."

He takes one of his dad's baseball caps off the coat tree by the door, the one from a Los Lobos concert, black with a grinning wolf, and follows her out to her car. When she pulls up in front of the library, Josh already has the door open, skateboard ready, backpack slung over his shoulder.

"You'd better call me if you can't get a ride home, Josh."

"I will. Thanks for the ride." He's out of the car before she can say what he knows she wants to say—that she'll wait until he's sure his friends are here. He slams the door and runs toward the library. Just before he goes in, he turns and waves because of course she's still sitting there. He gives her a thumbs up and goes inside, praying she'll leave and not park the car and follow him inside. He feels bad about lying to her, but he's going to be a sophomore in September, and she needs to stop babying him. He walks to the magazine racks, finds the latest issue of *Guitar Player*, and sits down where he can watch the door. After five minutes, he figures it's safe to leave. She's gone.

It's two miles from the library to downtown. Main Street is clogged with people. He slides his board behind camera crews from Channel 7 and Channel 11 and snakes his way through a group of muscled men wearing red MAGA hats. A lot of people are carrying 'Take Back America' signs. Some wear shirts with the initials RAM, which Josh thinks at first means they're Rams football fans, but there's a tree with some kind of telephone pole running through the middle. When he looks closer, he realizes it's a sword.

The kids from school are clustered on the corner in front of Zubie's Surfboards with hand drawn signs, among them, Monique's purple Love sign. He flips off his board and steps up on the sidewalk near Monique. She has her back to him, but Brittany sees him right away.

"Oh, great. What are you doing here, Cart Boy?"

Monique whips around. "Did you tell Tyler you were coming?"

"I didn't tell anyone anything." As he glances around the crowd, trying to figure out which guy Monique is with, he hears chanting start further up Main Street. A crowd of men streams out of Cyclone's Bar and joins the even bigger crowd on the sidewalk.

"The same thing happened in March," a guy in a Lakers hat with a camera slung around his neck tells Monique.

"What happened in March?" Josh asks. This must be the boyfriend. He looks older and Josh wonders where Monique met him.

141

"Cyclone's handed out free drinks that day too," Camera Guy says. "People got stupid drunk and started fighting."

Josh holds his skateboard against his chest. "We should probably go."

Brittany looks at him, incredulous. "It hasn't even started yet. No one invited you to come, Cart Boy. Run on home if you're scared."

"I'm not scared," he says as the crowd from the bar surges into the street. Josh backs up against the window of a bathing suit store, gripping his board across his chest. He can't believe it when Brittany grabs the sign from Monique and charges into the crowd, Monique and Camera Guy following, as if they're gladiators.

He yells at them to come back but his voice is lost in the noise, and he immediately loses sight of all three of them. Everyone is angry and loud. He can't stay much longer, especially if he has to skate all the way home, but it doesn't feel right to just leave the girls here.

He hears a dull thud. People scream. Paramedics push through the crowd toward Cowabunga Tacos. He sees Monique now, coming toward him, Brittany behind her, crying.

"What happened?" Josh hates when girls cry.

Brittany holds up her phone. "Some asshole broke my phone."

Monique's eyes are angry. "The police shot something at that guy with the camera."

"Is he alright?"

"I don't know."

Brittany stares at her phone. "I'm pretty sure it wasn't a real bullet, Monique. And the paramedics came right away. My mom's going to kill me. This phone is brand new."

"You can tape the case back together," Monique says. "Why did you cross the street anyway? You should have stayed on the corner with me."

"I wanted to check the emblem on that woman's shirt. I think those people were from the Rise Above Movement."

"You mean that tree thing with the sword through it?" Josh asks.

"You saw it too? I didn't know those people would be here today."

"Who are they?" Josh asks.

"They're violent." Monique sounds exasperated. "Which means you shouldn't be staring at their shirts, Brittany. I just hope that guy's okay."

"What happened to your sign?" Josh asks.

"Some old woman threw it in the trash." Monique is on her tip toes now, trying to see over the crowd. "I can't believe they shot him."

She must really care about this guy. "Who is he anyway?"

"He said he's working for a newspaper," Monique says.

"Let's just go home," Brittany says.

"Could you maybe give me a ride?" Josh says.

Brittany scowls. "Why? You have your skateboard."

They hear glass break further down the street. People cheer.

"Let's get out of here," Monique says. "Come on, Josh."

He follows the girls to Monique's car, expecting the Camera Guy to reappear but there's no sign of him.

"Get in the backseat, Cart Boy," Brittany says. She waits impatiently for him to figure out where to put his backpack, board, and legs.

"Drive down by the pier," Brittany says. "I want to see if that asshole who broke my phone is still there."

Monique shakes her head. "We're staying away from the pier."

Josh keeps a vigilant eye on the cross traffic as Monique makes her way through the crowd on Main Street, but she's a careful driver. The neighborhood is quieter once they get away from downtown.

"Why was that guy so angry at me?" Brittany asks. "I didn't do anything to him."

"Why did you even want to come to this thing?" Monique asks.

"I thought we could make a difference," Brittany says. "I thought adults would listen if a bunch of kids showed up."

Monique shakes her head. "That's really naive Britt."

"Our sign was naive. Love Trumps Hate makes us sound like hippies. Next time we're using something more direct."

"There's not going to be a next time for me," Monique says.

"But there's another protest in San Diego next week-end," Brittany says. "I was hoping you would drive."

"This was enough for me," Monique says. "I have plans next weekend."

Plans with the camera guy, Josh thinks.

Brittany groans. "Are you going to that coffee shop again? I never see you anymore."

"I see you every day in the pool, Britt. And I was here today."

"I appreciate you coming," Brittany says. "I know it's not your thing."

"What coffee shop?" Josh asks. "Did you get a job?"

Monique gives him a sharp look in the rear-view mirror. "It's none of your business."

Sometimes Monique is worse than Brittany. "Where do you know that guy from anyway? The one with the camera?"

"I already told you," Monique says. "He was just there. We don't know him."

Why can't she just be honest? "Your mom said you were meeting someone today. She thinks you have a boyfriend."

Monique's eyebrows go up. "When did you talk to my mother? Did you tell her I was coming down here?"

"Of course not. I saw her today when I was working."

"I didn't tell her where I was going. Why would she think I'm meeting someone?"

"Why would she ask Cart Boy about your love life?" Brittany says. "That's weird. She could have asked me."

"There's nothing to tell," Monique says.

"So, you don't have a boyfriend?" Josh asks and of course his voice breaks.

Brittany squeals. "Why? Are you planning on making a move?" She looks at Monique and they both laugh hysterically for way too long.

"Josh is kind of cute," Brittany tells Monique. "And at least he has a job." She turns and looks at him over her sunglasses. "How much does that grocery store pay you anyway?"

"Minimum wage," he says. Monique didn't answer his question.

"My parents don't want me to work until I'm out of college," Brittany says.

"Not everyone gets a hundred dollars a week for an allowance, Brittany," Monique says.

Brittany gets a hundred dollars a week! "Albertsons isn't that bad." Josh can't believe he's actually defending his stupid job. "I'll get a raise after six months."

"God, how depressing," Brittany says.

Brittany's dad owns three bars, and her mom is a lawyer. Monique's parents bought her a brand-new car, and her dad drives a Tesla. "Get over yourself," Josh says. "Not everyone has money."

"Brittany's job is being a bitch," Monique says. "Everyone knows that."

"So, what's your excuse?"

"Wow," Brittany says. "That's a rude thing to say to the person who's giving you a ride home. You need to apologize."

"No," Monique says. "He's right. I'm sorry, Josh. We were rude to laugh at you."

He doesn't want an apology. He wants her to tell him the truth about the boyfriend. She pulls into their tract and drops him off. He watches them drive away as the church bells chime five times. At least he's not that late getting home.

"How was the library?" his mom asks when he walks in the door. "I thought you'd come home with a stack of books."

"I couldn't find what I was looking for."

"Give me the list. I'll reserve them for you online. I'll request extra copies for me too, so we can read them together."

This summer can't get any worse. Now he's going to be stuck doing book reports with his mom until school starts again.

CHAPTER NINETEEN
KEITH NELSON

On Sunday, Keith gets a text from Wayne reminding him about the free beer at Cyclone's, so after his gym workout he puts on the hat and drives downtown. The red hat still feels lucky. Cliff is on vacation, and no one at the gym has asked him about renewing his membership. He took Granny C and Fay some fresh strawberries, and Fay made smoothies. When he checked his phone later Kiri, the guy with the available garage, had left a message that he can move in next week. In the meantime, he's discovered a new place to sleep in a Lutheran church parking lot. Eric hasn't called him back into his office again. And now he finds a free place to park just off Main Street.

He joins a throng of people wearing red hats like his. There's a buzz of energy in the air. A man in front of the post office blasts "Proud to be an American" on his cell phone. A pretty redhead with a clipboard stops Keith. "We're collecting donations for the 'Take Back America' foundation," she says, giving him a dimpled smile.

"Take it back from who?"

Her green eyes narrow. "The liberals. The media. They're trying to replace us with illegals. We need to secure a future for our children. Don't you want to contribute?"

"I don't have any children," he says. "And I'm a little short on cash right now."

"We take credit cards."

"I'm a little short on credit too." He wants to stick his finger in the dimple on her cheek, just to feel her skin, but she's already turning around to talk to some other guy in a golf shirt wearing an expensive-looking watch. She has a good body but too many lines around those green eyes. Further down the sidewalk, Wayne stands outside Cyclone's Bar, waving him in.

"Drinks are on the house right now, bro."

Keith fist bumps Wayne and follows him into the bar. "Who's buying?" he asks as Wayne flags down the waitress and holds up two fingers.

Wayne points to a thin-faced man wearing glasses sitting in the corner of the bar. "He's one of the fight club sponsors. Glad you made it."

"Sure thing. So, what's new?"

Wayne's smile fades as they slide into a booth. "We had to put Bella down." His eyes redden. "Broke my heart. She was a good girl."

"What happened? She wasn't that old."

"She had cancer." Wayne wipes his eye. "Vet said it's common in pit bulls. They couldn't do anything. It really sucks, man."

"Sorry, Wayne."

The waitress sets four beers down. "You wanted two each, right?"

"You're a sweetheart." Wayne hands her a five-dollar bill.

Keith takes a sip. His mouth puckers at the bitterness. "What is this?"

"Double Bastard Ale. Eleven percent, dude. When it's free, we go top shelf." He drains half the glass. "I need this today, bro. I'm ready to cut loose."

The bar is loud. The guys at the table next to them chant "USA, USA." They're all clean cut, military types. From Wayne's fight club gym, Keith guesses.

"Good thing you showed up today," Wayne says. "Guarantees you a spot on the Virginia trip."

He should have known there'd be strings attached. Nothing is free, not even a hat made in China. "What's going on in Virginia?"

Wayne shakes his head. "You live under a rock or something, bro? Don't you watch the news?"

"I watch sports mostly."

"There's a bunch of stuff going on back east. Libs are trying to rewrite our history. I keep telling you to join my gym. You'd learn something."

A couple of the men at the table next to them nod. "Those statues in Charlottesville are part of American culture," one of them says. "You guys will be at the meeting next week, right? We've got the latest info about what you can bring on the flight. We're going to pick up the rest of our supplies at Walmart after we land."

"Excellent," Wayne says. "The fight club's mobilizing, Keith. You need to get ready."

"I just came for the beer, Wayne. Seriously. I can't get time off work."

Wayne leans forward. "Keep your voice down. I already vouched for you, so don't blow it. All we're going to do today is stand in front of the pier and show the world there's some real Americans left in Wellington. We can talk about Virginia later. You need to be part of this."

"Lock her up. Lock her up." Everyone in the bar is chanting now.

"Today won't be like last time?" Keith says.

"That was epic, right?" Wayne finishes his first pint and belches.

After the election, Wayne talked him into going to a pro-Trump march on the beach. Wayne got riled up and punched one of the *Herald* reporters in the back. The man's knees buckled, and he face planted in the sand, dropping his notebook and pen. Wayne disappeared into the crowd. One advantage Wayne has, being on the smaller side and anonymous looking. Keith booked it back to his car immediately. People tend to remember him.

"The guy who gave me this hat said you took a shit in front of the *Herald's* office. Is that true?"

Wayne laughs and starts his second pint. "Damn straight, it's true. I used the front page to wipe my ass afterwards. It's what they deserve for trying to shut down our free speech."

"Dude! That was you?" A man at the next table gives Wayne a high five. "You're my hero."

"I got no problem with anyone expressing their opinion," Wayne says. "But if you tell me I can't express mine, I got a big problem. Anyone who wants to start a fight, I can fight. I'm not a pussy."

Keith works on his beer. He doesn't like IPAs, and this is more alcohol than he's had in a long time, but it's free and he's not a pussy either. His dad would hate him being here with Wayne. His Dad wouldn't like him wearing this hat either. He straightens the brim.

The thin-faced man over in the corner must have made some signal because everyone stands. Wayne finishes his pint and most of Keith's second beer as the bar empties. Outside, the sidewalk is packed with men wearing MAGA hats and T-shirts. A few people have on shirts with Nazi insignia. There are other emblems too, one Keith has never seen before with a sword stabbed through the center of a tree. The crowd chants "USA, USA." Someone kicks over a *Herald* news rack.

Keith drops back, feeling the alcohol. He counts badges. Wellington cops, Citrus County Sheriff, police from every neighboring city. The officers' eyes are invisible behind their sunglasses, but their expressions are all the same—stony slabs of granite, like his father's face. He should get some coffee and head to his car. None of this has anything to do with him.

Wayne turns. "Come on, man. Keep up."

"Too many cops."

"You worry too much, dude. Law enforcement's on our side today." Wayne points across the street to a crowd of what look like high school kids, carrying hand drawn signs. "There's the ANTIFA assholes."

"What does ANTIFA stand for again?" Keith says.

An older woman ahead of them turns around. She also has a tree with a sword emblem on her shirt. "Anti-fascist lib-tards," she says. "Don't you watch the news?"

Keith remembers learning about fascists in high school, but he never thought they were a good thing. This must be something different.

"Come on," Wayne says. "Let's cross over before the light changes." Just as Wayne steps off the curb, a young girl holding a Love Trumps Hate sign in one hand and a purple cell phone in the other comes out of nowhere and steps right in front of them. Keith maneuvers around her, but Wayne trips over the curb and goes down hard on one knee. "Fucking bitch," he yells, jumping up right away. "Watch where you're going."

"Sorry," the girl says, lowering her sign. "I didn't see you."

Wayne's face is red. "Are you blind as well as stupid? You're on the wrong side of the street with that sign." He slaps the phone out of her hand, and it drops to the sidewalk. "You need to pay attention to where you're going instead of looking at your damn phone."

"What did you do that for?" The girl is crying now.

"Here's something else for you to cry about, snowflake." The tree emblem woman grabs the girl's sign, snaps it over her knee, and jams it into a trash can. The crowd cheers.

A young Mexican kid wearing a Lakers cap raises a camera. "Put that fucking camera down, beaner boy," Wayne says. "Nothing to see here."

Keith is glad the kid has enough sense to lower the camera lens.

Wayne says, "Let's go."

Keith starts to follow, but now the kid with the camera turns and takes a photo of the line of cops. Kid's got no sense after all, Keith thinks. One of the cops steps back and says something to another cop, and they both look at the camera kid, who has just turned his back and is talking to the blond girl. And then, the kid winces and holds his hand to his temple.

"Oh my God!" the blond girl screams. "You're bleeding."

The kid staggers over to the wall in front of Cowabunga's and sinks down to the sidewalk. When he takes off his Lakers cap, streams of blood trickle down the side of his face. The blond girl kneels next to him. Keith turns as a taller girl pushes through the crowd, yelling, "Brittany, where are you?" Her face is familiar, something about her eyes.

Who is she? he wonders as he hurries to catch up with Wayne. "I think that cop just shot that kid with the camera."

"It was a rubber bullet, dude. That's what cops use now. Beaner boy will be fine. Might have a headache tomorrow. Might want to start wearing a helmet to these things if he's going to go around sticking his camera in people's faces. But regardless, he doesn't belong in Wellington."

These kids are none of his business, Keith tells himself. He follows Wayne across the street to the pier and they join the men who were sitting next to them at Cyclone's. Wayne seems to be best buddies with all of them. Keith catches bits of their conversations. More about the upcoming Virginia trip, how you can't fly with knives, how it's important to look clean cut.

"You'll need a haircut," one of them tells Keith.

"I'm not cutting my hair," Keith says.

"You'll need long sleeves," someone else says. "No tattoos."

"I don't have any tattoos." Keith can't find the tall girl or her blond friend among the young people across the street. The men he's with start yelling at the kids and move forward. The kids step forward too, and the crowd swarms into the intersection, stopping traffic. Car horns blast. People are in each other's faces now, screaming and starting to shove.

Keith smells adrenaline and sweat, feels the energy coming out of everyone's pores. He steps off the curb, just for a minute he tells himself, but immediately a kid jumps in front of him, dressed all in black, wearing a ski mask that completely covers his head. A fucking ski mask? How can he breathe? The kid doesn't even say anything, he just stands there and stares at Keith through the mask with his dark creepy eyes.

"Get away from me." Keith says, but the kid doesn't move. He tries to go around him, but the kid jumps in front of him again. "What is wrong with you?" Keith says.

The kid doesn't answer. Instead, he grabs Keith's forearms with both hands. He's wearing black leather gloves, like he's some kind of cat burglar or something. It's ridiculous. "Don't fucking touch me." Keith tries to shake the kid off, but he won't let go, so Keith pushes him away, not hard at all, but the kid's so much smaller that he flies backwards and lands hard on the street. He bounces up and is in Keith's face again, staring at him with those creepy eyes. What kind of fool does this?

"I told you to get out of my way," Keith says. When the kid doesn't answer, Keith slams the side of his head with a blow so hard he can hear it. Even as loud as the crowd is, he hears it. He feels it too, from his knuckles to his gut. "I warned you," Keith says.

The kid steps back and touches the side of his head with his black gloved hand, then drops to his knees and curls forward.

"I warned you," Keith says again.

"I got you, man!" Wayne is next to Keith now, kicking the kid in the ribs.

"It's cool, Wayne. We should go." Wayne doesn't hear him. The kid says something too, but Keith can't understand him.

"What was that?" Wayne's eyes are lit up like Christmas, his mouth a cruel sneer. "What did you call us?"

The kid lifts his head. "Fucking racists."

Wayne looks at Keith. "You going to let him get away with that?"

Wayne starts kicking the kid again, so Keith joins in, but the kicks don't connect in any way that is satisfying. Two against one doesn't feel right. The kid is too small. When he staggers to his feet and stumbles off, Wayne pounds his fists on his chest like a gorilla and does the same stupid Tarzan yell he used to do when they were kids on a field trip to the zoo.

Keith wants to punch Wayne now, but a cop is watching them. Wayne pushes onward through the crowd and whacks a man carrying an Impeach Trump sign in the face. That dude was old, Keith thinks as someone shoves him from the back. He whirls around. The man raises both hands and grins. He's one of the guys from Cyclone's, Keith realizes. The man skips into the intersection like he's on a playground at recess. When Keith turns back around, the cop is gone.

Keith steps up on the sidewalk. His heart pounds, his blood races. "I have to pee," he says, although no one is listening. "I'll be right back." Wayne is nowhere in sight. It's probably wise to keep some distance from Wayne right now. Main Street looks like a battlefield. He hurries down the stairs to the public bathroom on the beach. "That was fucked up," he tells his reflection in the bathroom mirror as he washes his hands. Why did that kid get in his face like that? He isn't a racist. He's not even sure the kid was Black.

He shakes his fingers dry and heads outside. His heart is still beating crazy fast. He watches the seagulls sitting on the sand, wings tucked under as if they're waiting for a meeting to start. He counts thirty-five gulls before his heart gets back to almost normal. He should find Wayne and the rest of them. They need him there. Wayne already vouched for him.

One of the birds hops on top of a trash can and pulls out a McDonald's wrapper. Two other seagulls immediately start a fight over it, pecking at each other with sharp beaks and claws. *Flying rodents*, Keith thinks. Garbage collectors, just like Wayne. His mouth is dry from the adrenaline rush and too much alcohol. He should rehydrate before he looks for Wayne. He heads into the Dairy Queen across the street. The two girls behind the counter are talking about the protest, hoping their manager will let them go home early. One of them points at the menu on the wall when Keith asks if they have juice or Gatorade. A bottle of water is as expensive as a soda.

"Just give me a Diet Coke then."

"All we have is Pepsi."

"Fine. Give me a Pepsi. But make sure it's Diet." Everyone in the Dairy Queen is staring at their phones while they wait for their orders, so Keith takes out his phone thinking Wayne might have texted him. There are no messages. He wonders if that Lakers cap guy with the camera is back on the street taking photos.

Did the kid in the ski mask have a phone with him? Keith didn't see one.

The kid's probably fine. Like Wayne says, he worries too much. The Dairy Queen crowd could also just be scrolling through messages from their friends or looking at pictures of their families. The girl hands him his drink and he goes back outside.

His boss Eric had pictures of his family on his desk. That's who the girl was. The daughter.

He hears glass breaking now, people screaming, and sirens. Time to go. He saw a flyer about a Sunday potluck on the bathroom wall of the Lutheran church where he slept last night. It's too early for dinner and he's not really in the mood to talk to a bunch of Lutherans, whatever they are, but it's something to do, someplace to be. He adjusts the brim of his red hat and heads toward his car.

CHAPTER TWENTY
JOSH KOWALSKI

"Josh," his mom says, looking up from her laptop Monday morning, her eyes angry over her glasses. "Come over here and explain this to me."

He sets his spoon down next to his second bowl of Cinnamon Toast Crunch, gets up, and stands behind her.

"That's Brittany, isn't it?" She has Facebook open to a video on the Wellic Wise page. Brittany is center frame, in front of Cowabunga Tacos, holding Monique's peace sign and her purple phone. A red-faced man in a Trump hat yells at her and slaps the phone out of her hands. Brittany bursts into tears. The man walks away, keeping his face turned away from the camera. Josh holds his breath, but he doesn't find Monique or his black wolf cap in the crowd.

Brittany looks tiny among those angry people. He reads the comments over his mom's shoulder. "Wrong place. Wrong time," @WBSURFBRO says. "Serves her right for not knowing where to stand," @BIKINIBABESUE says.

His mom shuts down the screen. "I thought Brittany was at the library with you yesterday."

He turns away from her and opens the fridge. "She didn't show."

"But Monique did?"

"Some other kids too. Mostly girls from the water polo team."

"Why didn't you tell me?"

"I didn't think it really mattered."

"This doesn't make any sense. Monique and Brittany have been inseparable since kindergarten. I can't believe she was downtown all by herself. That was dangerous."

Josh keeps his head in the refrigerator. "There were kids from school there too. I mean, in the video."

"Those kids could have been hurt. What are you looking for?"

"Bagels. I'm still hungry. I thought you hated Trump."

"I don't like him. But that protest was violent. Those kids shouldn't have been down there."

"I can pick up groceries at work today. We need more milk too. And cereal."

"We're out of milk already? How is that possible?" She stands. "I'll leave you some grocery money. You should have told me that Brittany didn't show up yesterday. I'm sorry she let you down. That wasn't nice."

"Brittany isn't nice. She says being a bitch is her job."

She gives him a stern look. "I don't like that word, Josh."

"I don't either, but that's what she calls herself. She's proud of it too."

"Why would she be proud of something like that?"

"I don't know, Mom. I don't understand girls at all."

"You don't?" She laughs and runs her fingers through his hair. "Stop growing up so fast." She puts her empty oatmeal bowl in the sink and heads upstairs to get ready for work.

He rinses the dishes and puts them in the dishwasher. Through the open kitchen window, he hears something shrieking a horror movie sound high up in the neighbor's pine tree. *Killy. Killy. Killy.* His mom comes down in her scrubs and picks up her keys.

"What's that noise?" he asks.

She stops for a moment and listens. "It's a kestrel."

"It sounds disturbed."

"It's a bird of prey. Hopefully, it'll take care of those grasshoppers. They're destroying my succulents. Pick up some fresh basil at the store too. I'm going to make pesto tonight." She kisses the top of his head.

As soon as she's gone, he finds the Kensingtons' phone number in his mom's old address book. He needs to talk to Monique in case his mom calls Mrs. Kensington to double-check his story, but he doesn't know her cell number. The way his luck's going, he expects Tyler or one of his parents to answer, and he can't think of one good reason that would explain why he's calling Monique. But she answers on the second ring.

"This is Josh Kowalski," he says in the deepest voice he can manage.

She laughs. "So formal. What do you want?"

"Did you see the video?"

"Of course, I saw the video. Brittany is grounded for the rest of her life."

"Um . . . did you tell anyone I was down there too?"

"No. Why would I?"

He hesitates and then says, "My mom totally freaked out when she saw Brittany. I told her I was at the library with you guys yesterday."

"What'd you do that for?"

"She doesn't like me going downtown alone. I told her you and Brittany were helping kids with the summer reading list."

"You're quite the little storyteller. She believed you?"

"You're a Junior Advocate, aren't you?"

"For the water polo team. Not for you! So how did you explain Brittany being in that video?"

"I just said she didn't show, and we didn't know she went to the protest. Are you in trouble too?"

"Not yet." Monique sighs. "It's probably okay. But don't start telling people we're friends. Because that would be weird." She hangs up.

He's pretty sure he's just made everything worse. He cleans up the kitchen, makes his bed, starts a load of laundry. When he takes out the trash the kestrel is still out of sight, shrieking its kill warning.

■ ■ ■

By Thursday, his mom hasn't mentioned the protest again. Josh reads online that there were fights, a few people were hurt, store windows were smashed, and a porta-potty got turned over, but no one died or anything. Maybe he's in the clear. After work he changes into shorts and a Foo Fighters T-shirt, goes out in the garage, and pounds his drum set. He misses Neil. He's mastered all the charts Neil gave him, and now he needs some new direction. He's even thinking about joining the lame-ass high school band in September.

During his second attempt at the drum solo from "When the Levee Breaks," he hears someone knocking at the front door. Unhappy neighbor, he figures and hits the drum skins harder. He hears the doorbell ring next. He beats the bass drum. And then someone knocks on the garage door, and he hears Monique's voice. "Josh, I know you're home." He puts down his sticks and goes into the house, opens the front drape, and peeks out the living room window.

She's alone. She has never once come to his house alone. Years ago, she and Tyler were invited to his birthday parties, but that was back in grade school. He checks his hair in the mirror. When he plays drums, he sweats; and when he sweats, the stupid pomade his mom gave him to keep his hair off his face gets even stickier. It looks like he's wearing a lopsided helmet. Monique's going to laugh at him. There's nothing he can do about it now though. He opens the door.

Monique brushes past him, waving a newspaper in his face. "Have you seen this?"

She rips opens the issue of the *Wellington Herald* and slaps it down on the coffee table. "That's me, right there." She points to a photograph, a wider angle of the Facebook video. Brittany's center frame, crying, her phone on the ground, Monique's off to the left. "If my mom sees this, I'm dead."

Monique lifts her hair off her neck and Josh smells lavender and wishes he'd taken a shower. At least he's not in the picture, but if his mom sees Monique, she'll know that he lied to her.

"It just came out today," Monique says. "We need to make sure no one else sees it."

"How? It's already published."

"It isn't like it gets delivered to every house like the *LA Times* or the *Citrus County Register*. It doesn't even cost anything. We'll find all the copies we can and destroy them." Monique leans forward and swings her hair toward the floor.

"That won't work." He tries not to stare at her upside-down torso.

"We have to do something. And this is kind of your fault for dragging me into your stupid lie about the library." She twists her hair into a knot, stands, and frowns at Josh's shirt. "You like the Foo Fighters?"

"I like their drummer." Josh points to the man standing next to Monique in the photo. "That guy looks familiar. I've seen him before."

"Really?" Monique leans past him. "Where?"

He smells lavender again and has to think for a second until it comes to him. "It's that Uber driver. The one who parks on Mountain Brook all the time."

Monique shrugs. "I've never noticed him." Her hair comes loose and falls around her face, catching the afternoon sun streaming in the front window. Red, gold, and brown. She flips forward again, bundles her hair in one hand, and slips a green rubber band around it. She stands. "Where do people pick up the *Herald* anyway?"

Josh feels a little dizzy. "There's a newsstand where I work. All the grocery stores have them."

"We need to get started then."

"We can't just throw away newspapers, Monique."

"Brittany's dad pulls them out of the racks in front of his bars and throws them in the trash all the time."

"That doesn't make it right. Besides, the *Herald* news racks are all over Citrus County. They're everywhere. Trader Joe's. The post office. Liquor stores."

"We can at least get rid of the ones at places our parents might go. Or their friends."

"This isn't going to work, Monique. I'm not doing it."

"It's not like we're stealing or anything. And you have to go with me. It'll go a lot faster with you in the car."

"Get Brittany to go with you. Or Tyler."

"Brittany's grounded and Tyler has too big of a mouth."

This is not only a complete waste of time, it's also a really bad idea. And she's asking him to help her. "Okay," he says.

"You can't tell anyone about this either."

"Obviously," he says. He follows Monique out to her car. The passenger seat is stacked with books. When Josh starts to move them to the backseat, Monique shrieks at him to leave them alone. She yanks the books away from him so quickly he barely has time to catch the titles on their spines. Poetry, it looks like. Shakespeare sonnets, Neruda, Ginsberg. She stacks them on the floor behind his seat.

"Are you going to summer school?"

"No," she says.

"You're just randomly reading poetry?"

"Why shouldn't I read poetry?"

"No reason. It's actually kind of cool."

"It's actually none of your business."

"I just asked a simple question."

"I'm sick of everyone thinking I'm just a jock, okay?" She starts the ignition and the car speakers come to life. A woman's deep, raspy voice, like she smokes cigarettes says, "I want to walk like I'm the only woman on earth."

"Is that rap?" Josh asks.

Monique snaps the volume off. "It's Kim Addonizio. She's a poet."

"Her voice is cool." When Monique doesn't answer, he adds, "No one thinks you're just a jock. Everyone I know thinks you're super smart."

"How many people do you know?"

"You want me to help you or not?"

"Sorry," she says. "Let's start at the Trader Joe's on Ackerman and work our way back."

Josh flips through the *Herald* as she drives and notices a poetry reading at the place in Buena Loma that Brittany mentioned. Coffee and Words. The last page still has the escort ads with the big-busted women in tiny bathing suit tops. His dick comes to attention. He folds the page over his lap as casually as possible, praying that Monique doesn't notice.

The rack at the Trader Joe's on Ackerman is empty, but they have better luck at the Ralphs on Pershing Street where there are fifteen copies. The liquor store in the strip mall has twenty. An old man smirks when Josh pulls out the entire stack. "Piece of shit newspaper. I hope you put it straight in the trash where it belongs."

"We're going to recycle them," Josh says.

Adam is standing out in front of the store where Josh works when Monique pulls up next to the rack. Josh jumps out and takes the full stack of papers from the rack then salutes Adam and climbs back in the car. Monique hits the gas and Adam walks into the middle of the driveway, puts his hands on his hips, and stares at them gape mouthed.

"He's going to get run over." Josh rolls down the window, leans out and yells, "Adam, Darlene's paging you. You'd better get back inside."

Adam turns around and scurries toward the store. They both laugh.

After that, it starts to be fun. Monique turns on the radio and Josh switches it to the classic rock station. By six o'clock the backseat of her car is loaded with *Heralds*. They drive to the industrial area off Gunner and find a big recycling bin behind an auto paint store. "Stairway to Heaven" is on the radio as Monique turns the car toward their neighborhood.

"All that glitters is gold?" Monique says. "What a cliché."

Josh is shocked. "You can't be serious. Don't you know who this is? Led Zeppelin!" He turns up the volume.

"Ooh, it makes me wonder?" Monique laughs. "There's nothing to wonder about. Those guys were full-on misogynist pigs."

"You don't know what you're talking about."

"Misogynist? It means sexist."

"I know what the word means, Monique. But this song is a classic."

"Classic asshole music."

"It's about being out on the road, searching for something. It's about dreams." He sounds like an idiot. "Never mind. I like it."

She looks at him. "Dreams or nightmares? You surprise me, Josh." She's quiet until the song finishes. "Do you ever dream about finding Mrs. Gorman dead?"

He hesitates, not sure how honest he should be. He never thinks about Stephanie Gorman at all, which probably makes him a terrible human being. "I'd never seen a dead person before. It was awful, but I couldn't stop staring at her."

"I've never seen a dead person either. What did she look like?"

He shrugs. "Purple and cold looking. Her mouth was open. She looked dead. You didn't see your grandmother?"

"No. They cremated her right away. I kind of wish I had seen her. It still doesn't feel real."

Monique's eyes moisten. He hopes she isn't going to cry. "I get that," Josh says. "What bothers me more is that Neil can't work with me anymore. I guess that's selfish."

"It is," Monique says. "But I'm glad you're still playing drums. You should start your own band. Forget about the Nashville Kings."

That's not a problem, he thinks, since David hasn't returned any of his phone calls.

"You could call it the Wellington Warblers," Monique says.

She's making fun of him, but at least she's smiling now. "That's weak," he says. "It sounds like a bluegrass band. I have a better idea. The Misogynist Zeppelins."

Monique's laughter is real and when she drops him off at home, she even thanks him for helping her. "It probably didn't do any good," she adds, "but at least we tried."

He has the lyrics to "Stairway to Heaven" stuck in his brain for the rest of the night.

CHAPTER TWENTY-ONE
JEANNETTE LARSEN

It's Sunday afternoon and Jeannette's taught cardio classes back-to-back all week, sandwiched in between tennis lessons, water aerobics, and a Zumba class. Felix and Gloria are coming over later, and Jeannette's looking forward to sitting in the backyard, listening to KJAZZ, and having a few cocktails. Maybe Bob will cook some burgers.

Felix and Gloria Ramirez were their across-the-street neighbors in their former neighborhood in Angel City. The Ramirezes are older but lively, always up for dinner out or a concert. The four of them have tickets for Tom Petty at the Hollywood Bowl in September. Felix and Gloria never had kids, which makes them easier to hang out with than couples with children. They knew Zack though and they came to his funeral. Gloria brought over her famous yakitori chicken and miso soup afterwards, and she and Felix sat with them for hours, knowing when to ask questions and when to listen.

When Jeannette asks Bob if they have enough charcoal, he says he'd rather put a picnic together and take the Ramirezes to the concert in Wellington Central Park.

"Okay," Jeannette says, "as long as we come home early. The new season of *Game of Thrones* starts tonight."

"Whenever you want to leave," Bob says. "Doug and his

crew are going to be there too. They might go out for drinks afterwards."

She should have known this would involve Doug, she thinks, as she changes into a pink tank top and a pair of black shorts. After Bob wrote a check to the service club, Doug invited them to a dachshund race at the German Village, a John Fogerty concert at the Citrus County fair, and the Farmer's Market on Main Street. Bob says it's generous of Doug to take them under his wing and give them a local's perspective, but the more time they spend with Doug and his friends, the less she trusts them. She's never asked Bob how much money he donated. Hopefully not a lot.

She ties a leopard print cardigan around her shoulders, in case it cools down later. When Felix and Gloria arrive, she gives them a quick tour of the new house. Bob loads the picnic basket and four chairs in the Suburban and they all pile in.

"You guys sure have had a lot of protests down at the pier lately," Gloria says as Bob pulls into Central Park.

"Wellington's always been kind of an outlaw town," Felix says. "There was a big punk scene here in the eighties."

Bob shakes his head. "I don't like the people these protests attract."

"I read it was ANTIFA that caused the problems at the latest one," Felix says.

"No," Gloria says. "That was a pro-Trump rally."

"There's nut cases on both sides," Bob says.

"And some of them are Bob's new best friends," Jeannette says. "You'll get to meet them today."

Bob gives her a warning look. "They're good people, doing good work for the community. You guys will like them."

"Wellington seems like a cool place to live," Felix says. "I heard so many great bands at the Grizzly Bear back in my day. Los Lobos, José Feliciano . . ."

"Wellington is cool," Gloria says. "Literally. It's nice to get out of the heat. It's at least ten degrees warmer in Angel City. And smoggier too."

The Central Park lot is nearly full, and Bob has to circle twice to find an empty space. Jeannette decides it's warm enough to leave her sweater in the car. Bob and Felix carry the chairs and picnic basket down the hill. She and Gloria follow behind. Doug's group is easy to find. They're all sitting in teak chairs around tables laid with white linen tablecloths.

"Wow," Gloria says. "How . . . elaborate."

Doug, Carla, Krystal, and Greg are with a bigger group today. There are at least ten children dressed in red, white, and blue outfits running wild around a young Filipina woman holding a baby in one arm, her other hand on the head of a toddler. The plates aren't paper, the utensils aren't plastic, and the food is much more complicated than the Cuban sandwiches and Maui potato chips that Bob put together. He makes the introductions, and they all sit down.

Gloria stares at Greg's red MAGA hat. "I warned you," Jeannette says under her breath.

Carla is wearing a sundress made out of an American flag. "Help yourself," she says in her usual chalk-screech voice, pointing to two large white coolers loaded with beer and wine.

"I didn't know we could drink in the park," Jeannette says.

"Isn't it great?" Carla passes around jumbo-sized wine glasses. "I'm not a fan of orchestras, but a little wine sure helps."

The strains of "The Star-Spangled Banner" begin. "Stand up!" the hyper-thin conductor on stage announces. "This is the home of the Wellies, and we believe in America. No Colin Kaepernicks allowed."

Jeannette looks over at Bob and says, "Seriously?" but Bob is staring at Krystal's tight red tube top and doesn't hear her.

"Kids!" Carla screeches. "Be respectful. Hazel, can't you do something?"

Hazel must be the nanny, Jeannette decides, as she watches the young woman attempt to corral the kids. Everyone rises and covers their hearts with their hands, except for one of the younger kids, who plops down on a blanket and opens an iPad. When the orchestra finishes, the crowd applauds, and they all sit down. The older kids race off toward the lawn, the kid with the iPad stays on the blanket, and Hazel hands Carla the infant and chases after the children.

"Keep them away from those people," Doug yells. He points toward the eucalyptus trees near the bathrooms where a group of people are clustered around bicycles. "I can't wait until the homeless shelter opens so the cops can arrest them."

"I don't understand why the city council approved a shelter," Carla says. "It'll just attract more of them."

"Because of that fucking judge," Greg says. "You can't arrest anyone for being homeless unless you already have a place to put them."

"Cover your ears, Donald," Doug says. "Uncle Greg's using bad words. Although he's speaking the truth." The child on the blanket ignores him. Doug opens another bottle of wine and fills everyone's glass.

"Donald's an interesting name for a child," Jeannette says.

"We've been fans of the President since *The Apprentice*," Carla says. "All our kids have meaningful names. Lindsay, Mitch, Sarah, Donald, and Laura."

"Laura Bush?"

Doug shakes his head. "Laura Ingraham. We're definitely not Bush fans anymore."

Jeannette looks over at Gloria, expecting a reaction, but Gloria isn't listening. She and Felix are telling Bob about their latest trip to Alabama. Felix is part of a team that travels around the country closing down Sears stores, and Gloria's started tagging along to keep him company since she just retired from the post office.

"You would not believe the collard greens we ate in Birmingham," Felix says. "They were braised in a wok with pork belly. And Alabama BBQ is stellar. They use this white sauce that's off the charts."

"Fattening too." Gloria pats her belly. "I need to get back to the gym. Now that I'm not carrying a route anymore, I'm starting to put on the pounds."

"We went to the recording studio in Mussel Shoals," Felix says, "where the Stones recorded 'Wild Horses.' Gloria bought me this T-shirt in the gift shop."

"We also went on a Civil Rights tour," Gloria says. "We visited that church in Birmingham where those four little girls died in a bomb explosion."

"God." Bob shakes his head. "I bet that was depressing."

"It was Gloria's idea," Felix says.

"I want to know more about our country's history," Gloria says.

"Good for you," Jeannette says. "I admire that." She feels eyes on them and glances over at Doug, who is listening intently.

"Excuse me," he says. "Where are you guys from?"

Felix and Gloria look at each other. "Across the street from where Bob and Jeannette used to live," Felix says. "In Angel City."

"No," Doug says. "Where are you really from?"

"I was born in Downey," Felix says, "and Gloria's from San Gabriel."

"What about your people?" Doug says. "I'm guessing they're not from around here."

Felix gives Doug a steady look. "My great grandparents were born in Michoacán, and Gloria's grandparents are from

Japan. She's second generation American and I'm third. Does that answer your question?"

Doug gives him a toothy smile. "Just asking."

"Why are you asking them and not us?" Jeannette says.

"Babe," Bob says. "Doug's just curious."

Gloria gives her a quick grin. "America's a melting pot. That's what makes it a great country."

"It's starting to get great again," Doug says. "We've got to protect our culture though, before it's destroyed."

"Well," Felix says. "I agree if you're talking about the true American culture. Rock and roll, man. We invented it."

"Cheers to that," Bob says.

Jeannette takes a big gulp of wine. She really should call out Doug's rudeness, but Bob and Felix and Gloria have apparently decided to ignore what he said. Felix starts to describe some musician he and Gloria saw in Alabama when Doug interrupts.

"You know anything about Virginia, Felix?"

"Not really," Felix says. "We're off to Georgia next. I'm looking forward to visiting the Allman Brothers' house in Macon. Gloria's doing some research."

"I was a huge Gregg Allman fan," Gloria says. "We're going to try to visit his grave."

Doug leans forward. "I've been following those stories about the Robert E. Lee monuments coming down in Charlottesville."

Greg is listening now too.

"Gloria's the history expert," Felix says. "You heard anything about that, hon?"

Gloria clears her throat. "Well, if you really want to know what I think, it's about time those monuments came down. In my opinion, Robert E. Lee was a traitor."

"Wow!" Greg sits back in his chair and shakes his head. "Someone's been watching too much CNN. You might want to expand your horizons a little."

Felix frowns. "Not sure what you mean, buddy. We switch back and forth between Fox and CNN all the time. We like to hear both sides."

"We do too," Bob says.

"We're all entitled to our own opinions," Gloria says. "It's a free country."

Jeannette pulls the cork from a wine bottle. Greg and Doug were both so awful. She should say something.

Gloria holds out her empty glass. "Before I forget Jeannette, we might have a conflict for that Tom Petty concert. Felix's scheduled to go to Tennessee in September. We'll know more after the Georgia trip."

The band starts another song, "Cabaret." That was about Nazis, Jeannette remembers, starring Liza Minelli. Doug asks Bob if he'd watched the US Women's Open.

"Trump was there," Doug says. "Thank God there was a lot of law enforcement. Those women were completely disrespectful."

"Elect a clown, expect the circus," Jeannette says.

"Excuse me?" Doug says.

"It was printed on one of the women's T-shirts," Jeannette says.

Doug tightens his smile and turns around to talk to Greg.

Gloria leans over and whispers, "We're not going to change these people's minds about anything."

"You're right," Jeannette says. "I'm just sorry you had to listen to all of that."

"We've heard it before," Gloria says. "At least we've diversified the crowd a little."

"True." Jeannette tries to smile and concentrate on the music. "Oklahoma," "Some Enchanted Evening," "Bali Hai." All the Broadway musicals her grandparents listened to when she was a child. A few monarchs flit from tree to tree. It's a beautiful park.

Bob's eyes are back on Krystal's tube top. Krystal is too busy studying her lipstick in a rhinestone-studded compact mirror to notice. Felix and Gloria try to decide if they should fly out of Citrus County or LAX. Carla and the other women discuss facialists. Hazel plays with the kids, who are climbing all over her, laughing, and falling down like puppies. None of their parents are paying any attention.

These children are not your responsibility, Jeannette reminds herself, and neither is the young woman, although she might have more in common with Hazel than anyone else. More than likely, Hazel's also working for minimum wage with no benefits or retirement plan. There's an enormous difference between their lives of course. She gets to live in a beautiful home she could never afford on the peanuts Citrus County Fitness pays. Because of Bob, she has healthcare. Because of Bob, she won't have to work until she drops dead.

"You look really tan," Gloria says.

"I've been teaching tennis all week." A man wearing a blue tank top stands at the crest of the hill near the parking lot, watching her. He almost looks like that guy from the gym. Wishful thinking, she supposes. Why would he be here? She blinks and looks again. It *is* him.

"I know I'm going to sound like your mother," Gloria is saying. "But you might want to up the level on your sunscreen."

Jeannette nods. He's still standing there. She waits until the last bars of "Bali Hai" finish and then says, "You're right, Gloria. I do feel a little sunburned. I'm going to get my sweater out of the car."

"Are you cold, babe?" Bob asks. "I'll go get it."

Jeannette shakes her head. "I'll be right back." Bob hands her the car keys. She hurries up the hill. The man in the blue tank top steps into the shade of a tree. When she gets closer, she nods and keeps walking. He matches her stride, a big grin on his face. Instead of the ponytail, his hair is loose today, catching the slight breeze. Her heart beats faster. This is madness, but the idea of fucking him in broad daylight to what now sounds like the theme song from *Cats* is thrilling. She pushes a button on the key fob and the lights on the Suburban flash.

"Hey neighbor," a woman's voice says to her right. "I thought I recognized your car."

Jeannette whips around. The woman who drives the blue Prius and lives down the street from them, with the son and the unfortunate front yard, walks toward her. She's alone, carrying a folding chair and the new John Grisham novel. "I'm Martha Kowalski. We haven't officially met."

"I'm Jeannette." The man in the blue tank top walks past them up to the next row of cars and stops. "I need to get my sweater," she adds, pointing at her car. "My husband's down there sitting off to the right side of the stage, if you want to join our group. Look for the big white coolers."

The woman holds up her book. "That's nice of you, but I usually just sit in the back and read. Enjoy the concert." Martha hurries down the hill.

Jeannette turns as the man moves closer to her car.

"Nice to see you again," he says. "Jeannette."

"I don't even know your name."

"Keith." He glances over at the Suburban.

She shakes her head. "Not now. And not here."

"When?"

"I'll call you. What's your phone number?"

He tells her and walks up the hill. She grabs her sweater from the car. The orchestra is playing "If I Were a Rich Man" from *Fiddler on the Roof* as she walks down the hill, mentally chanting Keith's phone number. There's a dead monarch butterfly on the sidewalk, its torn wings like shattered stained glass. Jeannette shivers and pulls the sweater over her shoulders.

"There you are," Bob says when she sits down next

to him. He looks at her quizzically. "You look gorgeous. New lipstick?"

"Same old, same old," she says. When Bob turns to get more wine from Carla, she grabs her phone, adds Rich Roofing to her contacts, and types in Keith's number.

The orchestra begins "Somewhere" from *West Side Story*. Carla stands. "I'm sick of these old fogey tunes. Let's go to the Surf King. Hazel can watch the kids at our house."

Bob looks at Felix. "You guys want to go with them? It'll be fun."

Gloria glances down at her T-shirt, now stained with mustard. "The Surf King's kind of fancy, isn't it?"

"I like this music," Jeannette says.

"There's two more open bottles of wine," Carla says. "You guys should finish them."

Doug's group leaves, and Jeannette pours wine into their four glasses.

"I feel sorry for Hazel," Gloria says. "That's too many kids to watch at once."

"She had them all under control," Felix says.

"I hope they pay her well," Gloria says.

"They're also giving her a place to live," Bob says.

"So she can work twenty-four seven," Jeannette says.

"You don't know that for sure, babe," Bob says.

"I've never met anyone with a nanny before," Gloria says.

"I didn't particularly appreciate that comment your buddy Greg made about us watching too much CNN," Felix says.

"It's okay, hon," Gloria says. "Don't make a big deal."

"Greg was just kidding," Bob says.

"No, he wasn't." Jeannette feels like screaming. "Why are you making excuses for these people? They're racist and rude and obviously taking advantage of a young woman who probably has no other options."

They're all staring at her. Maybe she was screaming.

"I wish you'd give them a chance," Bob says. "They've been nice to us."

"You know what would be really nice, *babe*? If you hadn't spent the entire afternoon staring at Krystal's tits." This is foolish, to pick a fight over Krystal now, when she was more than ready to fuck Keith in broad daylight fifty yards up the hill. She should just shut up. Except she didn't fuck Keith, and Bob shouldn't be looking at anyone except her like that. "Did you like how you could see her nipples through that tube top, Bob? That was really nice, wasn't it?"

Bob stands. "Someone's had a little too much wine."

"We've all had a lot of wine," Gloria says. "Maybe we should find some coffee."

"I can drive," Bob says. "You guys ready to go?" He folds up his chair.

Felix and Gloria stand and look at each other. "Maybe we should call an Uber."

"Nonsense," Bob says. "I'm fine to drive." He grabs the cooler and heads up the hill toward the car. Felix carries the chairs. Gloria follows. Jeannette lags behind. The butterfly is gone.

Maybe, after they're home and Felix and Gloria jump out of the Suburban, say goodbye and speed off, Bob will tell her he's not interested in Krystal because he loves her, and she should know that. Maybe she will tell him she's not worried about Krystal, take his hand, and lead him back to their dark bedroom. Or maybe he will lay her down on the living room rug and make love to her with all the lights on. Maybe for once they will say what they're really thinking.

Maybe if she were a different woman something would finally change.

CHAPTER TWENTY-TWO

KEITH NELSON

Wednesday afternoon, the girl on the elliptical next to Keith glances over and does a double take. She's cute too, smooth skin, no freckles. He smiles, guessing it's his red hat. It still feels lucky. Maybe if he'd worn it to that concert Jeannette would have invited him to the backseat of her car again. At least he knows her name now. And she'd asked for his phone number. His life is turning around. He moved into the garage in Garden City yesterday afternoon after buying a blow-up mattress, sheets and towels, a microwave, and a tiny fridge from Walmart. He slept there last night, woke up a few times, but got more hours of sleep than he has in months.

The girl next to him takes off one of her earbuds. "You're that guy," she says. "From the video?"

"Sorry," Keith says. "I don't know what you're talking about. Video of what?"

"On Facebook. From the 'Take Back America' march? Downtown Wellington?"

He looks over his shoulder to see if anyone is listening. Wayne's never said anything about a video. Wayne only wants to talk about how epic the day was. How they'd both scored major points with the club and their spot on the Virginia team is set.

"Where on Facebook did you see this video?" Keith asks.

"Wellie Wise Community Forum, of course!" She grins. "Thanks for representing us Wellies. High five!" She raises her right hand.

Keith taps her palm with his, and she puts her earbud back in. He runs faster on the elliptical. Because of his stupid old phone and cheap ass provider, he's always the last to know anything. When the girl leaves, he abbreviates his work out and takes the world's fastest shower.

Cliff waves him down as he heads out the door. "I'm going to need your credit card today."

"Next time," he says. "Gotta go." He tries to connect to Facebook in his Honda, but the tiny hourglass just spins. He gives up and calls Wayne, but Wayne doesn't answer and Keith's too antsy to leave a message. He feels like everyone in the parking lot is looking at him.

The third time Keith hits redial, Wayne picks up. "I'm working," he says. "What's up?"

"Did you know there's a video on Facebook of us at that protest?"

"You can't even see my face," Wayne says.

"But you can see mine?"

"Oh, yeah."

"With that kid in the ski mask?"

"No." Wayne laughs. "It must have been right after that blond girl tripped me. The picture of you in the *Herald* is much better."

"I'm in the *Herald* too?"

"No one reads the *Herald*, bro. That girl needed to be a taught a lesson."

"She was there with my boss's daughter. I could get fired if he finds out."

"For what? Standing on a sidewalk? That video's about to disappear anyway if it hasn't already." There's a loud beeping noise as the garbage truck backs up.

"This is messed up," Keith says. Eric might look at Facebook or the *Wellington Herald*. Even if he doesn't, other people from the office might recognize him. Some cop might see it too. Keith lowers his voice, even though he's in his car with the windows rolled up. "What about that kid in the ski mask? Is there a video of him too?"

"Not that I know of. No one's come forward to complain. You should be proud, Keith. You did good. We both did. The club is happy. We're on the Virginia list."

"I can't get off work to go to Virginia."

"Maybe you'll get fired." Wayne laughs. "Problem solved."

"That's not funny."

"I'm working, dude. We'll talk later."

If his parents aren't home from work yet, he can probably use their laptop to find this video, see how bad it is. He drives past their cul-de-sac. The trash cans are out on the curb, which means his father isn't home yet. His dad always pulls them off the street the instant he comes home from work. It used to be Keith's job and his dad would go ballistic if Keith didn't bring them in immediately.

He makes a U-turn and drives by again, trying to see if there are any lights on in the kitchen. It's hard to tell from this angle so it doesn't register at first that there's a For Sale sign planted in the middle of the small lawn he used to cut every Saturday morning. He slams on his brakes and whips the car around.

Lisa Kensington's name and photo is right above the phone number for Sandcastle Realty. He didn't know Eric's wife was a real estate agent, but that explains why she's so worried about where people park. There's one of those lockboxes on the front door too, which means he's locked out. He takes out his phone and punches in his mother's number. He doesn't bother saying hello when she answers.

"Were you just going to move and hope I didn't notice?"

"This all happened really fast. We decided to downsize and then we got three offers immediately. It's been kind of crazy."

He lets the word downsize sit in his head for a second. "What are you going to do with my stuff?"

"Nothing is final yet. And you don't have much here that belongs to you."

"My weights. My bench. The bag. The mats. All of that is mine."

She sighs. "We're going out to look at property next Sunday afternoon. Why don't you come by then?"

"You mean while you're gone?" She doesn't answer. He'd like to reach through the phone and shake her, remind her that he's her only kid. "Property where?"

"Temecula, maybe. We haven't decided for sure."

"Temecula? That's a long commute. What about Granny C?"

"She has a live-in. She's doing fine. Boeing made us an offer. We're going to retire."

"I didn't know that either."

"Like I said. It's happening really fast, Keith. We were going to tell you. Temecula's just an idea. We went to a wedding out there last month and it seemed really nice. I'll leave the garage unlocked next Sunday. And you need to put in a change of address with the post office. You should have done that a long time ago."

He hangs up. His intestines feel knotted, and he needs a toilet. He speeds out of the track, drives to the Mobile station with the 7-Eleven inside where they'll let him use the restroom if he buys something. It doesn't do any good to complain about how filthy the toilet is. He's already tried. He pays for an overpriced bottle of Gatorade, gets the restroom key from the clerk, does his business, and washes his hands as best as he can even though the water's cold and there aren't any paper towels. Shaking his wet hands, he goes back to his car, which feels like a jail cell. He drives over to Church Park, parks his Honda near the lake, and gets out.

His parents have probably seen the video too, he thinks, as he leans against the hood and sips his drink. He's surprised his mother didn't bring it up. She probably would have if he'd given her a chance. She doesn't want to see him. She wants him to come by to get his stuff on Sunday when they're not home.

There's no way the bench and the weight rack and everything else will fit in his car. He'll have to make more than one trip. He wonders if Eric's wife will be there, hosting an open house. It isn't like he has fond memories of living in that place, but the idea of Lisa Kensington showing strangers his old bedroom makes him sick to his stomach.

Over by the lake, a little girl throws breadcrumbs at some Canadian geese while her mother stares at her phone. The birds are gigantic, aggressive, sharp-beaked, and they're not supposed to eat bread. The little girl is fearless. She laughs as she chases the geese across the grass. There's so much bird crap everywhere because of all the junk people feed them. He imagines how grimy the kid's shoes are going to be. Serves the mother right for not paying attention. "Hey," he yells. "Read the sign. You're not supposed to feed those birds."

The woman looks up and swallows hard, then puts her phone in the back pocket of her jeans. "Chelsea," she yells. "Come hold mama's hand."

The little girl races toward her mother. "Mommy," she says. "Who is he?"

"Come on, sweetie, let's go home." The woman speed walks to her car, dragging the now crying little girl behind her, her feet nearly flying off the ground.

He should leave too, Keith thinks, but he can't make himself get back in his car. He walks over to the picnic table underneath the eucalyptus trees in the back of the park, finds a bird poop-free spot on the bench, and sits down. From here, his Honda looks even smaller. Wayne has that huge truck. He could ask Wayne to help him move the weights. They could take care of everything in one trip. And once he has it set up in his garage, he won't need a gym membership. Keith starts to feel better until he notices a man on a bicycle veer off the sidewalk and head across the grass straight toward him. Ray Murdoch, the nosy old man who lives behind his parents.

"Hey Keith," Ray says when he gets closer.

"How's it going?" Keith says.

Ray gets off his bike and sets the kickstand. "My mother's in the hospital."

"Sorry," Keith says. He remembers hearing Ray's mother's complaining voice. Miss Vicky. She must be a hundred years old by now.

Ray's eyes are bright red. "She tripped over a throw rug and broke her hip. I was home too." He shoves his hands in the pockets of his shorts and rocks back and forth from his heels to his toes.

"That sucks," Keith says.

"I spend all my time worrying about her when she's alone, and then she falls down right in front of me."

A fire truck comes out of the Hefner Street Station and turns on its siren.

Ray clears his throat. "It's been a lousy summer. I guess you heard about Neil Gorman's wife."

"What about her?" Keith says. He knows who the Gormans are. They have a grey-striped cat. Now that he thinks about it, he hasn't seen the old Gorman woman out on her front porch or the cat lately.

"Heart attack," Ray says. "Neil Gorman has Alzheimer's. He's in a care center. And you probably heard about that woman drowning in her pool in that house where the real estate agent lives?"

There's no reason to tell Ray he works for the real estate agent's husband. An ambulance passes the park now, lights flashing, sirens blaring. "They always send two," Keith says. "Why is that?"

"Worst case scenario," Ray says. "They never know what they're getting into. When I called 911 after my mother fell, they sent at least twelve paramedics. The neighbors all came over too, people I've never even talked to. It was overwhelming. I'm used to keeping a lower profile."

"Me too."

"I worry about you, Keith." Ray glances over at the Honda. "If you ever need to talk, you know where I live."

"Talk about what?"

"I read that Wellington's opening a shelter."

"I don't need a shelter. I've got a place now, in Garden City."

Ray's face breaks open in a giant smile as if it's the best thing he's heard in a long time. "Terrific!" he says. "I'm really glad to hear that."

It's pathetic, how happy Ray is to hear about him finding a place that's just a garage. It's his garage though, which means he actually has someplace to go instead of this crappy park. Why does he keep coming back here? Kiri might even have decent Wi-Fi. Keith stands. He should go find out. He pulls his keys from his pocket.

"I'll let you get on with your bike ride, Ray. Catch you later."

CHAPTER TWENTY-THREE
LISA KENSINGTON

Lisa doesn't remember driving home she is so angry. She rushes into the house, drops her purse on the floor, rips through the latest issue of the *Wellington Herald*, and slaps it down on the counter next to where Monique is sitting, reading a book, pretending to be completely innocent. She stabs her finger at Monique's photograph. "What were you doing there?"

Monique's face goes pale, but she lifts her chin, defiantly. "Protesting that asshole in the White House."

Tyler gets up from the couch. "Let me see." He leans over Monique's shoulder and cackles. "Oh, man! You're in deep shit, sis."

"Someone in this family needs to stand up for our country," Monique says.

Tyler snorts. "And that's you? What do you know about our country, Pickle Brain? You've spent your entire life soaking your head in chlorine."

"Shut up. You're the one with brain damage."

"Both of you stop it," Lisa says. "Did you know about this Tyler?"

"You might not have noticed, Mom, but Monique doesn't exactly confide in me."

Lisa hears a small amount of hurt in her son's voice, which surprises her.

Monique looks surprised, too. "You're never interested in what I'm doing."

The smirk has already returned to Tyler's face. "Because you're boring. I have a life." Tyler heads back to the couch and picks up his phone.

"Why were you reading the *Herald*?" Monique says.

"Because they're going to publish my essay." Lisa hasn't told her family about her interview at the *Herald* this afternoon, not even Eric. The editor loves her essay. He wants her to write another. They're even going to pay her. She'd floated out of the office and pulled the latest issue off a stack by the door, thinking she should familiarize herself with recent articles. There was her daughter's face on page six. Thank God Monique's name wasn't in the caption.

"*You* wrote an essay?" Tyler's laugh is derisive. "About what?"

"Don't be rude, Tyler," Monique says. "That's great, Mom. I'm really proud of you."

"They'll probably rescind their offer once they realize it's you in that photo."

"Why would that matter? How would they know it's me anyway? They didn't print my name."

"It matters because you lied to me and went to a riot."

"It wasn't a riot when I was there. And I didn't lie to you. You never asked me where I was going."

Everything always gets twisted around into being her fault. "We'll talk about this when your father gets home. Go to your room."

"Jesus, Mom. I'm not ten years old. You can't just order me to my room."

"Watch your language, young lady."

Monique picks up her book and fills her water bottle from the fridge spout. "I'm choosing to go to my room now because I want to, not because you're making me."

"I could give you some ideas of what to write about, Mom," Tyler says once Monique has slammed the door of her bedroom shut. "You could take some pictures of me wrestling. Maybe get a few shots of my trophies too. It'd be good publicity for my team. And you could interview me about what music is trending this summer. FYI, it's not that Fogerty dude Dad wanted to see."

"Everything in this world doesn't revolve around you, son."

Tyler gives her one of his charming smiles. "Just trying to help."

■ ■ ■

"I'm kind of proud of her," Eric says when he comes home from work. "My parents were always protesting too. She takes after them."

"Proud of her! She could have been hurt. Or arrested. And we didn't even know she was down there."

Eric squints at the picture of Monique and pats his shirt pocket. "I must have left my reading glasses at the office."

"There's a pair in the kitchen." She calls down the hall-way, "Monique! Your father wants to talk to you."

Eric comes back wearing glasses and picks up the *Herald*.

"We need to take away her car keys," Lisa says. "For the rest of the summer."

"That's not fair," Monique says as she comes down the hall. "I didn't do anything."

"Huh." Eric points at the photo. "That guy looks like my employee, Keith."

"Who?" Monique says, looking over Eric's shoulder.

"Keith?" Lisa snatches the paper away from Eric. "The ex-con who works for you?"

"Ex-con?" Monique says.

"It sure looks like him," Eric says. "I never took him for a Trumpster though."

"Oh my God." Lisa doesn't trust her feet to hold her. She pulls out a barstool from the counter and sits. "Did you ever talk to him about why he was parking in our neighborhood?"

"He said he was waiting for his mother," Eric says. "His parents live a few streets over from us."

"I'm well aware of that, Eric. They're my clients. I thought you said Keith didn't live with his parents anymore." She'd seen no sign of a son when she did the walk through with the Nelsons.

"He doesn't," Eric says. "He's got his own place now."

Lisa turns to Monique. "So, this is who you've been sneaking around to see."

"I'm not sneaking around to see anyone, mother. Especially not that guy. He's old. Where do you get these stupid ideas? Josh told me you hunted him down at Albertsons trying to find out who I was going out with."

"There's no reason to be rude, Monique," Eric says. "Your mother's upset."

"You should be upset too!" Lisa says. "And I did not hunt Josh down. I simply asked him to help me find the frozen meatballs." They both look at her as if she's deranged, which is infuriating, although right now she feels deranged. "I need you to be honest with me, Monique."

"I've always been honest with you." Monique looks her straight in the eye.

Lisa feels a slight pang of guilt. Monique's the child they have always been able to trust.

"Let's all calm down," Eric says. "This does seem a little farfetched, Lisa."

"Calm down?" Lisa says. Eric will do anything to avoid conflict. "The *Herald* prints a photo of your daughter at a riot with an ex-con who works for you and has been spying on us, and you want me to calm down?"

"I know why you're freaking out," Monique says. "You're afraid the *Herald* won't print your essay now."

"The *Herald* is actually going to print that essay?" Eric says.

"Don't sound so surprised. They might not print it now."

"I wasn't with that guy. I don't even know who he is. And it wasn't a riot when we were there."

Eric shakes his head. "She's right, hon. Maybe we just need to set stricter boundaries."

It almost sounds as if Eric thinks she's the one who needs boundaries. "Why aren't you ever on my side?" Lisa asks. "If you won't do this, I will. Hand over your keys, young lady."

Eric's lips tighten.

"Fine," Monique says. "I'm sick of being Tyler's chauffeur anyway. You can drive him around for a change." She grabs her purse, pulls out the keys, throws them down on the table, and goes back to her room, slamming the door behind her.

"I think you're being a little too hard on her," Eric says.

"You want to just let her run wild?"

"We can have both kids be clearer about their schedules. Don't we have their phones on trackers?"

"You say *we*, but you really mean *me*. I'm the one who tracks them. I'm the one who always has to play the bad parent. These are your kids too, Eric."

"What do you want me to do?"

"You need to fire Keith."

"I can't fire him for standing on a public street."

"Next to our daughter at a riot! Isn't that a violation of his probation?"

"He's not on probation anymore. I really don't think he knows Monique. But I'll talk to him."

"You'd better do more than talk to him. He's a creep who's been scoping out our house and stalking our daughter."

"We don't know that for sure."

"You're naive."

Eric holds up his hands. "Maybe I am. At least Monique did the right thing. When it got dangerous downtown, she left right away."

"She shouldn't have been there in the first place."

"At least she believes in something. Isn't that good?"

"And I don't? Is that your point?"

She can tell Eric has more to say, but now Tyler comes in the house from the backyard, glassy eyed again, carrying his duffel bag. "What's up with Monique? She says she can't drive me to practice tonight."

"I have a roast in the oven," Lisa says. "And you didn't tell me you had practice tonight."

"You didn't ask," Tyler says.

"I'll take you," Eric says.

They file past her to the garage and get in the Tesla. Lisa yanks the roast out of the oven and throws it in the trash. "Fix your own dinner," she tells the empty room. Six church bells chime. The water faucet drips. The buzzer on the dryer goes off. Across the room in the china hutch, her blissful face in the wedding photo mocks her.

"Oh, for God's sake." She takes the roast out of the trash, wipes off the potato and carrot peelings, and puts it back in the oven. Her family won't notice.

■ ■ ■

The make-up sex is good, but Lisa can't sleep afterward with Eric's snoring. She tiptoes down the hall and cracks open the door to Monique's bedroom. Monique is curled up on her side under the blankets, her phone charging next to her bed on top of a small leather journal Lisa's never seen before. She could retrieve them both and find out exactly what Monique has been up to, but she doesn't want to be that kind of mother.

Maybe she did overreact, but this is such bad timing. The *Herald* might decide she has too much baggage. Why can't she have this one tiny bit of success for herself? She closes Monique's door, walks back down the hallway, opens the slider, and steps into the backyard. Normally she enjoys being outside at night. She likes the idea of the cinder block wall enclosing their property, turning it into a small compound of the people she loves. But tonight, the fog has rolled in and the concrete around the pool is cold on her bare feet. She stares at the water, remembering exactly how Betsy looked, floating face down.

The pool will be gone as soon as she can find a contractor to fill it in. She's decided not to worry about the potential impact on their property value. Not everyone wants a house with a pool anyway, especially one where someone drowned. She shivers in her thin nightgown and hurries past the pool to the workshop. The door creaks a little as she pushes it open. Tyler is sprawled across the bed, snoring as loudly as his father. His sheets are twisted around his lower torso, the bare skin on his chest smooth and supple. Her beautiful son.

She hears nails clicking on the patio near the swimming pool and turns. A possum limps toward an avocado that has fallen from her neighbor John's tree. When it stops and stares at her, she can see a scar on the crown of its head. It doesn't have a tail either, and it's missing part of its right hind leg. Lisa's heart thumps. It would be just like Betsy to come back to haunt her as a crippled rodent. She'll talk to John tomorrow. He needs to get that avocado tree trimmed.

CHAPTER TWENTY-FOUR
JEANNETTE LARSEN

Jeannette follows Keith through the gate on the side of the garage, past three garbage containers lined up in front of a wooden fence covered with night blooming jasmine. The sickly-sweet fragrance is nearly nauseating.

"Nice surprise," Keith says, "you calling me tonight."

"I had some free time."

"I was really glad I ran into you at that concert. I've looked for you a couple of times at the Seaview gym."

"I mostly teach in South County now."

She waits while he unlocks the side door, noting the chipped white paint on the doorframe, and then follows him into the garage. He leaves the security screen open and turns on a fan, which only moves the stifling air back and forth. Summer in Wellington Beach has been cool so far, but Garden City is much further inland and at least ten degrees warmer. The garage feels like a convection oven.

"Like I said, it's not much." Keith turns on an overhead fluorescent light that hums, flickers, and pulses.

Jeannette remembers the sound of shrieking violins from the shower scene in *Psycho*. "It's fine," she says. It's not fine. She smells bleach, roach spray, and cigarettes now, in addition to the jasmine and the garbage cans. It was a mistake to

191

come here. She should go home. She made that one-time-only rule for a reason.

"Did you have any trouble parking?" Keith asks. "I should have told you to park behind my car. I try to stay away from the jacaranda trees. Those purple flowers are sticky. They'll ruin your paint job. They bloomed late this year. Usually, they're done by now."

She didn't notice the jacaranda trees. She can't even remember what kind of car he drives. She never intended to call him. She's only here because she's angry with Bob. She'd raced home to make dinner after teaching back-to-back aerobics classes, but as soon as she pulled the meat loaf out of the oven and set the table, Bob called and said his team was taking Amy out to celebrate her birthday. "I'm sure I told you," he'd added.

She is sure he didn't. "Have fun," she said. "Tell Amy happy birthday for me."

She heard him swallow, unsure of her tone.

"We're going to Houston's," he said. "You could meet us there if you want."

"I just got off the freeway, babe. I can't stomach the idea of getting back on it right now."

"I probably won't be home until after ten. It's a big group and you know how the service is at Houston's."

10:00 p.m. She'd wondered if that meant he was sleeping with Amy. "I'll watch a movie or something. Mostly I just want to take a shower." She'd wrapped the meatloaf in foil and put it in the fridge. Then she took a shower and called Keith.

"Would you like a beer?" Keith says now. "Or a glass of water?"

"No thanks," she says. "Where's the bathroom?"

"Inside. No one's here right now. My roommates don't speak much English, but they're friendly. And clean."

"Mexican?"

"Cambodian. They cook a lot of fish. The smell takes a while to get used to."

She smells the fish now as she looks around her. A sisal mat covers the floor. There's a microwave on top of a miniature white fridge in one corner and a blow-up queen-sized mattress in the other. There's an orange crate next to the bed with a lamp and a phone charger plugged into the same extension cord as the fan. There are two plastic chairs and a small plastic table. Plastic boxes are neatly labeled: socks, underwear, and gym clothes. He's rigged a closet pole off a shelving unit, hung with blue dress shirts, black slacks, and blue-striped ties. The bottom two shelves hold bags of protein powder, packages of rice cakes, a large can of oatmeal, and a blender. The amount of thought, time, and energy he's put into this pathetic setup is completely depressing. Her closet is bigger than the space Keith calls home.

"Maybe I will have a beer," she says.

She sets her pink canvas Coach bag on the plastic table and sits down. The middle shelf holds a stack of books. *In Search of Excellence, Barbarians at the Gate, Liar's Poker.* All the books Bob read years ago when he first went into management. She remembers packing them up when they turned his office into Zack's nursery. She takes a sip of beer. She won't think about Zack right now.

"Self-improvement books," Keith says. "My grandma gave them to me." He nods at a framed photo of an older woman in a loose Hawaiian dress on the top shelf.

"Is that her?" Jeannette says,

"Granny C. She's going to be eighty at the end of August."

She doesn't want to make small talk with this man. She's never thought of him having a mother, much less a grandmother. An eighty-year-old grandmother means his parents could be in their late fifties, which means he might be in his late thirties. He doesn't look that old though. She's getting a sinus headache from the jasmine. She doesn't want to calculate age differences.

"I need to use the bathroom," she says. Inside the house, the smell of fish is stronger, but everything is spotless. She wonders if Bob is having sex with Amy right now. If she confronts him tonight when she gets home, will he tell her the truth?

When she returns to the garage, Keith is stretched out on the mattress with a big grin on his face, naked except for a red MAGA hat.

"Are you kidding me? You're a Trumpster?"

His grin disappears. "Not really."

"Then why the hell are you wearing that ridiculous hat?" She picks up her purse. "I never should have come here." She needs to get home before Bob does.

"Someone gave it to me." Keith takes the hat off and tosses it across the floor. "It's supposed to be a joke."

"It's not a joke. Don't you know what that hat stands for?"

"It was free."

"What's your deal anyway? Are you just not that smart?"

A quick flash of anger crosses his face, and the tendons in his neck flex all the way down his torso. He has a giant erection, and she imagines he could get angrier, which is disturbingly erotic. She sets her purse down on the table. "I shouldn't have said that. I'm sorry."

"Nothing I haven't heard before."

She unzips her dress, steps out of it, and hangs it over one of the plastic chairs. "I don't have much time."

■ ■ ■

Afterwards, he watches as she puts her clothes back on, then stands and reaches for his shorts. "I'll walk you out to your car."

They might run into his neighbors, she thinks, and she doesn't want to be introduced to anyone. "That's not necessary. I'm fine on my own."

"How old are you anyway?" he asks.

The questions stings, considering he's just seen every inch of her body in this god-awful fluorescent light. "How old do you think I am?"

"I'd guess, early thirties?"

She smiles, relieved. "Same as you, then."

"Oh man!" He looks wounded now. "You really know how to hurt a guy. I'm only twenty-four."

Twenty-four. The blood rushes out of her head. Five years older than Zack. She could be his mother. She picks up her purse from the table. "I need to get going." Where is Keith's mother? she wonders. And why aren't his parents helping him?

"I know this is a weird setup," Keith says. "But one of the housemates is leaving at the end of the year. I'm in line for his room."

"Something for you to look forward to I guess." This will never happen again. She will delete his phone number as soon as she gets in the car. Her Tinder app too. This foolishness has gone on too long.

Keith picks up the Trump hat from the floor and opens the side door. The jasmine/garbage smell is even stronger now. He lifts the lid of one of the trash bins and throws the hat away. "Does that make you feel better?" he asks.

"It should make *you* feel better." She'll tell Bob everything tonight. Come clean. They need to be honest with each other. She lets Keith kiss her before she gets into her car and watches him in her rear-view mirror, standing in the road as she drives away, broad grin still on his face.

Before she confesses to Bob, she should probably make an appointment with her gynecologist. Once she's sure she's disease-free, she will tell Bob everything.

She hopes she hasn't already lost him. It might be too late.

CHAPTER TWENTY-FIVE
KEITH NELSON

Thursday at the Bug Guy, Keith sits at his desk feeling like he's forgotten something. Ever since he threw away the red hat, his luck has changed. This morning he didn't have time for a shower because his roommates tied up the bathroom too long. He barely got to brush his teeth. He's going to have to talk to Kiri about setting up a schedule.

Grace comes out of Eric's office and heads straight toward him. This time she looks really nervous when she says Eric wants to see him. This time the *Wellington Herald* is spread out on Eric's desk.

"You're standing next to my daughter," he says. "Why is that?"

Keith moves closer. He hasn't seen the photo yet so it's not hard to pretend to be surprised. "I didn't see her there," he says. "I didn't even know there was going to be a protest. My friend invited me to meet him downtown for a beer."

"I can't fire you for what you do on your time off, Keith. I can't fire you for your politics either. But if I catch you anywhere near my daughter again. I'll not only fire you, I'll press charges."

"I don't know your daughter."

"Keep it that way. You can go back to your desk now."

He's not fired, not yet anyway, but when he walks by Grace's desk, she glances up at him and shakes her head. "I don't understand why you were part of all that nastiness," she says.

"I just met a friend for a beer."

"You need to make some new friends." She turns away and avoids him for the rest of the day. None of the people he works with will make eye contact either. He's not all buddy-buddy with them anyway so he doesn't really care, but Grace has always been nice to him, and he misses her smile. It's a long day. He's glad when he can clock out, get in his car, and go home to his garage.

■ ■ ■

Except he doesn't go straight home. It's like his Honda is on autopilot as he once again finds himself heading toward Wellington and turning into his parent's tract. Both of their cars are in their driveway. The For Sale sign is still in their yard with Lisa Kensington's smug face plastered above the Sandcastle Realty phone number.

He drives by Eric's house and slows down. The garage door is wide open, a white Mercedes is parked next to Eric's blue Tesla, and there's a green VW in the driveway. The Mercedes looks like something a realtor would drive. The VW must belong to one of the kids.

The door from Eric's garage to his house is also open. It would be simple to walk right in and announce that he's calling a Bug Guy family meeting, that he's never met the daughter and didn't kill the grandmother. He likes imagining Eric's shocked expression, but that would only get him fired, and Granny C has always told him not to leave a job until he has another one lined up. He has nothing lined up except a blow-up mattress in a garage. He makes a U-turn and heads to Garden City.

■ ■ ■

Sunday afternoon. Wayne is late. Keith paces inside his parents' garage. At least Lisa Kensington isn't having an open house today. At least his mother left the garage unlocked, although the door to the house isn't, which means he can't even go inside to pee.

Wayne finally backs his red F-150 into the driveway just before 5:00 p.m. "Dude!" he says when he sees the For Sale sign, "Your parents are moving? Where?"

"I don't know. Maybe Temecula."

"Temecula's awesome. I wouldn't mind moving out there."

"Why?" Keith asks.

"Tina loves wineries. She's always bugging me to take her and her girlfriends out there to get wasted."

"I'd be up for hanging out with a few wasted girls next time you go."

"Those girls are wild. Last time, one of them followed me into the head and let me fuck her from behind. Tina was right outside the door too, sipping chardonnay, with no clue."

He can't always tell if Wayne is telling the truth or not. "Everything's stacked and ready to go," he says. "One trip up and back, just like I promised."

"I hope so," Wayne says. "Just because I have a truck, every-one expects me to drop everything and help them move."

Wayne already said this before when Keith called. "I'm buying drinks afterwards," Keith says. "Wherever you want." He said that before too, but now it'll be dinner time before they finish, which means he'll also have to spring for food.

"Where's your car?"

"Around the corner on Hillside. You know how the neighbors are about parking here." Even now, Keith can feel eyes behind the shutters across the street watching them.

"I've got all the stuff piled up there in the corner. I took the weights off the rack to make it easier to move."

Wayne lowers the tailgate, looks at him, and scowls. "You're not wearing the hat."

"This woman I'm seeing isn't much of a Trump fan."

"Then you need a new woman. Got your bags packed for Virginia?"

"I'm not sure I can get the time off work." He picks up the weight bench. "So, what's going on with that video?"

"It's been taken down and taken care of." Wayne climbs in the truck bed. "Be careful not to chip my paint, dude."

"Taken care of how?" Keith heads back to the garage and picks up the weight rack. He's fairly sure stuff on the internet never gets taken down. That's why he never posts anything.

"I know the guy who runs the Wellie Wise Facebook Page. He talked to the woman who posted the video. She deleted it."

"There could still be more videos. That guy in the ski mask . . ."

Wayne interrupts. "He was asking for it, bro. He confronted you. I saw the whole thing."

"Someone else probably did too. Someone else probably has it on their phone."

"No one's come forward to complain. Except for a few store owners who got their windows broken."

"I didn't see any of that happen."

"So, you're good. We're both good. You worry too much, dude."

"What about that blond girl and the broken phone?" Keith carries the weights to the truck.

"You mean that bitch who tripped me and dropped her phone?" Wayne stacks the weights on the rack. "No one cares about her. Her father owns three bars in Wellington. He can afford to buy her a new phone."

"How do you know all these people?"

"I know people who know people. You'd know them too if you came to the meetings. Most of them are cool dudes. They're paying for our airfare to Virginia."

"Why would they do that?"

"They appreciated what we did at the protest. You're going to need a haircut before then."

He's not cutting his hair, but he's not telling Wayne that right now when Wayne's doing him a favor. They load the mats, kettle balls, and punching bag in the back of Wayne's truck and get in the cab.

■ ■ ■

"This is where you're living?" Wayne says. "Seriously?"

"It's the house with the Jacaranda tree," Keith says. "Back up in the driveway though. The flowers on those trees are sticky. They'll mess up your paint. They really should have finished blooming by now. It's global warming, I guess."

"Global bullshit," Wayne says. "You sure about this place?"

Keith gets out of the truck, goes around to the side of house, and unlocks the garage door. Everything looks tidy. The fish smell isn't bad today. He punches the garage door opener. "I'm going inside to pee," he tells Wayne. "I'll be right back."

When he comes outside, Wayne is still standing next to his truck. "You actually bring women here?"

Keith grins. "One in particular. She's hot. You'd like her." He unloads everything and carries it into the garage while Wayne just stands there watching him. When Keith says he has a six pack of beer in his fridge, Wayne shakes his head.

"This neighborhood doesn't feel safe. We don't exactly fit the profile, dude."

Keith looks at the houses around them. They're on the small side, mostly one story, some with bars on the windows.

There are a lot of cars parked on the street and in the driveways. A few parents stand in their front yards, watching their kids play. They're mostly Asians and Mexicans, which he guesses is what Wayne means about not fitting the profile. "We can go somewhere else to have a beer. Let me lock the garage." They get back in Wayne's truck and head toward Wellington. Wayne remains silent.

"So where do you want to go?" Keith finally asks.

Wayne spews out a laugh. "I can't believe you're seriously living in a garage in Little Hanoi."

"Actually, my roommates are Cambodian."

"What's the difference, dude? You couldn't find any place else? I mean, it's a garage in a fucking ghetto. You don't even have a toilet."

"I use the one in the house. It's not that bad. And it's what I can afford."

"Where were you living before exactly?"

"With my parents most of the time. Sometimes I slept in my car."

Wayne laughs.

"What's so funny?"

Wayne laughs harder. "I can't picture you sleeping in that piece of shit Honda."

"It's not a piece of shit. And I'm not sleeping in it anymore."

"And this is better? Holy shit, Keith. What happened to you?"

"You know what happened. I'm paying off attorneys and court fees."

"Ancient history."

"To you," Keith says. "You didn't do any time."

"Are we going there again? Unbelievable. I didn't do time because I'm not the one who got himself arrested."

"I'm not the one who ran."

"Whatever, dude. At least you're working now."

"For minimum wage. Whatever happened to getting me on where you work?"

"They're supposed to be hiring again next month."

"You said that before."

Metallica is on Wayne's sound system. Keith turns up the volume. "I'm your pain," the singer growls.

Wayne doesn't say anything else; he just laughs occasionally. When they turn into his parents' tract, Keith has already decided to tell Wayne to forget the beer. He's not in the mood to hang out with Wayne tonight. He'll go home and set up his weight bench, take a shower, and go to bed early.

CHAPTER TWENTY-SIX
JOSH KOWALSKI

Josh sets his skateboard on the rim of the Kensingtons' empty swimming pool, sits down on the edge, and stares at the mossy green puddle in the bottom. "You guys should leave it like this. It looks cool."

Monique glances at him over her book. "Not happening. My mom's already hired someone to fill it in with dirt."

Tyler lights the bong on the table next to his chaise lounge, takes a deep inhale, and blows out a white cloud of smoke. Tyler doesn't usually smoke out by the pool, but the senior Kensingtons aren't home this afternoon. "My dad tried to drill holes to get rid of the rest of the water, but the drill bit broke off."

"Which totally freaked him out," Monique says. "He's convinced the pool is haunted."

Brittany pulls a bottle of dark purple nail polish out of her backpack and sets it down on the patio table. "Your parents really should have buried Betsy."

"I know," Tyler says. "We didn't even get to say goodbye to her. They took her straight to the crematorium and we never saw her again."

"That's just wrong." Brittany takes the bong from Tyler. "Personally, I want a huge funeral, a purple casket, and a gravesite overlooking the ocean with a purple granite headstone. And I want purple roses delivered every week."

"Duly noted," Monique says. "Purple is your signature color after all."

"Betsy never even liked the beach," Tyler says. "I don't get why Dad wants to dump her ashes out in the ocean."

"What would you rather do?" Monique asks. "Put her in your bong and smoke her?"

Josh and Brittany laugh, but Tyler's eyes go wide. "That's a messed-up thing to say, Monique. Jesus."

Brittany takes a hit and hands the bong back to Tyler. "We need to figure out what your signature color is, Monique. I'm thinking dark green, like your car."

"I'm thinking black," Monique says, looking down at her book.

"Why?" Brittany says. "Because that's what your poet friends wear?"

Tyler snickers. "Poet friends? What are you Chlorine Heads talking about?"

"We weren't talking to you," Brittany says.

"I think writing poetry is cool," Josh says. When Monique glares at him, he runs his fingertips over his head. His scalp itches. It's not even a week since he used his dad's old electric razor to buzz off his hair and it's already starting to grow back.

"Black is practical," Monique says. "I need something new to wear to Betsy's funeral anyway since my mom's decided I look terrible in all of my clothes."

"Lisa doesn't know what she's talking about," Brittany says. "Her look is definitely dated. And I can't believe she thinks you need a boob job."

"Shut up, Brittany." Monique snaps her book closed. "I should never tell you anything."

Josh is sure he hasn't heard right because there's nothing

wrong with Monique's boobs. His ears burn just thinking about them.

Tyler, in mid-exhale, bursts into sarcastic laughter followed by a raspy cough. "You're finally getting a boob job? About time."

"I'm trying to have a conversation with your sister," Brittany says. "And her boobs are fine."

You're right, Josh thinks, and then he worries he's said that out loud. Tyler is still laughing.

"Although if Lisa's going to pay for bigger ones," Brittany says, "I say go for it."

"I'm not discussing this right now," Monique says.

Brittany shakes the bottle of nail polish. "Anyway, there's a party in the Marina tonight. What are you going to wear?"

"You're both supposed to be grounded," Tyler says.

"I'm aware of that, Tyler," Monique says. "Mom probably hired you to sit here and watch me all day."

Tyler crows, "How does it feel to no longer be the perfect angel? I'm the good kid now."

"I'm not grounded anymore." Brittany opens the nail polish. "And you shouldn't be either. I mean, neither one of us did anything wrong."

"You went to a riot with Dad's ex-con," Tyler says.

"That is not true, and you know it," Monique says. "That guy was just there. And now he's ruined my summer."

"We still have more than a month left," Brittany says. "My mom is so sick of me staying home, she put money in my Uber account and begged me to find something to do tonight."

"Are you serious?" Monique says.

"Once again, being a bitch pays off," Brittany says.

Josh watches her stroke polish on the nails on her left hand. The color is so purple it's almost black. He thought the plan was for all of them to hang out tonight. He'd even loaded a few rockets, a package of sparklers, and a couple of firecrackers in his backpack from the stash his dad left behind, thinking it'd be cool to light them at the bottom of the empty pool once it got dark.

Technically, he's supposed to be grounded too, but his mom's working a twelve-hour shift today and won't be home until after midnight. She still doesn't know he was at the protest, but she saw the photo of Monique in the *Herald*. Now, because he lied to her, he's only allowed to go to work and come straight home after. That's why he buzzed off his hair. He thought his mom would be pissed, but she says she likes it. He'd hoped he'd get fired, but Darlene likes it too.

"Come on, Monique," Brittany says. "We'll Uber to Buena Loma, you can read your poems in that coffee shop, and then we can hit the party."

"Wait a minute." Tyler leans forward. "Who do you know in Buena Loma?"

"Monique's reading some of her poems this afternoon," Brittany says.

"Sounds bogus to me," Tyler says. "Where are you guys really going?"

Brittany taps on her phone screen. "An Uber can be here in ten minutes. You're already grounded. What else can Lisa do to you?"

"I'm trying to get my car keys back, Brittany. My mother doesn't give up as easily as yours does."

"Lisa can be pretty relentless." Brittany blows on her nails. "Which means you probably are going to end up getting that boob job."

"Nope," Monique says. "Not happening. And I already said I didn't want to talk about it."

Josh's ears get hot again. He scratches his head, feeling the contour of his skull as he studies the shape of the empty pool. "You know what would be cool? Have a party and set up a band in the deep end."

"That's actually a good idea, Cart Boy," Brittany says. "Maybe Betsy's ghost would leave. Especially if you hire my brother's band and his skinhead drummer."

"Shut up about the ghost," Tyler says.

"I'm not a skinhead," Josh says. "And I'm not their drummer either."

Brittany stands. "Are you seriously not going with me tonight, Monique? Because I found something totally outrageous for you to wear."

Monique groans. "You can't keep buying me stuff, Britt."

"It was on sale at Nordstrom Rack. No big deal."

It must be nice, Josh thinks, to be Brittany and David, and have so much money you can buy clothes for other people and own a five-thousand-dollar guitar that you don't even know how to play.

Brittany leaves and Monique goes inside. Tyler puts his phone down, lies back, and stares up at the sky. Josh looks up too at a Southwest plane heading north toward Los Angeles.

"You ever just want to get away?" Tyler asks. "Like in that stupid commercial? I mean, before your life starts sucking any more than it already does?"

"What sucks about your life?"

Tyler frowns at his phone. "Nothing really. But we're going to be sophomores, which means we'll have to figure out where we're going to college, and then we'll have to get jobs and our lives will basically be over."

"I'm not even sure I'm going to college." Brittany left her nail polish. He reaches for it.

Tyler snorts. "Of course, you're going to college. What else are you going to do? Work at Albertsons for the rest of your life?"

"You don't have to be rude. I'm not sure my parents can afford college."

Tyler looks at his phone again. "Get a loan, dude. That's what everyone does."

"I'm not everyone."

"Thank God for that."

Josh paints both his middle fingers. "Looks cool, don't you think?"

"It looks stupid. Are you going to start wearing eyeliner now too?"

Josh flips him off and sets the bottle back on the table. "You could also turn the pool into a skatepark."

"I could see that." Tyler puts his phone down. "Let me borrow your board for a sec."

"No way. You haven't ridden in a while. And you'll get it all slimy."

"You go then."

"I don't know. Betsy's ghost might get pissed off."

"Shut up about the ghost."

Josh walks down the steps, sets his board down, and skates over to the deep end of the pool. He circles the bottom twice, gaining momentum, climbing higher on the walls with each revolution, until he's almost sideways.

Tyler whoops. "Awesome, dude."

He's flying and laughing, but when he tries to do a flip, the wheels of the board catch on a plastic light fitting and the board flies over his head. Josh crashes down hard on both knees.

"Didn't hurt." He jumps up. He's only bleeding a little.

They switch off. Tyler's reflexes are slower at first, maybe because of the weed, but then it's annoying how quickly he gets the hang of it. His core strength is greater than Josh's and his balance is steady. Tyler spins around the top curve of the pool, nearly perpendicular to the ground, a grin on his face Josh hasn't seen since grade school when they were the same height and weight and were best friends.

They each fall a few times. The wheels of the board get wet. By the time they're both out of breath from laughing, most of the murky water is either on them or splashed on the sides of the pool.

"That was rad," Tyler says.

"Why did you get rid of your board anyway? You used to skate all the time."

"We're not kids anymore. We're going to be sophomores."

"I brought some fireworks," Josh says. "For later. When it's dark."

Tyler's phone chirps. "Finally," he says. He reaches for it and punches out a text, then stands and picks up his bong. "I need to get moving."

"I thought we were hanging out."

"We did hang out. And now I have to go."

"You're not inviting me?"

"You don't know these kids, Josh. You wouldn't have any fun."

"You mean I wouldn't fit in."

"You can't keep randomly stopping by, expecting me to drop everything and entertain you."

"That's rich. All you do is get stoned."

"Whatever. If you want to stay and skate, go ahead. I don't have to be here."

It sounds like Tyler thinks he's doing him a big favor. "I have stuff to do too. I have other friends, you know."

"Good. I'm glad to hear it. We'll hang out another time."

Josh slams his board into the side gate on purpose as he leaves and turns around to see Tyler's reaction, but Tyler's already gone back inside.

The church bells chime five times as Josh rolls down Tyler's driveway. He rides around the neighborhood, aimless and angry, too restless to go home. Where is Tyler invited that he isn't? Noah's, maybe? He skates across Eckerd Street to Noah's house, but there's no one home. He heads to the skate park and does a few tricks, but there's no one to watch him. He skates to the Church Park, which is empty, and then back over to the Kensingtons' house. The Tesla is parked in the open garage, the white Mercedes and the VW are in the driveway. Tyler's probably left by now to wherever it is he's going. Josh rolls past Ray's silent house. He guesses Ray's at the hospital. His mom told him Miss Vicky broke her hip.

Josh is almost in his driveway when he realizes the grey Honda parked in front of Ray's house is that guy's car. The one he thought was an Uber driver, the ex-convict who got Monique in trouble. He turns around and passes the Honda again. He's never seen it empty before. Everyone has something else to do tonight, even the ex-con. Everyone except him.

The back windows are rolled down a half-inch and there's a towel stretched out on the backseat that looks crusted and dry. One of the firecrackers in his backpack has a fifteen second fuse, which makes it even more illegal. His dad warned him to leave those alone. "Too dangerous," he said. Fifteen seconds gives him time to make it down the street and up his driveway before it goes off. He's not going to do this, of course. The car would probably blow up and set the trees on fire, and then the entire neighborhood might burn down because of him.

A small voice underneath his heart whispers, "Do it anyway." The dragon Zippo lighter his mom doesn't know he has is no longer in the pocket of his shorts, it's in his hand. The firecracker is out of his backpack in his other hand. The voice moves up into his chest where it feels urgent and warm. "Do it now." He lights the fuse and slips the firecracker through the car window. The voice screams "Go" and counts down the seconds. "Fourteen, thirteen, twelve." Josh pushes off on his board and flies down the street like a rocket. "Eleven, ten, nine." He passes the house with the twin BMWs. "Eight, seven, six." He rolls up his driveway. "Five, four, three." He flips off his board and pulls out his house key. "Two, one. Lift off."

He rushes inside and slams the door behind him, heart thumping like a bass drum. It won't take long for sparks to ignite, red and gold. They'll scorch the towel and explode into flames that will leap from the backseat to the front and then move toward the engine. He'll be able to hear it, everyone will, all over the neighborhood. Monique and her parents, maybe even Tyler, wherever he is. The fire trucks will be coming soon. The Hefner Street station is right around the corner.

He listens. Silence. Maybe it's good the fire trucks aren't here yet. It'll give the fire a chance to burn longer. More oxygen, more heat, more fuel. It could burn forever. There should be sirens by now. He stares out the living room window. That firecracker was probably too old. It was a stupid thing to do, like everything he does, one more idea that turns into a big fat nothing. He goes upstairs. From the open window of his bedroom, he can see two people standing on the corner and now he's pretty sure he smells something burning. His heart picks up tempo as he hurries back downstairs and goes outside, expecting to see emergency vehicles rounding the corner, scorched trees, the burned-out shell of a car in front of Ray's house, panicked neighbors in the street.

Ray is in front of his house, coiling up his garden hose. *Ray was home?* Josh freezes. *Shit. He probably saw me.*

There's a brick on the ground next to the Honda and the back passenger window is broken. The two people he saw on the corner are halfway down the street. They're just out walking their dog. Josh turns around, hoping to go back inside before Ray sees him, but Ray calls out his name. Ignoring him would look suspicious, he decides, so he walks slowly down the street. "What happened," he says as casually as he can make his voice sound.

"Somebody threw a firecracker in the backseat," Ray says. "Luckily, I got to it with my hose in time."

"That was lucky." Josh's heartbeat is back in overdrive.

"Not really. I had to break the window to put the fire out and the backseat is torched. But I guess it could have been worse."

It should have been worse, Josh thinks. *This whole street is supposed to be on fire right now.*

"I don't think I've ever seen you walk before," Ray says. "You're always flying around on that skateboard."

"I walk sometimes."

"You know whose car this is, don't you?"

"I don't think so." Two crows dive from the telephone wire across the street, down to the ground, and fight over what looks like a pizza crust.

"It's Keith Nelson's car. Peggy and Tom's son? They live behind me. I'm guessing they kicked him out a few months ago. He was sleeping in that car for a while."

One of the crows squawks. Josh feels the hairs on the back of his neck rise. "I thought he was an Uber driver."

"So, you have seen him before."

"I don't know him. Is the car ruined?" How much does it cost to replace windows and car seats? A lot probably.

"The backseat's a mess and he's going to have to get the window fixed. I wonder where Keith is. I guess I should go tell the Nelsons what happened."

"Okay. See you later, Ray."

"Is your mom home?"

His heart drops to his stomach. Ray saw the whole thing. "She's working tonight."

"Could you tell her they moved my mother into a rehab facility? She'll be home in a week or so."

Or maybe Ray didn't see anything. "I'll let her know."

Josh goes home feeling nauseous. He heads up the stairs to take a hot shower, exhausted, wondering if maybe he's getting the flu. He dries off, puts on a clean T-shirt and boxers, and brushes his teeth. Ray would have said something if he saw him do it, wouldn't he? Josh stares at himself in the bathroom mirror for a long time, wondering when he became this person, then turns off the light and goes to bed.

CHAPTER TWENTY-SEVEN
KEITH NELSON

It's nearly 7:00 p.m. when Wayne turns on Hillside and pulls his truck up behind Keith's Honda. "What the fuck happened here, dude?"

Keith is already out of the car, running toward the Accord. The rear passenger window has a hole punched through it. The towel on the backseat is toasted; the seat itself is charred and soaking wet. He pulls a note out from under the wiper blade.

"Someone tossed a firecracker in my backseat," he tells Wayne. "One of the neighbors broke the window to put out the fire." He opens the door. The burned upholstery reeks. He never should have left the back windows cracked, but the towel he'd used to clean his weights wasn't quite dry, and he'd thought parking in front of Ray's house was safe. Stupid, stupid, stupid.

"This could have been a lot worse, dude," Wayne says. "You're actually lucky."

"Lucky? How am I going to get to work?" Keith slams the door. "Who would do something like this?"

"Some kid messing around." Wayne laughs. "At least you don't have to sleep in that thing anymore. You have a garage in Garden City. You're ready for new wheels anyway, aren't you?"

"This isn't funny. I can't afford a new car. I just bought a fridge, microwave, and all that shit for my new place."

Wayne comes closer. "Seriously, dude. The universe is telling you it's time for a change in vehicles and a different place to live." He laughs again. "You need to pay attention."

"The universe? What the fuck are you talking about?" When Wayne laughs harder, Keith pushes him in the chest. "Shut up."

Wayne rocks back on his heels, then catches his balance, a stupid snarl on his face. "Don't tell me to shut up. You live in a garage and your car's a piece of shit. I bet that bitch you're seeing is a whore. Why else would she fuck you?"

Keith swallows hard and cracks his neck from side to side. Wayne didn't mean that. "Take it back," he says. "You're supposed to be my friend."

Wayne spits out a laugh. "We were never friends, dude."

"Hey, Keith," Ray Murdoch's voice says in the distance. "You okay?"

Keith feels the veins in his forearms strain against his skin. "Why would you say that, Wayne? I'm the one who defended you every time you got beat up."

Wayne spits on the street. "No one else wanted anything to do with you after you stabbed that girl in the eye."

Ray's voice again, asking if he needs help. Keith's eardrums are pounding now. "You know that was an accident."

Wayne's lips curl. "I'm only helping you today because I feel sorry for you. Tina told me to stay away from you. You're a loser."

Keith punches Wayne hard in the jaw.

Wayne staggers back and his eyes fill with tears. "What'd you do that for?"

"Keith, come inside." Ray Murdoch walks down his driveway toward them.

"Stay out of this, Ray."

"You should leave," Ray tells Wayne. "Before I call the cops on you."

"Call the cops on *him*, you fucking geezer." Wayne wipes his eyes and touches his jaw, which is starting to swell. "Keith's the criminal. You don't know half the shit he's done." Wayne opens his truck door. "You and me are finished, man. You can forget about Virginia."

"I was never going to Virginia anyway. You're an idiot to trust those guys."

"Oh, yeah? We'll see who can trust who. You're going to regret this."

"Come in the house," Ray says. "The woman across the street is watching from her front window."

"Let her watch," Keith says as Wayne drives off. "Maybe she saw who did this. Did you?"

"No," Ray says. "I heard a pop and ran outside. Who was that idiot?"

"You don't remember Wayne?"

"I don't blame you for hitting him. Come inside for a minute."

Keith puts his hands on top of his head. He doesn't want to go inside Ray's house, but he doesn't want to get in his stinky car either. "I don't want to bother your mother."

"She's still in the rehab center." Ray turns and starts up the driveway. "She's doing great though."

"That's right. She broke her hip. You're dealing with stuff. I should go."

"She won't be home until later this week. Come inside."

Keith follows Ray up the sidewalk, flexing and curling the fingers on his right hand.

Ray opens the front door. "You want some ice for that?"

"It's okay. I won't stay long."

"I have a buddy who does upholstery. I bet he'd give you a fair price to replace the backseat."

"The window's fucked up too."

"Yeah. That might be expensive. You have insurance?"

"The deductible's pretty high. But I guess I should call them."

"Let me talk to my buddy about the upholstery. He might know someone who does glass."

What's Ray's trip? Why is he acting like he cares? "Can I use your bathroom?" Keith says. "I need to wash my hands."

"It's down the hall. Are you hungry? My neighbor brought over some lasagna."

He hasn't eaten all day. "I like lasagna."

"I'll heat it up. There's a case of Dr. Pepper in the garage fridge. Grab a couple."

Keith runs cold water over his knuckles in the bathroom sink then walks down the hall to the garage, opens the door, and takes inventory. There's a bicycle, an older model blue Camry, and neatly stacked boxes. More empty space here than in the garage he's renting. Next to the washer and dryer is a fridge loaded with Dr. Peppers.

When he goes back in the house with the drinks, Ray holds up a bag of ice. "For your hand. Let's sit on the patio. It's cooler outside. We don't have AC."

He follows Ray past the hutch with those little statues Wayne tried to steal years ago. Ray slides the door open, and they sit down at the patio table and open their sodas.

"What did your friend mean about Virginia?" Ray asks.

"I don't know. Wayne's all involved with some idiots at his gym. And he's not my friend anymore." Keith takes a sip. "What is Dr. Pepper anyway?"

"Some people say it's carbonated prune juice." Ray laughs. "My mother loves it. It'll grow on you."

Keith stares at the cinderblock wall between Ray's house and his parents. It's weird to be sitting here. He remembers following Wayne over that back wall. Probably shouldn't bring that up right now.

Ray looks at the wall too. "I went over to your parents' house to tell them what happened to your car, but they weren't home."

"They're out in Temecula looking at property today. I guess they're going to retire and move."

"Good for them. So, how's your new place? You all settled in?"

Keith takes a long sip and decides he doesn't need to impress Ray. "It's actually a garage. I don't even have a bathroom to myself. My roommates cook way too much fish, but it's clean. And it feels safe enough to me."

"Maybe it's where you need to be for now. Lasagna should be warm soon. Grab another Dr. Pepper if you want. I'll give my buddy Louie a call."

When Ray pulls out his phone, Keith tries not to laugh. It's an even older model than his. Louie, it turns out, knows someone who knows someone who works in a junkyard. He says a Honda Accord window might take some time, but he can get one.

After he and Ray eat, Keith pulls the Accord into Ray's driveway. They punch out the broken window and Ray finds a piece of cardboard and some duct tape. They tackle the backseat next. There are four bolts holding it in place, and it takes them a while to figure out how to unscrew them. Keith pulls the seat out, and the two of them carry it into the garage and set it down. They're both sweating.

"You sure your mother won't mind?" Keith asks.

Ray laughs. "Oh, she'll mind all right. But she needs something to complain about."

"Why are you doing this for me?"

"I'm the one who broke the window. Give me your phone number. I'll let you know when Louie is ready to start work on your car."

■ ■ ■

When he gets back to Garden City, the only place to park is under the jacaranda tree but ruining the Honda's paint job seems the least of his worries tonight. Kiri is sitting with a group in the front yard. Keith's tired of talking to people, but he forces himself to stop and say hello. He recognizes the two other housemates, Nimo and Prak, but not the woman with the pretty oval face and the long black hair sitting next to Kiri.

Kiri pulls a Bud Light out of a cooler and hands it to him. "Sit down. Join us." He points toward an empty lawn chair.

The young woman lifts her chin. "What happened to your car?"

Nosy, he thinks. "Somebody thought it'd be funny to throw a firecracker in my backseat."

"You have enemies?" Her dark knowing eyes shine in the streetlight.

"Who doesn't?" He hides his swollen hand under his forearm. "I'm getting it fixed."

"Forgive my sister," Kiri says. "She asks too many questions. This is Chenda."

Keith sips his beer and tries not to look at the woman, but he can feel her eyes examining him. He finishes half of the can and stands. He'll go take a shower since all the housemates are outside. "Thanks for the beer."

"Nice to meet you, Keith," Chenda says.

He heads toward the garage. It feels like she's still watching him.

■ ■ ■

After his shower, Keith stretches out on the blowup mattress with a baggie full of ice on his right hand. He hears his housemates laughing, chattering in some language he supposes is Cambodian, but he's tired enough it could also be English. He smells cigarettes. Kiri told him when he moved in that they play mahjong at night, that it's a friendly game, they only bet quarters, and Keith is welcome to join them. Keith told Kiri he didn't like card games. He needs to save his quarters. He has no idea how much junkyard windows cost or what Ray's buddy Louie will charge him for reupholstery.

He wonders if the sister is playing cards too.

Chenda.

The air mattress squeaks a little when he stretches out his arms and legs, but it's comfortable enough. He can smell the jasmine now. Like Ray said, maybe this is where he needs to be. He'll figure out the rest tomorrow.

**SANDCASTLE
REALTY**

LISA KENSINGTON

*Prestige Haven Homes,
Where Your Home Is Your Castle*

JULY 28, 2017 | (800) WB4-EVER lisa.kensington@Sandcastlerealty.com

THE RIPTIDE UPDATE

The current plans for the redevelopment of the Riptide Apartments call for 180 parking spaces, which is completely ridiculous. There will be 120 units if the plan is approved and we all know those people have more than two cars, not to mention work trucks and gardening trailers. We can't let this plan go through. However, attendance at the City Council meeting last week was disappointing. A few concerned citizens (including yours truly) spoke, but the council seems to think this is a done deal. It's not. Attend next Monday's City Council meeting at 6 p.m. sharp. Show up and speak out.

Helpful Household Tips

" *Everyone's busy these days. To keep track of important meetings, create a daily planner and set reminders on your phone.* **"**

In Case You Didn't Know

If you don't live in the house you are parked in front of, or if you are not guests or employees of the owners of the house you are parked in front of, then you should not leave your car there. We need to get on top of this now, especially if the City Council is successful in forcing this housing project down our throats.

PRESERVING THE CHARACTER OF WELLINGTON BEACH

Low-income housing is not the right fit for Wellington Beach. Here's some supporting data from the 2016 US Census Bureau. 82% of Wellington Beach residents are native US born citizens. The median Wellington Beach household income is $88,000. 60% of registered Wellington voters cast their ballot for Donald Trump in 2016 and 71% of residents are white.

The proposed Riptide housing project would definitely not be in harmony with the surrounding Prestige Haven neighborhood.

CHAPTER TWENTY-EIGHT

LISA KENSINGTON

Lisa leaves her latest newsletter on the front porch of the two-story, four-bedroom, one and three-quarter bath model on Hillside West. The new people have been here a few months already, but they haven't done anything with the yard and their trash cans are still sitting on the curb, two entire days after pickup. It wasn't her listing. She would have explained how things are supposed to work in this tract.

The garage door opens and a black Suburban backs out. The woman driving rolls down the window. "Can I help you with something?"

She doesn't sound friendly at all. Lisa arranges her best realtor smile. "I'm Lisa Kensington, with Sandcastle Realty? I don't believe we've met. There's going to be an estate sale over on Summertime Lane. You might want to stop by."

"We don't need anything," the blond woman says.

Lisa keeps smiling. "We're also hosting a neighborhood garage sale later this month. It's a good opportunity to get rid of stuff you don't need anymore. I know sometimes after people move to a new house, they look at all the boxes they need to unpack and—"

The woman cuts her off. "We don't have anything to get rid of either."

"Well, that's great," Lisa says. "Good for you. Most people aren't that organized."

The woman squints and looks up at the sky. "That's a huge bird."

Lisa follows her gaze. "It's a blue heron. I see them all the time down at the wetlands."

"I've heard that's a nice place to walk."

"If you park on Pershing and walk to the bridge and back, it's a four-mile loop."

"I'll have to remember that." The woman hesitates. "I'm Jeannette Larsen. And my husband is Bob."

"Welcome to the neighborhood."

"I'm late for work." Jeannette backs out of her driveway and speeds off.

She's in a hurry, Lisa thinks. She'd wanted to mention the city council meeting tonight, but Jeannette didn't give her much of a chance. She remembers the Suburban now, she'd followed it out of the Albertsons parking lot last week and watched it move into the turning lane without signaling and streak in front of two oncoming cars. *Reckless*, Lisa thinks now. *What's that all about?*

Further down Hillside, Ray Murdoch is outside watering his mother's roses. He glances at her and turns his back, obviously hoping she won't stop and talk to him. What an old grump.

"How's your mother, Ray?" Lisa says when she gets closer. "Martha told me she broke her hip."

"Thanks for asking." Ray's face softens a little. "She's at a rehab facility. I can tell she's feeling better because she's complaining all the time."

"These houses really aren't designed for older people, are they? Are you guys thinking about moving?"

Ray snorts. "I guess you're always angling for another commission."

"No!" Lisa says. "I didn't mean it that way. I worry about seniors living here. I want them to be safe. We already lost Stephanie Gorman, and then our Betsy...." Her voice breaks and her face feels hot. "I'm sorry," she says, fanning herself with the newsletters. "I didn't mean to get emotional."

"I'm sorry too," Ray says. "I didn't know Betsy, but that must have been awful."

"Thank you. It was. Anyway, Neil Gorman's estate sale is next weekend." She hands him a newsletter. "We're expecting a big crowd."

"Seems like Joni Gorman might want to wait and see how Neil does before she sells everything."

She could have waited a little longer before she got rid of Betsy's things, she supposes. Gone through them more carefully, saved the pearls for Monique. "Joni doesn't think Neil will ever be able to live on his own. Alzheimer facilities are expensive. And that house is supposed to be Joni's inheritance."

"Some people think everything is about money," Ray says.

He must think I'm as greedy as Joni. "Some people have their children's futures to worry about."

"Joni doesn't. I don't either. But I see your point."

She watches as the blue heron lands gracefully on the roof of the house next door. Ray turns to see what she's looking at. "A heron landing on a roof is supposed to be good luck," she says. "One of the Tongva elders told me that at the anniversary celebration last year. Can you believe it's been almost twenty years since we saved the wetlands from development? Remember how they had plans to drain it and build a shopping center?"

She's proud of stopping that, proud of protecting the last remnants of open spaces for her children. Just like she's trying to preserve the value of the Prestige Haven neighborhood. She should put that in her next newsletter.

"Those people have a fishpond in the backyard," Ray says. "I'm guessing that's what the bird's after."

"If they leave feathers behind it's even better luck."

"Well, it's not my yard, so it wouldn't do me any good."

What a grouch. She hands him a newsletter. "I'm sure you've heard about the city council's plans for the Riptide apartments," she says. "We need to stop that from happening."

"Doesn't bother me. People need to live somewhere."

"They haven't planned nearly enough parking. You'll never be able to park in front of your own house."

"I park in the garage. I might need to live in those units once my mom is gone."

"No, you won't. You'll inherit this house."

"Not necessarily. My mom might leave it to PETA or Greenpeace."

"She wouldn't do that." Ray just likes to argue. She could explain about the increase in crime and the impact on police and fire and the school systems, but this isn't what she wants to talk to him about. "Do you know the people who live in the house behind you? The Nelsons? Their son Keith works for my husband."

"I didn't know that. Another one of your listings, I see."

"It is. I'm actually a little too busy these days. How well do you know Keith?"

Ray shrugs. "I know who he is."

"Did he have some kind of a falling out with his parents?"

Ray's lips tighten. "How would I know? None of my business. Why don't you ask the Nelsons if you're so interested in their son?"

He knows something, she's sure. "You're right. It isn't my business either. Just thought you might have noticed something. I know you're home a lot. I used to see Keith sitting in his car, but I haven't seen him around lately. Any idea where he went?"

"Nope."

"Have you ever seen Keith talking to any of the neighborhood kids?" Like my daughter, she almost adds, but she doesn't want to give Ray the idea she doesn't have her kids under control.

"No," Ray says. "I haven't."

"Do you think you might be watering those roses too much? We are in a drought after all."

"Wellington sits on top of an aquifer. My mother loves her roses, and they need water."

"Say hello to Miss Vickie for me. I hope she gets well soon." She turns and heads toward the next house. Ray definitely knows more than he's saying. Keith is a problem, and she is right to worry about him.

■ ■ ■

It's date night and Lisa's turn to pick the restaurant. Their favorite sushi place has a huge crowd and a half hour wait. The hostess apologizes and gives them a buzzer. "Let's get a drink at Knuckleheads next door while we wait," Eric says.

When they walk into the bar, Lisa recognizes two of the four men sitting at a nearby booth. Greg Oppenheimer is the top realtor in the Wellington Marina, and she's met Frank Palmer, one of the city planners, before, at a benefit for the wetlands. The other two men have their backs to her. One is dark haired, the other, large and blond. The bartender sets two coasters on the bar and Eric orders gin and tonics.

"You know what I saw last Saturday?" the blond man in the booth is saying. "A coyote walking down the middle of my street at ten thirty in the morning. Like he owned the neighborhood! I couldn't believe it. Is that normal?"

Greg Oppenheimer catches Lisa's eye and smiles. "You'd better get used to that," he says.

"Too bad we can't poison them," Frank Palmer says. "Or even better, shoot them."

"Christ!" Eric says under his breath.

"Well, I don't know about that," the blond man says. "That coyote was a good-looking animal. And they were here before we were."

"That's what people say when they first move here," Greg says. "You'll change your tune. Isn't that right, Lisa?"

"Don't leave your small children or pets outside unattended." Lisa steps closer to the booth. "Hi Frank, Greg. You remember my husband, Eric?"

"Sure do." Greg raises his glass. "You're kicking butt over at Sandcastle these days, Lisa. I've been following the comps. Your numbers are impressive. And I love your newsletters."

Lisa smiles. This is a huge compliment coming from Greg. "The market's good right now."

"Enjoy it while you can," Frank says. "That housing project is about to take a dump on your property values."

Her smile freezes. "We're still hoping we can stop that."

Greg shakes his head. "That ship has sailed, Lisa. The Riptide's coming down and it's only going to get worse. The city council's in closed sessions right now, approving permits for another project near the high school."

"I didn't know that," Lisa says. "Is it legal for them to meet secretly?"

"It's what they do," Frank says. "We need to recall the entire council."

"It's date night," Eric says. "We both promised, no work talk."

Greg points to the buzzer. "You guys aren't eating here? Knuckleheads has the best fish tacos in Wellington."

"We're having dinner at the sushi place next door," Eric says. "It's one of our favorites."

The blond man glances over his shoulder and smiles. "I'll keep that in mind," he says. "My wife and I love sushi."

"There's always a big crowd of Asians in there," Frank says. "I guess that's a good sign."

"It's a sign we'd better watch out for kamikaze drivers in the parking lot when we leave." Greg nods at the blond man. "Like your Chinese friend from the concert? What was her name?"

"Gloria? She's not Chinese."

Greg shrugs. "They were an odd couple. You don't see too many Mexicans with Chinks. Their kids must be mutts."

"Jesus, Greg," Eric says. "What a thing to say."

Lisa turns around and whispers, "Let it go, honey."

"Finish your drink," Eric says. "And let's get out of here."

"Felix and Gloria are good people," the blond man says. "Nothing odd about them."

Greg laughs. "Don't get all defensive, man. I didn't mean anything."

"How about another round of Fireballs?" the dark-haired man in the booth says. "My day sucked. I got reamed by Carter Welch. The downtown merchants are not happy about all those broken windows."

Lisa glances over her shoulder at the mention of the city attorney.

"The idea was *one* free beer," the dark-haired man continues, "not endless rounds."

"Yeah," Frank says. "Things got a little out of hand. Some of the guys were overserved at Cyclone's. But we all know it was ANTIFA who broke the store windows and beat people up."

"Are you talking about that protest at the pier?" Lisa says. "I didn't hear about people getting beat up."

"It was a 'Take Back America' rally, not a protest," the dark-haired man says. "And it got hijacked by people who don't belong in Wellington. Left-wingers. Inlanders. ANTIFA. They broke windows and pushed people around."

"Disrespectful," Greg says. "They weren't locals of course."

"On a lighter note," Frank says. "Walmart's got a nationwide sale on tiki torches. Great timing, right?"

"You guys having a luau?" the blond man asks.

The other men laugh. The timer for the sushi restaurant buzzes.

"Saved by the bell," Eric says.

"See you guys around," Lisa says as Eric pays the bill.

"I told you that protest was dangerous," she says when they're outside the bar. "Monique is lucky she left when she did."

"I stopped listening after that first remark Greg made," Eric says. "I've never liked him or Frank. I wouldn't trust anything they say. I hope you don't expect me to go to their luau."

"We have to go if we're invited, honey. I'm sure you have work colleagues you don't like either, but you still do business with them. Greg's a big deal and Frank works for the planning department. And that dark-haired man obviously knows Carter Welch. I can't believe the city council is already signing off on another housing project. It's so depressing."

Eric takes her hand. "Let's go have a nice dinner."

"Okay. But I bet anything your ex-con was part of that violence."

CHAPTER TWENTY-NINE

RAY MURDOCH

Ray waves at Lisa as she heads into the sushi place with a man he assumes is her husband since they're holding hands. "That's the realtor from my neighborhood," he tells Louie.

"Does she know anything about that affordable housing complex going in near you?"

"I know she's against it," Ray says as he opens the door to Knuckleheads. "Why?"

"I'm thinking I might apply," Louie says. "The space rent for my trailer is going up seventy-five bucks a month. I can't afford that. It feels like they're trying to force me out."

"What a world," Ray says.

"I can't even remember the last time I was in a bar," Louie says as he follows Ray inside.

"Knuckleheads is a restaurant too. They're supposed to have good fish tacos. Thanks for looking at that car seat."

"It's not going to be that much work. Getting a new window might take some time." Louie smiles at the waitress. "How are you doing tonight, darling?"

"Just fine," she says. "You can sit over there. I'll bring you some menus."

"You need to stop with that darling business," Ray says as they walk toward an empty booth.

"I'm harmless," Louie says. "She knows that."

Ray glances at the four men in the next booth before he sits down. Sometimes he sees people he recognizes, but these men aren't familiar. One of them facing him looks like an old surfer, sun-streaked long hair, overly tanned. The guy next to him wears glasses and has a thin rat-like face. They both ignore him. The other two have their backs to him. One is bigger and blond, the other dark haired. It looks like they've been here awhile, judging from the pitchers of beer, empty shot glasses, and half eaten plate of nachos.

"How many miles are you up to now on that bike?" Louie asks as Ray slides into the booth.

"I did twenty yesterday," Ray says. "Down to the Pelican Pier and back."

"That's terrific. I'm proud of you, buddy."

"I could go a lot further if I didn't have to plan my routes around places to stop and pee."

"Speaking of which," Louie says, standing. "I'll be right back."

"The city council wants names, and they want arrests," one of the men behind Ray is saying. "It can't be anyone involved in fight club either. I'll talk to Wayne Connor. He knows a lot of people, and he was down there in the action."

Fight club, Ray thinks. *Wasn't that a Brad Pitt movie?*

"I'm not sure about Wayne," another man says. "He's got a short fuse."

"We need people with short fuses," the first voice says. "As long as they're willing to take orders."

"We should have another conversation with Wayne," one man says. "I'll invite him and his friend over to the house on Saturday for a barbecue. You guys should come too. Bring your wives."

Keith's friend Wayne sure seemed to have a short fuse, Ray thinks. Louie is back.

"It sucks getting old," he says. "I think I have to pee and then I can't."

The waitress overhears and grins as she hands them menus. "What can I get you gentlemen to drink? We have a special on pitchers tonight."

Louie laughs. "Our beer drinking days are behind us, darling. Ten years sober last month," he adds.

"That's wonderful," the waitress says. "I just got my five-year chip. How about a pitcher of iced tea on the house?"

"That's nice of you, sweetheart," Louie says.

Ray expects a lecture on calling women darling and sweetheart, but it doesn't come. They order fish tacos. Louie pulls out his phone. "I'm going to email my friend at the junkyard about that Honda window."

"I don't know how you can type on something that small. Why don't you just call him?"

"He never hears his phone ring." Louie squints at the screen.

Ray knows that Louie can't do two things at once, which means there will be no more conversation until the email is sent. He thanks the waitress when she brings the pitcher of tea and pours two glasses.

"They're taking down the statue of General Lee," one of the men at the booth behind him says. "It's government over-reach, plain and simple. You haven't been following that story?"

"Not really," the man directly behind Ray says. The big blond guy, he thinks. "I mean, I've heard some Southern states took steps after that church shooting in Charleston. That was terrible."

"Too bad Roof didn't take out more of them," one of the men says.

Ray nearly chokes on his iced tea. Surely, he's misunderstood.

The big guy sounds horrified too. "Excuse me?" he says.

"Dylan Roof," the man says. "Remember him?"

"That kid who shot up that church in South Carolina?"

When the man doesn't say no, Ray carefully sets his iced tea glass down on the table, a bitter taste in his mouth. He hasn't misunderstood anything. "Are you listening to this?" he whispers to Louie.

Louie holds up his index finger. "Just a sec. I'm almost done."

"They're letting the illegals take over," one of the men behind him says. "They want to replace real Americans like us with minorities they can control. We have to step up now before it's too late. We're the last line of defense."

Defense against what? Ray wonders.

"I didn't realize you guys were so . . . political," the big guy says.

"Political" isn't the right word, Ray wants to tell him. "Reactionary racists" is more like it.

"It'd be great to have you sponsor the trip," one of the men says.

"I've already made a donation," the big man says. "A substantial one, too."

"That money went toward our educational programs and mentoring," another man says. "And we appreciated the contribution. There'll be plenty of opportunities later on if you can't help us out this time."

"What the hell kind of education and mentoring are you guys offering?" The back of the booth shudders as the big guy stands. "I need to get out of here."

Louie looks up from his phone.

"You haven't finished your beer," one of the other men says. The big guy strides away from the booth and out the front door, slamming it behind him.

"What was that all about?" Louie asks.

The men behind them laugh. Ray turns around and looks at each of their three faces, committing them to memory for some purpose he's not sure of.

"Can I help you with something, old-timer?" the surfer asks.

"You guys from around here?" Ray asks.

"Born and bred," the dark-haired man says. "Why do you ask?"

"Just curious," he says. He turns back to Louie. "Like I said before, I don't understand this world anymore."

"Must be having a senior moment," the surfer guy says behind him.

"No reason to be rude," Louie says when the men laugh again. Louie leans forward. "I've got your back," he says. "Those guys might be younger and faster, but we have nothing to lose."

Ray almost laughs. "Don't be ridiculous."

The waitress brings two plates of tacos, rice, and beans. "Can I get you anything else?"

Louie grins. "How about some Cholula and your phone number?"

"Eat your tacos," Ray says. "Before we both make fools of ourselves."

SANDCASTLE REALTY

LISA KENSINGTON
Prestige Haven Homes,
Where Your Home Is Your Castle

AUGUST 4, 2017 | **(800) WB4-EVER lisa.kensington@Sandcastlerealty.com**

THE PROBLEM WITH THE RIPTIDE PLAN
There Aren't Enough Parking Spaces!

We all know that crime increases when people can't park in front of their own houses. Imagine your teenage daughter parking two blocks away, walking alone through the streets, being assaulted by some stranger. Imagine those strangers wandering our streets, breaking into our cars. A homeowner is entitled to curb space in front of their own house. Attend next Monday's City Council meeting and voice your opinion.

Helpful Household Tips

❝ *When walking alone, make sure to carry some sort of self-defense tool, like pepper spray, a taser, or a personal alarm.* **❞**

In Case You Didn't Know

The house on the corner of Paradise Court and Mountain Brook (the one with all the beautiful multi-colored plumeria trees) is for sale. This is one of the nicest floor plans in the Prestige Haven tract, a sunken living room, four bedrooms upstairs, and two and half baths. We'll miss the original owners, but we understand. Prestige Haven homes were designed for young families. If you are sailing into your golden years and need to make some changes, I can recommend several assisted living places and group homes.

KNOW ANYONE WHO WANTS TO LIVE IN WELLINGTON?

If you have friends and family who would fit in to our Wellington lifestyle and are ready to enjoy the sand, surf, sun, and subtle sophistication that still encapsulates what the City of Wellington Beach is all about, please give me a call at 1-800-WB4-EVER. I have some great listings available.

GET READY FOR THE GARAGE SALE!! Saturday, August 19th. Your trash might just be some other neighbor's treasure. I'll supply the signage.

CHAPTER THIRTY

JEANNETTE LARSEN

In the morning, when Jeannette shows Bob the newsletter about the garage sale, he's excited. "It'll be a chance to get to know the neighbors," he says. "Make some new friends."

New friends are part of the agreement they made last night after Bob's confession. Jeannette had panicked when he came home with tears in his eyes. He smelled like he'd been drinking, and she'd thought for sure he'd either found out about all the men or was leaving her for Amy. Or both. She started to say she could explain everything, but he stopped her and said he'd made a terrible mistake. He'd just met Doug and his friends at a bar, and they'd said horrible, racist things.

"I never should have given them money. Service club, my ass."

"How much did you give them?" she'd asked.

"Five thousand dollars." He spit out the words. "For *mentoring*. Fuck! Can you imagine what kind of mentoring those monsters do?"

Five thousand dollars? Jeannette let the amount sink in.

Bob went on about how she was right all along about Doug and his friends. They were just using him. He should have listened to her from the beginning.

"I was afraid you were going to tell me you'd slept with Amy," she'd said when he'd finished.

"God, no," he said. "Why would you think that? She's young enough to be my daughter."

After that, there was no way she could tell him about her Tinder account or Keith or any of the men. What good would it do anyway? He was already devastated. Confessing that she'd cheated and lied to him might clear her conscience, but it would surely break them apart forever. They've already lost so much. They need to move forward.

Neither of them got much sleep last night, but this morning, she's ready for a fresh start. She pours two cups of strong coffee. "You want to be part of this garage sale, babe? I could call that realtor woman and see if she needs help."

"Some kid would be happy to have all of those clothes out in the garage," Bob says.

Zack's clothes, he means. She tried to give his things away once before; loaded them in her car, dropped them off at the Salvation Army, and made it two blocks before she turned around and went back. She had to wrestle the bags away from the volunteer. She still needs to open them occasionally and breathe in Zack's scent, just for a minute.

"We could offer donuts and coffee," she says. "That would attract a crowd."

"That's a great idea," Bob says. "Everyone loves donuts. Let's do it."

After Bob finishes his coffee, kisses her, and leaves for work, she goes to Target, buys two giant plastic storage tubs, brings them home, and marks the top and sides of each box "XMAS Decorations" with a black Sharpie. It's always been her job to decorate for Christmas. Bob will never look inside these containers. She'll tell him she donated Zack's clothes if he asks.

She feels something watching her and glances over her shoulder. A hummingbird sits on an overhead electrical wire, its ruby throat glowing in the sunshine. It's strange to see the tiny creature completely motionless. "Don't you dare tell anyone what I'm doing," she says.

She pulls the bags off the shelf and takes out Zack's shoes and clothes. The T-shirt from that band with the unpronounceable name Zack loved so much, and she could never stand. His red baseball jersey that matched the ones she and Bob wore when they all went to the stadium together. The brand-new Converse sneakers he never had a chance to break in. Size twelve low-top, black, Jack Purcells, created in collaboration with some Japanese designer Jeannette had never heard of.

When Zack bought the shoes home, she was a little shocked at the price he'd paid considering they were made from canvas. Her first instinct was to suggest he return them. Once she looked closer though, she could see the design was sleek and sophisticated with its contrast white stitching. The smile on Zack's face was pure sunshine. "I know it's a lot of money," he'd said, "but you should be down with this. These are limited edition."

The shoes had a name. Vampire or Zombie, Jeannette can't remember now.

A voice behind her says. "We brought you some banana bread."

Jeannette turns. The hummingbird is gone, and a woman stands in the driveway, a teenage boy next to her, two thin silhouettes against the late morning light. It's the woman down the street who lives in the house with the yard that's half dirt and mostly weeds. The woman who'd stopped her from fucking Keith at that concert. She's forgotten her name, but she really should thank her.

"Banana bread?" The woman holds up a loaf wrapped in wax paper. "To welcome you to the neighborhood. Sorry it's taken me so long. I'm Martha and this is my son, Josh." She extends her right hand.

"I'm Jeannette." She should shake the woman's hand, but that would mean releasing the shoes, which she is apparently incapable of doing right now. "I remember you from the concert."

"Oh." Martha smiles. "I didn't think you would. I got there late, but the music was okay. If you like show tunes."

Jeannette nods.

"Are you getting ready for the garage sale?" Martha says. "We should get rid of a few things too."

"No," Jeannette says as the boy moves in closer. He's buzzed off his hair, a style she normally doesn't like, but it suits him. His eyes stand out. They're a nice hazel color and his brows frame them perfectly. He has a circle of freckles on his right cheek like a kiss.

"Those are the shoes I was telling you about, Mom. The Werewolf."

Werewolf, Jeannette remembers. *That was the name.* "How old are you, Josh?"

He stands up a little straighter. "Sixteen."

"Do you need help with those boxes?" Martha asks.

Josh steps forward. "I'd be glad to help, ma'am. Where would like me to put them?"

"I don't need any help," Jeannette says, her voice much too harsh she realizes, when Josh takes a big step back. "I mean, thank you. I can manage."

"Well," Martha says, "I'll just put the banana bread over here." She sets the wrapped loaf on top of the brand-new dryer next to the brand-new washing machine. "Front loaders," Martha says. "How do you like them? My old washer and dryer are about to give out on me."

"They're okay," Jeannette says. "As long as you get the stands too."

"I've heard that." Martha's gaze lingers. "This red is such a nice color."

There's something wistful in Martha's voice that makes Jeannette wonder if maybe she can't afford a new washer and dryer right now.

"Well." Martha turns. "Welcome to the neighborhood. We should get going, Josh."

"What size shoe do you wear, Josh?" Jeannette had no intention of asking this question and Josh looks as surprised as she feels.

"Twelve," he says. "Like my dad."

Jeannette notices a small shadow cross Martha's face at the mention of the dad and that's when she decides. "Try them on. You can keep them if they fit."

He looks at Martha who shakes her head. "No. That's much too generous."

"Please," Jeannette says. "You'd be doing me a favor."

"You want me to roll those trash cans in for you?" Josh says. "I could take them out for you next week too. Every week from now on. And I'm really good at weeding."

Jeannette laughs and holds out the shoes. "Okay. We have a deal."

CHAPTER THIRTY-ONE
JOSH KOWALSKI

Josh glides his board up Ray's driveway, not noticing the grey Honda parked next to Ray's car until he jumps off. He freezes as Keith lifts his head from whatever it is he, Ray, and some skinny old man Josh has never seen before are working on inside the garage. Ray stands, but Keith and the other man look back down at what Josh can see now are pieces of the backseat of a car. The backseat he set on fire. Each man has a section, and it looks like they're ripping the cushion seams apart. *Keith has to know I'm responsible*, Josh thinks. *Ray must have told him.* He looks at Ray's face for some kind of confirmation, but Ray is smiling at him.

"We could use another set of hands," he says. "That's Louie and this is Keith."

Josh stays frozen in the driveway, waiting for Keith to rise, enraged, charge toward him and smack him across the face, but Keith simply glances at him and says, "Hey. What's up?"

"What do you have there, Josh?" Ray asks.

Josh looks down at his hands and remembers he's brought his mom's pasta. He didn't want to deliver it. He's been avoiding Ray's house all week, but today he couldn't think of an excuse his mom would believe. He holds up the container and swallows hard, his mouth completely dry. "Fettuccini."

"Excellent," Ray says. "We'll be hungry later. Take my place, Josh. Turns out I'm useless at this. My fingers are too old and stiff."

"I have stuff to do," Josh says. "I'll just leave this and go."

"Stay awhile," Ray says. "Never hurts to learn something new."

Louie glances over at the low cinderblock wall between Ray's house and the one next door. "Those little gators are back."

Josh turns in time to sees two alligator lizards with bright yellow eyes facing off.

"They were doing pushups earlier," Louie says.

"Establishing their territory, I guess," Ray says.

The lizards streak down the wall and are gone.

Louie gives Josh a gap-toothed grin. "What's up with your hair, son? You're not one of those protestor skinheads, are you?"

"Protestor? No!" Josh scratches the prickly hair on his scalp. He buzzes it with a trimmer every other day now, but it grows back too fast.

"Josh here is a musician," Ray says. "He plays drums."

"Cool," Louie says. "You in a band?"

"I'd like to be." Leave, he tells himself. Leave now.

"He works at Albertsons too," Ray says. "Quite the entrepreneur. You could add upholstery to your resume, Josh. Louie's made a career out of it."

"It pays my rent," Louie says. "And keeps me in groceries. Like I was saying. It's a good thing it wasn't the front seat, Keith. Hell of a lot more complicated. Backseats are easy."

"Easy for you, maybe," Keith says. When he stands, Josh cringes, but Keith is only lifting his arms overhead and twisting from side to side. "This is hard work." He looks at Josh. "Someone threw a firecracker in my backseat. In case you were wondering what happened."

He doesn't say this sarcastically and his face is calm. *Calm before the storm*, Josh thinks.

"Help us out, Josh," Ray says. "You can use my ripper. Hand over the pasta."

Go home, Josh tells himself, but his legs move toward Ray like he's some kind of zombie.

Ray takes the container from him. "Sit." He nods at the empty chair next to Keith. "I'll go put the noodles in my fridge and get us some cold drinks."

"I can't stay long."

"Every little bit helps." Louie stands, pulls his phone out of his pocket, and walks over to Ray's washer. "We need some music to inspire us." He props his phone up against a plastic jug of liquid Tide and Led Zeppelin pours out of the tiny speaker.

"I've been the best of fools," the singer wails.

Keith shows him how to hold the seat cushion in his left hand and the seam ripper in his right. *This is insane*, Josh thinks. *Keith could easily reach over and stab me right in the jugular vein.*

"You just start pricking out the threads until the seam comes apart," Keith says. "See what I'm doing? One little prick at a time."

Louie laughs. "That's what she said."

Keith laughs too.

Josh picks up Ray's section of the cushion. John Bonham's drums match his heartbeat. He keeps his head down, but his eyes are sideways on Keith.

"Turn that up," Keith says.

"You like Zeppelin?" Louie asks.

"I'm more of a Metallica fan," Keith says, "but Zeppelin's okay."

"Metallica's basically Zeppelin on speed," Louie says. "Which works for me since it doesn't look like the Zep's getting back together anytime soon."

Josh takes a breath. "It wouldn't be the same anyway, without John Bonham."

"What?" Louie says. "You've heard of Led Zeppelin?"

Ray comes out with four cold Dr. Peppers. "Josh knows a lot about music. He was working with Neil Gorman for a while."

"Neil Gorman," Louie says. "Name sounds familiar."

"He was the drummer for Electric Catfish," Ray says. "He used to live over on Summertime Lane."

"Electric Catfish!" Louie grins. His teeth are disgusting. "They used to play at that club in Goat Hill. The Cuckoo Clock?"

"No, the other one," Ray says. "Kaleidoscope."

"Man, I haven't thought about Kaleidoscope in ages," Louie says. "Remember that bartender with the nose ring? She had a big crush on you."

Ray passes around the Dr. Peppers. "That was a long time ago."

"Back in our drinking days," Louie says. "Right after Nam."

"You guys were in Vietnam?" Keith says. "What was that like?"

"Ancient history," Louie says. "That Catfish band was hot. You're lucky, Josh, learning from someone like Neil."

"My dad played drums too. But then he quit." Josh's voice cracks a little. "And then he left." His eyes burn. He wasn't planning on saying that at all.

Keith looks at him. "I used to wish my dad would leave. I finally left instead."

"I'm going to lose my worried mind," the voice on Louie's phone wails. Drums crash and the song finishes.

Josh clears his throat. "Zeppelin's the kind of band I want to be in one day."

"I didn't think kids these days appreciated good music," Louie says. "You sure you didn't get talked into signing up for the Marines, son? That hair style looks like something they'd do to you."

"I'm only sixteen. And it's not a hair style. I just buzzed it."

The men all laugh, even Keith.

"Sixteen!" Louie shakes his head. "You got your whole life out in front of you. Stay out of the service, son. That's my only advice."

Josh normally doesn't like people calling him son, but Louie seems okay.

Keith sits down next to him again and opens the Dr. Pepper. "I didn't like the taste of this stuff at first, but it's starting to grow on me."

"Keith was telling us about his new girlfriend," Ray says.

Keith's face is immediately bright red. "I never said she was my girlfriend."

Josh almost laughs, he's so surprised at how embarrassed this big guy seems.

"What's she like?" Ray says. "What kind of work does she do?"

"She's smart," Keith says. "She supervises at a machine shop in Garden City."

"Sounds like a keeper to me," Louie says. "What about you, Josh? How's your sex life?"

"What?" Josh says.

Ray laughs. "Ignore Louie. And don't take advice from either one of us about women. Louie's a confirmed bachelor and I've been divorced longer than I was married."

Louie finds more Zeppelin on his phone. Josh starts to relax. The lizards return and show off for a while. They've just about finished ripping the rest of the backseat cover apart when Ray looks up and quickly rises. Two Wellington Beach police SUVs pull in front of the driveway. Two officers jump out of each vehicle.

Louie stands. "What's this about, Ray?"

"I'll talk to them," Ray says. "You guys stay here."

Josh jumps to his feet, ready to run. Ray set him up, he's sure, inviting him to join them, pretending they needed his help. Ray must have called the cops when he went inside to put away the pasta.

Ray walks out of the garage. "Can I help you gentlemen with something?"

What a phony, Josh thinks. *Ray knows exactly why they're here.*

The cop wearing mirrored sunglasses says, "We're looking for Keith Nelson."

"What?" Josh says.

"That's me." Keith stands. "What do you want?"

The cops walk forward. "We have a warrant for your arrest," Mirrored Sunglasses says as he pulls handcuffs out of his pocket.

"For what?" Keith says.

"Vandalism, property damage," Mirrored Sunglasses says.

"I don't know what you're talking about," Keith says.

Your car. Josh opens his mouth, but no words come out.

The cops surround Keith. One of them says, "You can make this easy or you can make it tough on yourself," like some bad cop show on TV. Josh's brain is spinning so fast he's dizzy, but Keith acts like he already knows the drill the way he automatically puts his hands behind his back.

"There's no need to cuff him," Ray says. "He's not resisting."

Why isn't Keith resisting? Josh finds his voice. "It was me."

Ray gives him a quizzical look.

Mirrored Sunglasses looks puzzled.

"The car," Josh says. "It was me."

Keith looks at him, and then at Ray. He shakes his head and laughs. "Perfect."

The cops raise their eyebrows at each other. Mirrored Sunglasses shakes his head. "There's nothing in the warrant about a car. What are you talking about?"

"He means we need Keith's car keys," Ray says. "He's parked in my driveway. We'll need the keys to move it later."

"The Honda?" One of the officers walks around to the side of the Accord. "You fixing it up to sell? My daughter needs a car for school."

A radio in one of the police SUVs squawks and the beefier of the four cops takes his receiver off his hip and listens. "We're on our way," he says.

"The car keys are in my pocket." Keith holds his hands up, palms open. "I can hand them over to Ray."

"Take them out slowly," Beefy Cop says. "And drop them on the ground."

Keith pulls out the keys and tosses them toward Ray. The cops quickly cuff him and walk him to the first SUV.

"Should I call your parents?" Ray says.

"You could try," Keith says.

"Where are you taking him?" Ray asks.

"Main Street station first," Beefy Cop says. "County afterwards."

"I'll follow you," Ray says.

"I'd wait for a phone call," Mirrored Sunglasses says. "It'll be a while."

One of the cops pushes Keith into the backseat. The two SUVS drive off.

Louie glances over at Josh and barks out a laugh. "Jesus H. Christ, son. You're the one who torched the backseat?"

Josh looks at Ray. "I thought you knew it was me. I figured that was why the cops showed up."

"You thought I called them?" Ray looks truly hurt. "You know me better than that, Josh."

"But you knew it was me."

"I didn't see you do it. I can't say I'm surprised though. It was one of your dad's explosives, wasn't it? He used to drive me crazy, all the things he blew up."

"Are you going to tell my mom?"

Ray shakes his head. "I'll leave that to you. I guess there's no hurry to finish this now."

"Keith's going to need a car when he gets out," Louie says. "And I got no place else to be right now."

They both look at Josh.

"Hangman, turn your head awhile," the singer on Louie's phone begs.

"I'd like to stay and help you finish it," Josh says. "If that's okay."

■ ■ ■

"Mom," Josh says when she gets home from work that night. "I need to tell you something."

She sets her purse and her lunch box on the counter. She's wearing the yellow scrubs with the green turtles printed on them, her work lanyard still around her neck. It's her third twelve-hour shift. She'll work another one tomorrow. And she still manages to smile at him.

"You didn't have to wait up for me," she says. She looks at him closer. "What's wrong?"

"I did something really bad."

CHAPTER THIRTY-TWO

LISA KENSINGTON

Lisa stands across Eckerd Street and watches the yellow excavator chew into the side of the Riptide apartment building. The machine reminds her of a giant ravenous praying mantis. The building seems to be made of cardboard; it comes apart so easily. She should go home. It makes her sick to watch this, but she can't look away. The workers aren't even attempting to recycle any of the materials. One of the men on the crew told her earlier this morning that the walls would be down by the end of the day.

"We'll bust up the foundation next," he said.

"What about the dust?" she'd asked. "What about the noise?"

"We keep the hoses going. That reduces the dust. In a week, everything will be gone."

When she reminded him about the drought, he asked her to move across the street. She shudders now as the roof caves in. The bulldozers and forklifts move in next. Lisa walks home, exhausted, as if she'd torn down the structure herself.

■ ■ ■

"I was wondering," Monique says after she's wolfed down the tuna sandwich Lisa made for lunch. "Would it be okay if I invited some friends over?"

Lisa pushes her own sandwich aside. "Of course!" she says. It's been such a dreadful day. She's been looking for a way to make up with Monique without having to admit she might have been wrong. Keith Nelson is obviously a dangerous man, but it's pretty clear to her now that Monique doesn't know him. "Your friends are always welcome here. I was just thinking we haven't seen much of Brittany lately."

"I mean new friends."

Does she mean the boyfriend? Lisa wills her expression to stay neutral as she takes a small sip of Diet Coke. "That sounds wonderful! What's his name? Or hers? That's fine if it's a girl. I'm a lot more open minded than you think."

"What I meant is, I'd like to invite some friends over for a poetry reading."

Lisa spews out her soda. "Poetry?"

"You don't like poetry?"

"Of course, I like poetry. I'm just surprised."

"I've been meeting with a group of poets at a coffee shop. At least I was before you took away my car. Would it be okay if they came here instead?"

"Are these kids from school?"

"No. It's all ages of people. All kinds too. There are a couple of veterans and older women, and a few kids from the Performing Arts School in Buena Loma."

How is Monique ever going to find a boyfriend if she spends all her time with old women and veterans and arty kids from an inland school? "I had no idea. Are you sure this is the best use of your time?"

Monique frowns. "What's that supposed to mean? I thought you of all people would understand. You've kind of inspired me. You're a really good writer. Even though I don't agree with you, I'm proud of you for expressing your opinion."

"You don't agree with my opinion?"

"I think we need that housing project. There's an older

vet in the poetry group who lives in a mobile home park. His rent is going up seventy-five dollars a month. He can't afford that. And maybe my high school teachers wouldn't have to drive in from Menefee every day. People need to live near where they work."

"People need to live where they can afford to buy." When did she get so cynical? "It's mostly that I don't want to see this neighborhood change, honey. Don't you love living here?"

"It's okay, I guess. But I won't ever be able to afford to buy a house here."

"We'll help you and your brother when the time comes. And Wellington Beach is more than just okay." Her voice falters a little and she takes a breath. "We have the beach— and before you say that I hardly ever go down there—it's important to me to know it's close by. We have a wonderful farmer's market, a beautiful library, the Nature Center. The wetlands. Monique, you and your brother and me pretty much saved the entire wetlands from development."

Monique smiles. "Dad says you should run for city council."

Lisa blinks. "He told you that?"

"I think he's right. You really care about this place. You're articulate. You say what most people here believe."

"Wow. Thank you, dear. That's really nice. But you know how people like to gossip, especially on social media. They'll blame me for your grandmother's accident."

"No, they won't because it was an accident. Most people have already forgotten about it."

"Some people can be awfully cruel."

"Not everyone."

"I'd like to meet your new friends. Can I hear one of your poems?"

"I'm still learning. How about I read you some poems by another poet who I really like?"

"I would love that."

When Monique goes to her bedroom, Lisa thinks that she could offer the car keys back now. There is really no reason not to. But Monique didn't ask, and she'd like to keep her home for as long as possible.

Monique returns with a book. "Have you ever heard of Lucille Clifton? She had seven kids, and she wrote thirteen collections of poems."

Oh, great, Lisa thinks. Another perfect woman to judge herself against. Monique is sharing this with her though, and that means everything.

"Read me your favorite one," she says.

CHAPTER THIRTY-THREE

KEITH NELSON

His mother is the one who bails him out. Keith can't believe it when he finds her sitting there the next morning in the waiting room at the Citrus County Jail. "Ray called me," she says as he follows her out to her Lexus. Keith doesn't even try to explain that he never did any of the things he's been charged with because what he actually did was much worse. It's only a matter of time before the kid in the ski mask comes forward.

"I won't be able to pay you back for a while," he says when he gets in her car.

"I don't expect you will."

"They set a court date. With my priors, I'm guessing it's not going to go well."

"Probably not."

He expects her to add something sarcastic, which he more than deserves, but she doesn't say anything. He waits a while and then says, "My car is at Ray's house."

She nods. "I didn't get Ray's message until this morning. We weren't home yesterday when the police called either."

So, it wasn't his parents who told the police where to find him. He'd spent most of the night sitting on a hard jail bench trying to figure out who it was. It had to have been Wayne then, Wayne and his new friends. He waits through a few more minutes of his mother's silence and then says, "Some kid threw a firecracker in the backseat of my car."

"Josh Kowalski. I know. He came over and apologized. His mother wrote you a check to pay for the damages."

"You can keep it. I owe you a lot more."

"It's made payable to you."

"Ray has a friend who's giving me a deal on reupholstering the backseat. I need to replace the window too. I guess it could have been a lot worse."

"Your father has cancer."

He suddenly has absolutely no idea where they are. The streets always look different from the passenger seat. The storefronts have Spanish names. Abogado. Fianza. Desintoxicación. "What did you say?"

"Pancreatic. Stage four. We just found out yesterday."

"Oh."

"We're going to take the house off the market. You should come by and see him."

"He doesn't want to see me."

"Maybe not, but you should still come."

"How are you doing?"

Her face crumples for a half-second. He touches her arm, but she lifts her right hand off the steering wheel and holds her palm up like a stop sign. "I can't talk about how I feel right now. I'll fall apart, and I don't have time to do that."

"Okay," he says.

She doesn't look at him or say anything until she drops him off at Ray's house. She pulls Josh's mother's check from her purse and hands it to him. "You should come by the house."

He should pick up the car keys from Ray, find out from Eric if he still has a job, get that window fixed. He needs to pay Louie, decide what to tell Kiri and Chenda. "I'll come by as soon as I get some time."

"You don't have much time left."

■ ■ ■

Keith's public defender, Thomas Washington, is a young Black man who wears glasses and is fresh out of law school. He has a lot of other clients and takes forever to return Keith's calls. He isn't free either. Keith has to pay him by the hour, which means he's digging himself into deeper debt. Josh's mother's check was generous, but he's not sure there's much point in fixing the car window. Once someone connects him with the kid in the ski mask, he won't need a car to drive or a place to sleep.

Thomas somehow convinces Eric to put Keith on unpaid leave. "This is good," Thomas says on the phone when he finally calls. "It looks better to the judge, you having a job. But Eric wants you to promise to stay away from his daughter."

"No problem," Keith says. "I don't know his daughter." He hesitates and then asks Thomas if he's heard about any other charges.

"No," Thomas says. "Is there something you need to tell me?"

Even though he knows all about client-attorney privilege, he can't explain to Thomas what he did to the boy in the ski mask. "Just let me know if you hear about anything else."

Kiri's going to wonder why he's home all the time. Chenda too. He'll tell her first, he decides. When her car pulls in Kiri's driveway that evening after work, he's waiting outside.

"I brought fried chicken for everyone," she says when she gets out of her car. "Help me carry it inside."

"I have something to tell you first." He explains about the arrest, his priors, his time served, what another conviction will mean. Her expression is impossible to read, which makes him even more nervous, so he keeps talking, about the free beers at Cyclone's, his boss's daughter in the photo, how crazy it got downtown. He doesn't tell her about the kid in the ski mask. Maybe he won't have to.

"You'd better tell my brother too," she says when he stops talking.

"He'll kick me out."

"I don't think so," she says. "Not as long as you keep paying rent."

"What about us?" he asks, which is stupid. He's not even sure there is an "us." It's barely been two weeks since she followed him into the garage and lay down next to him on his mattress. They've only slept together twice.

She studies the ground and then shakes her head and looks at him. "Better to stop for now. Let's go inside. The chicken's getting cold."

For now, he thinks as he follows her in the house. Maybe he hasn't lost her yet.

■ ■ ■

"My sister has a big heart," Kiri says later, out in the garage after Keith tells him. "You'd better not break it."

It was stupid to think Kiri didn't already know about him and Chenda. "She doesn't want to see me for a while."

"Good," Kiri says. "She doesn't need trouble."

She doesn't need me then, he thinks. He's a fool to believe whatever this is between him and Chenda could work. He never should have told Ray about her either.

"The Angels game is on," Kiri says. "Let's go inside and watch with the others."

But Chenda, Nimo, and Prak aren't watching the game when he and Kiri sit down on the living room couch. There's a *Breaking News* story on the screen.

"Where is this?" Kiri asks when the camera pans a long line of white men carrying tiki torches, marching together on a dark city street. Keith guesses there are at least five hundred of them, all wearing white golf shirts and khaki-colored pants. Their hair is clipped short and they're mostly clean shaven. "Jews Will Not Replace Us," they chant.

"Charlottesville, Virginia," Chenda reads from the bottom of the screen. "All of this because of taking down a statue? What does that have to do with Jewish people?"

"Blood and Soil," the men on the screen chant now. "Blood and Soil."

"This is like some Nazi horror movie," Prak says.

"Holy fuck," Keith says as a familiar face fills the screen. Wayne, with a fresh haircut in a white golf shirt, grins right at the camera. Keith feels Chenda's eyes on his hands and realizes he's clinching his fists.

"Look at that," Nimo says as one of the marchers swings a lit torch at a woman standing on the sidewalk. A fight starts.

"Change the channel," Prak says. "The Angels game should still be on."

Kiri clicks the remote. The Angels are playing the Mariners in Seattle. Normally the housemates all talk at once, laugh at each other, cheer when the Angels score, yell at the screen when they strike out. Tonight, no one says anything, not even in the ninth inning, when Mike Trout scores the go-ahead run from second base and the Angels win, six to five.

Kiri turns off the TV.

"I'm tired," Prak says, standing. "I'm going to bed."

"Me too," Nimo says.

"How do you know that man on TV?" Chenda asks, after Prak and Nimo leave the room.

Keith knows better than to ask which man or to try and change the subject. "I went to school with him," he says. "His name is Wayne. He's the one who reported me to the police."

Chenda's dark eyes are on fire. "You need to report *him* to the police. They're going to be looking for him."

He's never seen her get angry before. "No one will believe me."

Kiri seems angry too. "He's a criminal, Keith."

"All those men are criminals," Chenda says. "You have to do something."

Her anger gives him hope, even if he doesn't deserve her. "You're right," he says. "I do."

■ ■ ■

What can I do? he wonders later, alone in the garage.

■ ■ ■

The next morning, Keith puts more duct tape on the cardboard in the Honda's busted-out window and heads east on the Riverside Freeway, taking the 15 south toward Temecula. The night he spent in jail, someone in the holding cell with him mentioned having family in Temecula, said he hated it out there. "Nothing but desert and grapes," the man said.

Temecula doesn't sound like his parent's style either. They aren't wine drinkers or desert people. His dad used to surf; his mother always complains about dry skin. Wayne likes Temecula though. He can still see that leering grin on the TV screen as Wayne marched through a city he doesn't even live in and terrorized people he doesn't know.

Keith takes the Rancho California exit. At first, Temecula looks exactly like Citrus County. There's a Target, a Ralphs, and a bunch of housing tracts. After a few miles, there aren't as many houses. The road narrows to one lane and starts to curve back and forth and climb up into the hills. Keith slows at a sign for Dorland Mountain, the wide-open gate an invitation. He turns right and heads up the steep road. At the top, there are a few simple cabins tucked underneath pine trees and an old RV parked in the center of what looks like a campground. The RV has a line full of laundry out front next to a picnic table with a camp stove.

He makes a U-turn, drives halfway down the hill, and pulls over. His cell phone barely has one bar. He gets out and looks off into the horizon at the open rocky land dotted with scrub brush. He smells sage and hears rustling in the brush, rabbits maybe. If he were going to walk out there, he'd need long pants and closed toed shoes. He'd have to watch out for snakes. The ground looks hard, maybe too hard for a shovel. A body left here overnight might get eaten by coyotes.

There's a stiff breeze picking up and Keith bets it will be cold here when it gets dark. He hears a dog bark and then a man's voice. "Duchess. Come back here." The guy in the RV, Keith guesses. He sounds old. He probably goes to bed early. Keith gets back in the car. On his drive home he notices a Walmart in Corona. There might be a dumpster behind it where he could toss Wayne's truck keys, cell phone, ID.

You have to do something, Chenda said.

He's never killed anyone. All he knows how to do is hurt people. He's strong, but he'll need to be even stronger to carry this plan through. He'll start running again, beef up his weight routine and his supplements, eat clean. Focus on what needs to be done and then do it. Figure out what happens next later.

THE RIPTIDE HAS BEEN RIPPED DOWN

The low-income housing project is now under construction. I'm very disappointed with the Wellington City Council. They've turned into puppets and accepted the State of California's decisions on how much and what kind of housing Wellington Beach needs, no matter what the concerned citizens have to say. Wellington deserves better leadership.

Helpful Household Tips

" *If you wouldn't buy it today if you saw it hanging on a department store rack, why do you have it around now? There is probably someone who wants it more and would wear it more than you.* **"**

In Case You Didn't Know

If you're thinking about remodeling, I always say you should put your money in kitchen and bathrooms and keep the colors neutral. You want potential buyers to be able to envision their lives in your space.

I have a list of contractors who have all worked in the Prestige Haven tract for years. They understand these homes. Mention my name for ten percent off plumbing fixtures.

PRESTIGE HAVEN GARAGE SALE

Despite the horrific recent changes implemented by our city council, life in Prestige Have goes on. We're having a neighborhood garage sale on August 19th. Dust off your old furniture, unused toys, and outgrown clothing and get ready to make some money. Have your goods out by 7 a.m. There will be free coffee and donuts.

CHAPTER THIRTY-FOUR
RAY MURDOCH

Saturday afternoon, Ray changes the channel from the CNN coverage of the Charlottesville march aftermath to a replay of Friday's Angels game. "It's not good for either one of us to keep watching that horror show," he tells his mother.

"I don't understand what this country is coming to," she says. "Your father spent four years of his life fighting Nazis. Now they're marching through the streets with tiki torches and running over women? And that idiot in the White House thinks they are all fine people?"

"I don't know what to say, Mom. I'm going to get some air. Your roses could use some water."

"Bring some in the house for me," she says. "This place needs cheering up."

Ray takes a vase out from under the sink, gets the clippers from the garage, and goes outside. He uncoils the hose and glances down the street, wishing Keith's grey Honda would turn the corner. Last night, he'd recognized Keith's friend Wayne, marching in the crowd, carrying a tiki torch, but he never saw Keith or any of the men from the Knuckleheads Bar. He heard Keith tell Wayne he wasn't going to Virginia. He should stop worrying about him.

Keith didn't want to talk about his arrest when he came by to pick up his car other than he'd been charged with vandalism and his mother had bailed him out. He also said that Josh's mother left him a check to pay for the damage to the Honda. Martha tried to give Ray a check too, but he wouldn't take it. "Fixing Keith's car seat didn't cost me anything except a few Dr. Peppers," he told her. "And I owe you more for all the pasta you feed us." Josh has been over every day, bringing him groceries and helping around the house so Ray doesn't have to leave his mother alone.

The country might be going to shit, but the neighbors have surprised him. The two little boys next door brought over pictures they'd colored with "Welcome home, Miss Vickie" scribbled at the top of the page. The woman across the street with the orange Fiat brought over a box of See's candy. The roses are flourishing too. The French Lace had a few aphids, but Gregorio recommended he try worm castings, which did the trick. The ruffled white petals flutter in the afternoon sea breeze. The Mr. Lincoln rose is a deep red, fragrant in the warm air. The Double Delight is in full bloom. He cuts a handful from each bush.

Lisa Kensington comes around the corner carrying another stack of her newsletters. "I heard your mother is home, Ray. How's she doing?"

"Twice as mean and even faster, thanks to the new hip."

"That's good news. I'm sure you noticed that the Nelsons took their house off the market. Terrible thing about their son."

"What about him?"

"Didn't you see the picture in the *Herald* of Keith at that riot downtown? He was arrested for vandalism. I was right about him being trouble."

Ray imagines Lisa is fond of being right. "I don't read the *Herald*. I read the *LA Times*. And I try to stay out of other people's business."

"Other people are my business." She holds out a newsletter. "The neighborhood garage sale is next weekend."

"I hate garage sales. What's the point of arguing with people over fifty cents? Might as well just give everything to the Salvation Army." None of this is true. He actually likes garage sales. There's just something about Lisa's overly earnest face that makes him want to argue with her.

"Most people like garage sales," Lisa says.

"Most people are idiots. You watch the news lately?"

"I'm taking a break from the news," she says. "Too much other stuff going on."

He's been thinking he should take a break too. The news only makes him feel useless. "How's it going with the Gorman house?"

Lisa exhales. "Joni's a bit of a challenge."

"I got that impression."

"It really should have sold by now, but she insisted on pricing it too high. She doesn't want to put any money into repairs either. The estate sale was a complete disaster." She half-laughs. "Sorry. I shouldn't gossip like this."

"I'm sure you'd rather fix it up, get the commission, and move on to the next sale."

Lisa's smile fades. "That's not what I meant at all. I try to help people get the most value for their homes. Especially when they're the original owners."

She studies the sidewalk and is quiet for a little longer than is comfortable, long enough for Ray to wonder if maybe he's hurt her feelings. He never took her for a sensitive type. "I don't really know what I'm talking about. I've never bought or sold a house."

Lisa's smile returns. "I'm here to help whenever you're ready."

"It's my mother's house. Up to her what she does with it."

"I'm glad she's on the mend. Maybe Joni will have better luck in my garage sale. That new couple offered to supply coffee and donuts. Have you met Jeannette and Bob?"

"Not yet," he says. "I'll bring some soft drinks," he adds, surprising himself because until the words leaked out of his mouth, he had no intention of even going to the damn thing. "I have a cooler. I'll buy a bag of ice too. I hope people like Dr. Pepper."

Lisa looks as astonished as he feels. "Thank you, Ray. Thank you very much."

A shadow crosses the sun and they both turn to look up. It's a crow.

"I haven't seen the heron lately or found any feathers," he says. "So much for good luck."

"I see herons all the time down at the wetlands. It's a wonderful place to walk."

"I'm not much of a walker. I've been riding my bike on the beach trail lately."

"I've seen you out on your bike. You look like you've lost some weight."

He sucks in his stomach. "Couple pounds." His face feels flushed. She's flattering him.

"Your roses are lovely, Ray."

"I probably water them too much."

"Lots of people are switching to drought tolerant plants. I might write an essay about that for the *Herald*."

Another reason not to read the *Herald*. Lisa's silly newsletters are bad enough. "You should talk to Gregorio about drought tolerant plants."

"Who?"

"You don't know Gregorio? He does half the yards in this neighborhood."

"I don't know any of the gardeners. The ones who do our yard are only there for ten minutes at most. I'm sure they don't know anything about plants. Thanks for offering to bring drinks, Ray. That's very nice of you."

That's me, he thinks. *Mr. Nice Guy.* He pulls a Double Delight rose from the vase. "Take this one home with you."

Her eyes widen. "Really?" She inhales the fragrance. "It's lovely."

He turns off the hose and takes the roses into the house.

"Were you whistling?" his mother says.

"I guess I was."

CHAPTER THIRTY-FIVE
LISA KENSINGTON

Lisa stares up at the sun through the special viewing glasses Susan brought for all of them. She Ubered to the house this morning from the Ritz-Carlton hotel and has been out in the cul-de-sac with Tyler and Monique ever since. "I had no idea you kids were interested in this," Lisa says. She'd had no idea they'd scheduled Betsy's service on the day of the solar eclipse either. "It looks like an orange toenail," she adds. "That's what my dad used to call the moon at this phase."

Tyler lowers his glasses. "That's the sun, Mom. The moon is in front of it."

"I know that, Tyler. I was making a joke. A toenail sun?" No one laughs.

"Or maybe a cheese wheel?" Susan says.

Of course, Susan has a more elegant comparison. She is the epitome of elegance this morning in her simple black linen dress that Monique immediately pronounced "totally awesome."

"Maybe you can take me shopping for school clothes while you're here," Monique says.

Lisa starts to say that Susan won't be here long enough to take Monique shopping, when Susan says, "I'd love to, Monique." And then she touches her fingertips to her bare neck and turns to Lisa. "Did you have any luck finding Betsy's pearls?"

"No," Lisa says. "I did not."

Susan sighs. "I just wish I had something of hers. I mean, besides her wedding ring."

"And the earrings," Lisa says. "That I saved for you."

Monique drapes her arm over Susan's shoulder. "You have us."

Susan hugs her back. "You remind me of my mother sometimes."

Monique grins. "My dad says that too."

"You don't look a thing like Betsy," Lisa says. "We should get going soon. Why don't you kids go get dressed?"

"We are dressed," Monique says.

Lisa considers her children's choice of clothing. Tyler's wearing shorts, but at least he's put on a shirt with a collar. Monique's black shorts are long enough to be classified as capris, but that white sleeveless top shows off every single muscle in her arms. Lisa sighs and decides to let it go. She smooths the new black and white tunic over her new white slacks. The slacks fit well, but she's not sure about the print on the tunic. The geometric design's a lot bigger than it looked online and definitely not as elegant as Susan's dress. She hopes Eric is ready. He asked her twice this morning if he should wear a dress shirt and tie instead of one of the three Tommy Bahama shirts he bought at Pelican Island. He's been pacing back and forth, picking up Betsy's urn (he finally decided on the blue one), and then carefully setting it back on the bookshelf. Lisa's afraid he's going to break it.

"The last time there was a total eclipse in the US was in 1918," Susan says. "Some people chase eclipses all over the world. Umbraphiles, they're called. Shadow lovers."

Lisa tries not to roll her eyes. Susan not only researched every obscure detail about solar eclipses, she also bought herself a fancy new camera. Eric bought the exact same model online last night when they came home after meeting Susan for dinner.

He comes outside now, wearing the grey mosaic print shirt. "Make sure you keep those glasses on," he says. "CNN just showed our idiot president staring right at the sun with no protection at all."

"I'm not surprised," Monique says.

"I read that a solar eclipse signifies change," Susan says.

What does that even mean? Lisa wonders, but Monique, Tyler, and Eric all nod in agreement as if Susan, a mid-level manager at the Social Security Office, is some kind of expert on astronomy or symbolism. "We should get going," she says. "Someone needs to bring out the urn."

"I'll do it," Monique says. "I could drive," she adds. "We're going to need two cars anyway."

"You're still grounded," Lisa says.

Susan lifts her eyebrows. "Uh oh. What did you do, Monique?"

"Nothing," Monique says. "Seriously. Absolutely nothing."

"We don't need to talk about this now." Lisa gives Susan a warning look. "There's more room in the Mercedes anyway. You kids come with me and Susan can ride with your dad."

"I'm going to change my shirt," Eric says. "I'll be right back."

"Hurry," Lisa says. Monique goes into the house and comes back with the urn. "I want to ride with Dad and Susan." When she offers the urn to Tyler, his face goes white. He wheels around and gets in the backseat of the Tesla.

Eric comes out wearing the blue mosaic print shirt. "All set?" he asks.

Lisa straps the urn in the passenger seat of her car. "Once again, Betsy, you're stuck with me," she says as she follows

Eric out of the cul-de-sac. "I guess you're kind of used to that though." Before she turns out of the tract, Lisa glances over at the empty place where the Riptide apartment building once stood. It looks like they're getting ready to pour a new foundation.

■ ■ ■

Thankfully, the captain takes charge of the urn immediately. "We like to check the contents first," he says. "We don't want any surprises."

"What kind of surprises?" Lisa asks.

"Occasionally the cremains clump together. Sometimes they're double plastic wrapped. We try to make it as easy as possible for the family."

The yacht is elegant and sleek. The haze has cleared, the ocean is turquoise green, and the air smells fresh. Once they're out on the water the wind picks up. After about fifteen minutes, the captain cuts the engine. "Who is going to sprinkle the ashes?"

They all look at each other.

"It's kind of choppy," the captain says. "Whoever does it will need to be able to kneel down comfortably."

"Kids?" Lisa asks, but they both stare down at the deck.

"You and I should do it," Susan tells Eric.

They move to the front of the boat. The flags on the mast snap in the steady breeze. The captain hands Eric the urn. "Make sure you release the ashes close to water," he tells Susan. "In the opposite direction of the wind."

"I want to say something first," Susan says. "It's a quote from Chief Seattle." She scoops out a handful of ash and lets it slip through her fingers. "To us, the ashes of our ancestors are sacred."

Lisa wonders if the captain found pieces of Betsy's gold fillings among the ashes and if that makes them even more sacred. She tries not to laugh. The boat is rocking now. Eric holds out the urn and Susan takes another handful of Betsy.

"Release them closer to the water this time," the captain says.

Susan kneels and tosses a big handful of ash into the ocean. "May this resting place be hallowed ground."

Hallowed ground? Lisa smirks. It's the ocean, for god's sake. Why in the world did Susan chose these words and why is everyone nodding as if Susan has said something incredibly profound? The waves rise and the boat slaps down on the swell.

"Careful," the captain says.

Susan manages to keep her balance as she takes the urn from Eric and dumps out the rest of the chunky gray ash.

"You did great." The captain hands Susan a lei of white plumeria and she tosses it overboard and stands.

Lisa leans over the railing. The ashes have dissolved. The flowers float for a moment and disappear. "That's it?" she says. "Betsy's gone?"

"We'll send you the exact coordinates of where the ashes entered the ocean," the captain says.

Lisa starts laughing, a guttural sound that is completely inappropriate, judging from the captain and her family's horrified faces.

"Mom?" Monique says.

The captain looks worried. "It's included in the package."

"It's just that . . ." Lisa can barely speak she's laughing so hard. "We'll never be able to find her." She drops to her knees, crying now, and then sobbing. "It's too late, anyway. I didn't even look through Betsy's things. I just got rid of it all. Monique could have worn those pearls on her wedding day."

"I don't even like pearls," Monique says. "Please don't cry."

Eric steps toward her, holds out his hand, and helps her up. He keeps his arm around her waist all the way down the stairs to the bathroom. She spends the rest of the boat ride splashing cold water on her face.

■ ■ ■

Lunch is at the Flying Fish Oyster Bar. After the server takes their menus, Lisa clears her throat. "I'm sorry I made such a scene."

"It's okay to cry, Mom," Tyler says. "We all miss Betsy."

Lisa turns to Susan. "I should have let you go through her things first."

"Yes," Susan says. "But I shouldn't have put all the responsibility on your shoulders."

"I know you all blame me for the accident."

"No, we don't," Monique says.

"Betsy drank too much," Tyler says. "Everyone knows that. No one blames you for anything."

"You took good care of her, honey," Eric says. "We love you for that."

They're all looking at her and nodding. Their dear, sweet faces. "I love you all too. But I should have been more careful. Kept Betsy away from the pool anyway."

"Lisa," Susan says. "I don't think anyone could keep my mother from doing whatever the hell she wanted to do."

"I'll drink to that," Eric says.

They all raise their glasses.

"The boat was nice," Tyler says. "I'm glad we did this for grandma."

They order every dessert on the menu and extra forks and spoons so they can share. Susan dips her spoon into a crème brûlée. "Tell me more about this employee of yours, Eric."

"He was arrested for vandalism and property damage at a riot in downtown Wellington," Lisa says. One more bite of coconut flan, she decides, and then she'll make herself stop.

"What happened to innocent until proven guilty?" Eric says, his mouth full of chocolate cheesecake.

"You never want to believe anything bad about anyone," Lisa says.

"He's always been that way," Susan says.

"Isn't that a good thing?" Monique asks.

"Not always," Tyler says.

"I don't understand why this person is still working for you," Susan says. "Are you worried about repercussions if you fire him?"

"Keith's not like that," Eric says. "He's odd, but he's harmless."

"Then why was he in prison?" Susan asks.

"A burglary, when he was younger," Eric says. "Got mixed up with the wrong crowd is my guess."

Susan shakes her head. "And now he's been arrested for vandalism and property damage. Those are acts of violence, Eric. I agree with Lisa. You need to distance yourself from him."

How unexpected, Lisa thinks, for Susan to be on her side.

Eric sighs. "You might be right. I've been thinking about going in a different direction anyway. There are call centers that do scheduling and answer phones. It'd probably be cheaper to just let Keith go."

"That's an excellent idea, honey," Lisa says.

"A win-win solution," Susan says, smiling at Lisa.

Lisa pushes the coconut flan toward Susan. "You need to try this. It's delicious."

CHAPTER THIRTY-SIX

KEITH NELSON

On Monday, Keith has just finished his morning run and weight routine when Thomas Washington calls and says the Bug Guy is eliminating his position, which means he's officially unemployed. Keith can guess why. Eric's daughter probably told him some lie to cover up her own story. She looks smart enough to lie. He showers, makes a protein shake, and then calls Granny C. Today is her eightieth birthday.

"Your dad's in the hospital again," she says.

He can tell she's crying. He's never really thought of his dad as being her son. "I'll come see you later," he says. He cashes Josh's mother's check and buys flowers from a freeway vendor, then stops by Ray's to leave money to pay Louie.

Ray's eyes widen when he opens the door. "Wow, Keith. You're looking fit."

"I bumped up my workouts."

"I can tell. Come in for a minute, say hi to my mom."

"Who's that at the door?" Ray's mother says from inside the house.

"You're busy." Keith hands him the cash. "Tell Louie thanks. I'll let you go."

On his way out of the tract, he passes the Kensingtons' house. The green Volkswagen is the only car in the driveway, the garage is empty, the door wide open. Maybe the daughter is home alone. He could talk to her, find out what she told Eric. Maybe he could convince her to tell her dad a different story that would help him get his job back. He parks around the corner, walks down the sidewalk, and up the driveway through the open garage. He will try his best not to scare the girl and make things even worse.

The kitchen door is unlocked. "Hello?" he says. No answer. It's almost like they want people to steal from them, leaving the house open like this. The girl must be outside. He heads back out to the garage, through the side door, and into the backyard toward the pool. "Hello?" he says, but the backyard is empty. He remembers Grace saying they were going to drain the pool and fill it in with dirt, so he walks over to see what that looks like.

"Holy fuck!" Keith nearly falls forward when he gets to the edge. The pool has been drained, leaving an empty concrete shell. The kid who blew up his car is lying face up in the deep end, a halo of blood around his head, a skateboard upside down next to him. When the kid moans, Keith's heart drops to his feet. "Holy fuck," he says again.

The kid opens his eyes and squints at the sun. "Am I dead?"

"I thought you were." He should get the hell out of here. "What happened?"

"I don't know. I guess I fell."

"Is anyone else here?"

"I don't think so." He sits up and looks behind him. "Whoa. That's a lot of blood."

"I don't think you're supposed to move after a head injury. Lie back down. You might have a concussion. I'm calling 911 and then I'm going to leave. You can't tell anyone I was here."

"I'm not really supposed to be here either."

"Your name is Josh, right?" Keith punches 911 into his phone. A woman's voice, stern and official. "What's your emergency."

"There's a kid named Josh in an empty swimming pool with a head injury," he says. "Skateboard, I think. On Paradise Court. No, I'm not the homeowner, I'm the one who found him. I don't know the address. There's a green VW in the driveway." He hangs up. "The paramedics will be here soon." He starts to leave, then turns. "Are you friends with the girl who lives here?"

"Monique? Kind of. You know her too?"

"I work for her dad. You don't recognize me? I'm Keith. We met at Ray's house."

"You look different."

"Do you know what she told her dad about me?"

"You mean about the protest? We never even saw you there. She's still grounded though."

"You were there too?"

"Don't tell anyone. My mom doesn't know. My head hurts. Maybe I should lie down."

"The paramedics will be here soon." Keith hurries out of the backyard, down the driveway, and around the corner to his car. His phone starts ringing as he opens the car door. He turns it off. They can probably trace 911 calls. They probably already have. He waits until the ambulance pulls into the cul-de-sac, watches to make sure the paramedics go to the right house. When they file up Eric's driveway with a stretcher, he starts the car. No one is outside in any of the front yards, but he sees a black Suburban heading toward him as he leaves the tract.

Jeannette stares at him, open-mouthed as she passes. He keeps his eyes trained straight ahead, pretending not to see her. He can't imagine what she would be doing here, but he doesn't have time to find out. One more good reason to stay away from this neighborhood. He'll take the flowers to Granny C and go straight home to his garage.

CHAPTER THIRTY-SEVEN

JOSH KOWALSKI

Josh opens his eyes and looks up at a circle of people in blue uniforms standing above him. There's a lot of them. They have him sit up. They wrap a bandage around his head and ask if his parents are home. "My mom's at work," he says. "I'm actually fine. You guys can go."

"You need to be checked out," one of them says. "You want us to call your mom?"

"I don't like to bother her at work."

"She'll want to know about this. Is her number in your phone?"

Josh groans. Judging from the size of the blood stain, he's not going to be able to hide the cut on his head from his mother anyway. He pulls his cellphone from his pocket, punches in her number, and hands the phone to one of the paramedics who puts her on the speakerphone and explains what happened.

"What do you mean he's in an empty swimming pool?" Josh can hear the panic in his mother's voice. "Is he at the Kensingtons' house?"

The paramedic looks at him. "You don't live here?"

He shakes his head.

"Let me talk to Lisa or Eric," his mother says.

"Your son's the only one here, ma'am."

"Are you serious? He's there alone? Did they leave their garage door open again?"

The paramedics exchange glances. He's going to be in trouble with the Kensingtons' now too.

"I'm a nurse," his mother says. "Can you just bring him to Wellington Regional?"

"We're on our way."

They load him on a stretcher and roll him down the driveway. He hears Ray's voice and lifts his head. He was supposed to bring Ray groceries later. Ray's mother must be home by herself. "Sorry, Ray," he says as they load him in the vehicle.

"No reason to be," Ray says. "What can I do?"

"Maybe get my board? It's still in the pool."

■ ■ ■

"How much do you remember," the doctor asks later, after a physical, an eye test, a CT scan, and an MRI that his mother insisted on even though the doctor didn't think both were necessary.

He explains that he was on his way to Jeannette's to bring in her trash barrels when it occurred to him this might be his last chance to skate in the empty Kensington pool.

"Was anyone home?" the doctor asks.

"I don't think so. I didn't go inside. Tyler said I could skate whenever I wanted to. I just fell. I haven't practiced that trick for a while."

"Who called 911?" the doctor asks.

"I don't remember," Josh says.

"The homeowners have liability," the doctor tells his mother. "You might want to talk to an attorney."

When they finally release him, a nurse rolls him outside in a wheelchair. His head is wrapped in an embarrassingly huge bandage.

"Martha!" a woman yells. She hurries toward them, a panicked look on her face.

His mother sighs. "It's Neil's daughter, Joni."

"I don't want to talk to anyone right now."

"Too late. Here she comes. Hi Joni."

"What happened to Josh?"

"He fell off his skateboard," his mother says. "I'm surprised to see you here. Is your dad okay?"

"He's having some tests done. Routine stuff. Radiology won't let me go in with him."

"I need to get Josh home," his mother says.

Joni looks like she might cry. "My dad talks about you all the time, Josh. He thinks of you like a grandson. Please be careful."

"She seemed kind of freaked out," he says as they pull out of the parking lot.

"Head injuries are serious. I'm freaked out too."

■ ■ ■

His mom watches him all night the first night, stays home from work and watches him all the next day. She keeps asking how he feels. He admits he has a headache. His ears ring a little. He's tired, but he doesn't feel nauseous, and his vision isn't blurry. She thinks he shouldn't play drums for a while.

The Kensingtons come over with Tyler and deliver a pineapple and bacon pizza. Mrs. Kensington explains she'd thought Monique was home the day of Josh's accident, and Monique and Mr. Kensington were both sure Tyler was home, and they'd all stepped out to do errands and left the doors wide open. "We obviously weren't thinking," she says.

Tyler says he's sorry. "That was a lot of blood, dude."

Mr. Kensington clears his throat and pushes his glasses up his giant nose. "We'll pay for your medical bills, of course."

"Good," his mother says. "My insurance won't cover everything."

"We figure it must have been our gardening crew who called the paramedics," Mrs. Kensington says. "Eric asked them, but his Spanish isn't good. Maybe they were too afraid to tell us. Who knows what their status is? They're probably illegals."

"Josh needs to rest," his mother says. After they leave, she says pineapple doesn't belong on pizza and throws the box in the trash.

Brittany texts him a disgusting video of Johnny Knoxville popping out his eyeball and writes, "Could have been worse, Stunt Boy." Stunt Boy is better than anything else Brittany's ever called him.

Monique stops by, in person. "I got my car keys back," she says. "If you ever need a ride to the doctor or something, I could take you. I know you work a lot, Mrs. Kowalski."

"That's very nice of you, Monique," his mother says.

Josh is so surprised he can't think of anything to say.

His mother tells Albertsons that he had a skateboard accident and needs some time off. She doesn't say anything about the Kensingtons' pool.

"Are we going to sue them?" he asks.

"I haven't decided."

"It was my fault, not theirs."

"You need to rest."

He says he doesn't remember who called 911 so often he almost believes it. He's not really lying. He doesn't remember hearing Keith call anyone. Maybe it wasn't even Keith. The man he saw looked like a giant from where he lay at the bottom of the pool.

His dad tells him on the phone that the Kensingtons should pay, big time. "They're liable," he says. "Let me talk to your mom."

"You want to talk about liability?" she says when Josh hands her the phone. "What about those fireworks you left behind?" She tells his dad about Keith's car and says, "Of course I work too many hours, how else can I pay the bills?" She says if he thinks his son needs more supervision, he should come home. His dad says something else, and his mother says, "He needs a father," and then she slams down the phone.

Ray returns his skateboard. "Something you might want to know," he says. "Keith Nelson came by my house the afternoon of Josh's accident to leave cash for the seat cushion. I heard the ambulance not too long after he left."

"Do you think he called them?" his mother asks. "Because Lisa Kensington is sure it was her illegal gardeners."

Ray frowns. "Gregorio is her gardener, and he isn't illegal. He doesn't work in this neighborhood on Mondays either. Doesn't she know that?"

"What would Keith be doing at the Kensingtons' house anyway?" his mother says.

They both look at him. Josh shrugs.

"Last I heard, Keith was working for Eric Kensington," Ray says. "And I know Lisa Kensington doesn't like him."

His mother scowls. "I don't like Eric or Lisa Kensington much right now either. I'm grateful to whoever it was that called."

Joni Gorman calls and says Neil wants Josh to have his old upright piano. She arranges the delivery, his mother rearranges the living room furniture, and the movers roll the piano inside.

■ ■ ■

"That's my favorite song," his mother says when she comes home from work that night. "Your dad used to sing it to me."

Josh knows this already, which is why he looked it up on

YouTube. "Did you know Paul McCartney's dog was named Martha?"

She half laughs. "No, I didn't know that. Play it again."

When he finishes the song, she has tears in her eyes. Maybe he shouldn't have told her about Paul McCartney's dog. "There aren't many songs about Martha," he says. "I'm sure dad didn't mean anything."

"I can't believe you've already learned how to play this. How did you figure out the chords?"

"On YouTube. I can teach you if you want." She wipes her eyes. He scoots over on the bench to make room for her. "You just break up the chords and put them back together again, using the same notes. Like this."

CHAPTER THIRTY-EIGHT
JEANNETTE LARSEN

Early in the morning before the garage sale, Jeannette decides the breakfast burritos from Sanchez Burrito Company, the coffee cakes from Albertsons' bakery, and the two gallons of coffee from Starbucks might not be enough, so she makes a quick run to the donut shop, keeping her eye out for Keith's grey Honda. She's been looking over her shoulder since the day she saw him drive past. A coincidence, she keeps telling herself.

Bob laughs when she sets the pink box on the table. "This might be too much food, babe. We don't even know how many people will show up."

"I want it to be nice." She fans out the paper napkins printed with tropical fruit that match the paper plates and coffee cups she bought online and smooths the fold in the coordinating pink tablecloth from Bed, Bath, and Beyond.

"It's perfect," Bob says. "You're perfect." He kisses her and runs his hand down her back and over her ass. "Last night was incredible."

She lets herself relax against him. "We've had a lot of good nights lately."

"I'm glad we're hosting this breakfast," Bob says. "It'll be good to get to know some normal people."

"I'm not sure how normal they are," Jeannette says. "Especially that realtor woman. There's something about her that irritates me." She watches a seagull hovering almost motionless above her, floating on an air current. "Not a cloud in the sky," she says as Gloria and Felix pull up and get out of their car. Gloria carries a mason jar full of sunflowers.

"From our garden," Gloria says. "You two look happy." She sets the flowers on the table and glances up and down the crowded street at all the shoppers in the neighboring driveways, browsing through racks of clothes, stacks of toys, and boxes of books and dishes.

"You guys aren't selling anything today?" Gloria says.

"We're just offering breakfast," Bob says. "Hoping to meet some neighbors."

"Well, I'm ready to shop," Gloria says.

"Have some coffee first," Bob says. "And something to eat."

"I'll take a cup," Felix says. "We brought you those tickets for the Hollywood Bowl."

"I really hate to miss Tom Petty," Gloria says. "He's at the top of his game right now."

"We'll find someone who'll enjoy them," Bob says

"No charge," Felix says. "As long as they're music lovers."

Lisa pulls up in a Mercedes with a hook-nosed man. "I'm Eric," he says, shaking Bob's hand. "Ooh, donuts!" Eric takes a maple bar from the pink box. "This all looks delicious."

"I really appreciate you guys hosting this," Lisa says. She glances at Felix and Gloria, raises her eyebrows, and looks at Jeannette.

"These are our friends," Jeannette says. "Felix and Gloria. They were our neighbors in Angel City."

"Oh, okay," Lisa says.

"Were we not supposed to invite anyone?" Jeannette says. "I thought you wanted a big crowd."

"It's fine." Lisa sighs. "Normally it's just locals. But I guess once those people start moving into that housing project, things will change anyway."

Felix and Gloria look at each other.

"I'm not sure what you mean by that," Jeannette says as an older man pulling a cooler and an even older woman pushing a walker come up the sidewalk toward them.

"That's Ray Murdoch and his mother Vickie," Lisa says. "I wasn't sure they'd come. Vickie just had hip surgery."

"I've seen him outside watering his roses," Bob says. He walks down the sidewalk to greet them and takes the cooler from Ray.

"We brought extra chairs," Lisa says. "Help me get them out of the car, Eric."

Gloria whispers to Jeannette, "Are we not supposed to be here?"

"I'm glad you're here. I don't know what Lisa's problem is."

Lisa and Eric set up the chairs. Ray and Vickie introduce themselves and sit down. Jeannette stretches her legs out in the sunshine, determined not to let Lisa spoil the day. For once there is no morning overcast. Last night she had a dream about Zack. She didn't recognize him at first because he was riding a skateboard, something Zack never did. He rolled up the driveway, jumped off, and said, "It's okay, Mom." She woke up more rested than she's felt in years.

"You look familiar," Felix tells Ray. "Did you use to work at American Tire in Angel City?"

"A million years ago," Ray says. "You have a good memory."

"I always felt like I got a square deal at American Tire," Felix says.

"I liked working there," Ray says, "even if they did only pay minimum wage."

"Minimum wage is his middle name," Vickie says. "You're a pretty woman, Jeannette. You have any sisters who might be interested in my son? He doesn't have any money, but he's a nice man. Most of the time."

Everyone laughs, including Ray. "Sorry," Jeannette says. "No sisters."

Martha and Josh cross the street. Jeannette's glad to see Josh is wearing Zack's Converse shoes. "I hope you're both hungry. We have a ton of food."

Lisa stands, visibly pale, a grim expression on her face. She walks over to Josh and gives him a bearhug, almost knocking the Los Lobos baseball cap off his head. Lisa hugs Martha next and hangs on for a long time, saying over and over how sorry she is. Bob looks at Jeannette and raises his eyebrows. She shrugs and mouths, "No idea."

Martha finally pulls away from Lisa. "What are your kids up to today?"

"They're both sleeping in," Eric says.

Josh adjusts his cap. He looks disappointed. *Poor kid,* Jeannette thinks, *spending his Saturday morning with all these adults.* "I like your hat, Josh. Bob and I are big Los Lobos fans."

"My favorite band," Bob says, "next to Tom Petty." He stands. "Anyone want coffee? I'll pour."

"You're a tall drink of water," Vickie says.

"Sorry, Bob," Ray says. "My mom's lost what little filters she ever had."

"I say what I think," Vickie says.

Bob winks. "I find that refreshing, Miss Vickie. More people should."

Vickie beams.

Jeannette smiles and then grips the arms of her chair when she sees a grey Honda cruise up the street. The car slows down and then stops. The driver glances at the rack of clothes in the driveway next door, taking inventory. He's dark-haired and bearded and speaks Spanish to the woman next to him, and he is not Keith. Jeannette exhales. There are a million grey Honda Accords. Of course, he's not Keith.

"I thought that was Keith Nelson at first," Lisa says. "But he's probably still in jail."

"Jail!" Jeannette says. Keith is a common name, she tells herself, and she never knew his last name.

"What's that?" Bob asks turning to look at her.

She can't think of one thing to say, but Lisa is quick to answer. "The Nelsons' son Keith drives a car like that. He was arrested after that protest downtown. With all his priors, I'm sure he's going to be locked up for a while."

Jeannette feels faint. "I think I need to move out of the sun."

"Come sit by me," Vickie says.

"I don't believe I know the Nelsons," Bob says.

"They live behind Ray and Vickie," Lisa says. "Their house was for sale, but they just took it off the market. Their son used to work for Eric. I'm not sure what's going on with the Nelsons or their son these days. Have you heard anything, Ray?"

"Nope," Ray says. "These burritos are delicious, Jeannette."

"They're from Sanchez Burrito Company." She never asked Keith where he worked. It can't be the same man.

"Isn't Keith the one you were helping fix his car?" Vickie says.

Jeannette tries to remember if Keith said anything about his car needing work. She sinks down in the chair next to Vickie.

"Why in the world would you help Keith with anything?" Lisa says. "He's a criminal."

"I don't think so," Ray says.

"We've known the Nelson family for years," Vickie says. "They're our neighbors."

"You need to be careful," Lisa says. "Keith's violent. Eric never should have hired him."

"He doesn't work for me anymore, hon," Eric says. "Let it go."

"What kind of work do you do, Eric?" Bob asks.

"Extermination," Eric says. "My company is called The Bug Guy. We're up in Angel City."

"You're kidding!" Gloria says. "We hired your company last year to get rid of our termites."

"It's a small world," Eric says. "Glad we could help you out."

Jeannette hopes it's not that small of a world. "Please everyone, eat," she says.

Josh loads his plate with two of everything.

"I used to be able to eat like that and never gain weight," Gloria says. "How old are you, Josh?"

"Sixteen," he says.

"Sixteen! You're inheriting an interesting world." Felix sits back with his coffee. "Speaking of which, I read in the *Register* this morning that some of those people who were part of that mess in Charlottesville are from Wellington Beach. We were wondering if you guys know any of them. Maybe those people we met at the concert in the park you took us to?"

Bob coughs. "We haven't seen them lately."

"We decided we didn't have much in common with those people," Jeannette says. Bob was in DC during the Charlottesville march. He'd called her, in shock, and they'd watched it together, disgusted on two separate coasts. "Did we pay for those torches?" she'd asked. "I don't know," he said. "Let's just try and put this behind us."

"I was at that concert too," Martha says. "The music was good."

Martha probably knows Keith too, Jeannette thinks. *She might even have seen me talking to him that day.* "Aren't there two hundred thousand people living in Wellington?" she says. "It would be a miracle if any of us knew those people who went to Charlottesville."

"Not really," Eric says. "We have a lot of nutcases in this town. I wouldn't be surprised if some of them were involved."

"We have a lot of concerned *citizens* in this town," Lisa says. "That doesn't make them nutcases."

Vickie looks at Ray. "You said you recognized someone in that march."

"I might have, Mom. I could have been wrong."

"I always see people I know," Gloria says. "Or that know someone I know. So does Felix."

Felix reaches for a donut. "Six degrees of separation. That Kevin Bacon thing."

"What's this about bacon?" Vickie asks.

"Kevin Bacon's an actor," Ray says. "There's a theory you can link him to any actor through no more than six connections."

"I don't mean connections to celebrities," Gloria says. "I mean to each other. Look at us. Ray installed our tires. Eric's company got rid of our termites. Martha was at the same concert we went to. People are more likely to be connected to each other than not."

"I'm not so sure about that," Ray says. "It doesn't feel that way to me these days."

"Me either," Jeannette says. She glances over at Lisa, who is glaring at two of the shoppers from next door as they walk up the driveway. It's the couple who were driving the Honda.

"We heard there was coffee and donuts," the bearded man says.

"You're at the right place." Jeannette stands. "We have burritos, donuts, coffee cake . . ."

Lisa clears her throat.

"How about some coffee?" Bob asks.

"Thank you," the man says. "Black is fine."

Jeannette loads two plates and Bob pours coffee.

"You'll have to take that to go," Lisa says. "This table is for residents only."

"What?" Jeannette says. "No! We can make room."

"You can sit by me." Gloria says.

"Locals only," Lisa says. "Do you understand English? Vamanos."

"Lisa!" Eric says. "She doesn't mean that," he tells the couple. "Please. Sit down."

The man looks at the woman. "It's okay," he says as they back down the driveway. "Thanks for the food."

"I'm surprised at you, Lisa," Eric says. "That wasn't very neighborly."

"Oh, please." Lisa's voice is bitter. "Those people aren't our neighbors, although they will be soon enough. You'd all better start learning Spanish."

Felix rises from his chair. "What exactly is your problem?"

Gloria stands too. "It's pretty obvious, honey. Her problem is us. We should go."

"No!" Bob says. "You're our guests. You don't need to leave."

Everyone is staring at Lisa now.

"I didn't mean you guys." Tears form in Lisa's green eyes. "I meant all those other people."

Felix looks at Gloria. "Want to go do some shopping, hon?"

"I'm really not in the mood to shop right now," Gloria says, "but I would like to take a walk."

"Lisa's been through a lot lately," Eric says after Felix and Gloria head down the street. "With Betsy and everything. And she's been working too much."

"Your newsletter didn't mention anything about residents only," Vickie says.

"It was implied." Lisa wipes her eyes. "It just makes me angry. I've worked really hard to stop this housing project from happening and it hasn't made any difference. This neighborhood is special. I don't want it to change."

"If there's one thing I've learned in my life," Vickie says, "it's that everything changes. Let's go home, Ray. We'll take some burritos if there's leftovers."

"Thanks for the food, Jeannette," Ray says.

"We should go home too," Martha says. Josh follows her across the street.

Jeannette makes plates to go for Ray and Vickie. Bob says he'll help Ray with the cooler. Eric says he'll give Bob a hand, leaving Jeannette alone with Lisa, who is furiously studying a spot of oil on the driveway.

"I should never have said any of that," Lisa says, eyes still trained on the driveway. "I spoiled everything. And I really didn't mean to insult your friends."

"You sounded like you meant it."

Lisa grimaces. "Sometimes I don't like myself very much."

"I feel that way too," Jeannette says. "But we all make mistakes, I guess."

I've made way too many, she thinks. She could ask Lisa about Keith, but what else is there to know about him, really? She sees Bob coming up the street with Eric, laughing about something. He looks happy and that's all that matters.

"I love the color of your hair, Lisa," she says. "It really shines in this sunlight. It brings out your green eyes."

Lisa is crying again. She reaches for a napkin. "Thank you," she says. "I'll tell my hairdresser."

Bob and Eric are back. "Everything okay?" Bob asks.

Lisa blows her nose and stands. "I'm going to find your friends and apologize."

"They'll appreciate that," Bob says. He looks at Jeannette. "Eric invited me to play golf next Saturday. If that's okay with you, babe."

"Of course," Jeannette says. "You've been wanting to find someone to play with. I think I'll pack up the rest of this food to go. Can you guys move the table closer to the street to make it easier for people to get to?"

"That's very generous of you," Eric says.

"We can't eat all of this," Jeannette says, "We have more than enough."

CHAPTER THIRTY-NINE
KEITH NELSON

Keith backs into Wayne's empty driveway and cuts the engine. He doesn't see Wayne's red Ford F-150, which means Wayne's still at work. He's not sure what Tina drives or if she's home or not. He glances down at the leather gloves and the twenty-pound weight on the floor of the passenger side. Tina might be a problem.

Wayne's street is lined with bottle brush trees. Keith stays in his car and watches hummingbirds zip in and out of the blood red blooms. The branches need trimming. Wayne won't like him parking the Honda in his driveway, so he will offer up the six-pack of Stone's Arrogant Bastard right away. Wayne will never turn down free beer, especially an expensive brand. Next, he'll apologize for hitting Wayne, say something short and simple that might sound like he means it. He'll ask Wayne if they can hang out for a while, get him to talk about Virginia. Wayne will be happy to hear that he saw him on TV.

He already knows Wayne won't invite him inside the house. He's never been further than the garage. Wayne will eventually go inside to take a piss. Keith will get the weight out of his car and put on the gloves. He'll stand behind the door to the house and wait. Force and the element of surprise should be enough. Wayne's truck and his Honda will almost

291

block the view of the garage from the street. There will be blood. He'll use his new sheets and towels to mop it up and the green padded moving blanket he found in Kiri's garage to wrap around Wayne's body.

He's left everything else he owns behind in payment, except Granny C's photograph. He has a full tank of gas and the three hundred eighteen dollars he withdrew from his savings account in his wallet. He should be able to lift Wayne with no problem. He's bench pressed two fifty every other day for the past three weeks. Wayne should fit in the trunk of the Honda next to the brand-new shovel, purchased this morning at Home Depot.

After it's done, he'll change into jeans, a flannel long sleeve, and Doc Martens. It's too hot for all of that now, but he'll be grateful for the extra layers tonight. He'll drive around until it gets dark, toss his bloody clothes in the dumpster behind the McDonald's near the freeway onramp. Another cruise out to Temecula, another right turn into the open gate on Dorland Mountain Road, a trip up the hill, a gift for Duchess the dog to find in the morning. Then he'll drive east, ditch his car somewhere, and get on a Greyhound bus. Find work roofing or digging ditches or hauling two by fours somewhere no one knows him.

That's as far as his plan goes. It might work. He could also be in custody by nightfall.

■ ■ ■

The red truck pulls in the driveway at 4:00 p.m. As expected, Wayne jumps out and yells, "What the fuck are you doing in my driveway?"

Keith gets out of his car. "I came by to say I'm sorry." He holds up the six-pack. "You want one of these?"

Wayne touches his jaw. "You owe me more than a beer, dude. I'm sending you my dentist's bill."

"That sounds fair," Keith says. "These are cold. You sure you don't want one?"

"I never said I didn't want one, dude. Pop one of those bad boys open. Did you find a new gym or something? You've really bulked up."

"Just working out in my garage."

"Tina's not home," Wayne says. "She went to Vegas for her sister's bachelorette party." He punches a button on his keys and the garage door opens. "I gotta take a piss." When Wayne walks past him, he stinks of garbage and sweat. "Wait till you hear what happened in Virginia," he says, the same leering grin on his face that Keith saw on TV. "This is just the beginning, dude." Wayne goes inside, leaving the door open behind him.

Keith hadn't expected things to get rolling so quickly, but he's as ready as he will ever be. He steps into the garage and sets the six-pack on top of the washing machine, then walks back to his car and opens the passenger door, his heart thrashing his rib cage. Is he really going to do this? He's known Wayne his entire life. He picks up the weight, reminding himself that Wayne has never been his friend, not really. All those years of defending him, agreeing to those stupid schemes, watching Wayne get away with everything while he took the blame. He won't get away with this either. He'll get caught because he always does, and he'll be locked up for the rest of his life.

"You have to do something," Chenda said.

As he turns to go back into the garage, his phone rings and he nearly drops the weight at the sound. No one ever calls him. He won't answer it, he decides, but then he looks at the display, hesitates, and clicks on the green icon. "Hey, Dad. How's it going?" His father's voice is so low he can barely understand him. He needs to get back in the garage and behind that door before Wayne returns, which will be any second.

"What's that, Dad?" He can see drops beading on the bottle necks of the beers sitting on the washing machine. He's going to lose his best chance if he doesn't hang up now. "I can't hear you." He listens for a few moments. "Okay."

The weight in his hand is incredibly heavy and when he sets it down in the car, the release of the tension in his arms and shoulders and neck is so overwhelming, he nearly weeps.

"Okay, dad. I'll be right there."

He closes the passenger door then hurries around to the driver's side. As he pulls out of the driveway, he glances over his shoulder at Wayne, standing alone in the garage now, holding an open beer in one hand, that same dumb look on his face he's had his entire life.

That's enough, Keith thinks. *I'm done.*

WHERE DID SUMMER GO?

You may have noticed that I haven't been publishing my newsletter as frequently. Life has gotten pretty busy in the Kensington household with the kids back in school. I'm sure it's the same at your house.

There's still time to put your house on the market before the holiday season starts.

The days might be getting cooler, but the Wellington Beach home values are red hot.

Call 1-800-WB4-EVER for a free estimate.

Helpful Household Tips

" *Making your bed every morning ensures you start your day with something accomplished. It makes a world of a difference to your mindset for the rest of the day.* **"**

In Case You Didn't Know

I'm running for City Council! I've given this a lot of thought and realized it's a natural progression of everything I stand for. I'm so disappointed that the Riptide housing project is going through, but I'll do my best to make sure no more of these housing projects are approved. I've always loved volunteering for my community and helping families make their dreams come true. Now it's time to protect those dreams. Vote for Lisa Kensington!

NOT IN WELLINGTON'S BACK YARD

I'm a little weary of the way the word NIMBY gets thrown around like it's a bad thing, marginalizing citizens who are simply concerned about traffic, demands on public schools and services, and the environment.

Years ago, there were plans to build a shopping center in the Wellington Wetlands. Concerned citizens like me didn't want that in their backyards. Call me a NIMBY if you want, but I'm proud of stopping that development and I'm proud of where I live.

CHAPTER FORTY

LISA KENSINGTON

Lisa sips coffee and reads the *LA Times* on her laptop. The FBI has arrested twenty-four-year-old Wayne Connor from Wellington Beach in connection with the violence in Charlottesville. They have a video of Connor attacking two counter protesters who were seriously injured. Connor is charged with violating something called the Riots Act and faces up to ten years in prison. There's a photo of him being taken out of his home in handcuffs. Wellington City Attorney Carter Welch is quoted naming Wayne Connor "a suspect of interest in the vandalism downtown during the Trump rally in July."

Lisa wonders if Keith Nelson is still a suspect of interest too.

Over on the Nextdoor neighbor app, @Dogmom22 has posted that Wayne Connor is a true patriot and the media is framing him because ANTIFA was responsible for the violence in Charlottesville. The people on the Wellie Facebook Forum also praise Connor and blame ANTIFA. Lisa closes her laptop. She's grateful that Monique is into poetry now and not politics.

She needs to get moving. Ever since she decided to run for city council, her already demanding schedule has gotten even crazier. She has a busy day ahead, shopping

for a new suit, filing paperwork at City Hall, and inter-
viewing campaign managers. Plus, Tyler has actually invited
his girlfriend, Leslie, over for dinner tonight. Eric promised
to come home early from work, but Monique is going to
the Hollywood Bowl with Josh Kowalski to see Tom Petty.
Monique insists it's not a date, that Josh got the tickets for
free from Bob and Jeannette. Lisa hopes it's not a date. Josh
is a year younger and a head shorter than Monique and he
would never be Lisa's choice, but maybe his mother won't
sue them if the kids stay friends.

She sent Martha, Vickie, and Jeannette flowers to apologize for her meltdown during the garage sale, explaining
that she was feeling desperate, defeated, and frustrated and
hoped they would forgive her. She definitely needs to be
more careful, going forward, about what she says to people.
They're not only potential customers, they're also voters. She
picks up the stack of newsletters and opens the front door.

The gardeners are loading their mowers, blowers, and
edgers into their truck. Usually, Eric deals with these people
because his Spanish is better than hers, but he left for work
early this morning. There's another crisis. The call center is
a disaster. Grace is threatening to quit.

The pool is gone, and their backyard is a pile of dirt. Eric
promised to talk to the gardeners about putting in grass, but
as usual, it's up to her to make it happen. Keep the words
simple and enunciate clearly, she tells herself as she heads
toward the truck. "Did my husband ask you about putting a
lawn in the backyard?" Judging from their blank expressions,
they don't understand. She tries again, louder this time. "Mi
esposa? The backyard? We need grass."

One of them comes closer. "We can help you with that."

"You speak English? I thought you were from Mexico."

"My dad's from Guatemala. But I was born at Hoag
Hospital in Pelican Beach."

"Really? My kids were born there too." She wonders how his parents could afford that. "Anyway," she says, "how long would it take you to put in sod? We need to do something. There's so much dust and dirt, and it's getting inside the house."

He nods. "If you want grass, you'll need a sprinkler system too. But I have some other ideas that wouldn't require so much water and maintenance. We could put in native grasses and some sages. Hummingbirds love them. We do hardscape too. Maybe a path of decomposed granite. And a fountain? I could draw up some plans."

Lisa frowns. He obviously doesn't understand. "I want grass. What's the Mexican word for sod?" She pantomimes a square.

"I know what sod is." He looks disappointed.

She didn't mean to insult him. There's a remote possibility he might even live and vote in Wellington. "I'm Lisa. What's your name?"

"Gregorio," he says.

Could it possibly be the same gardener Ray mentioned? "Do you know Ray over on Hillside West?"

He smiles. "Ray's a good man. He has beautiful roses."

"He uses too much water."

Gregorio nods. "I've just about convinced him to install a smart controller sprinkler system. The controller monitors the weather forecast and then adjusts accordingly. It's tied in with weather satellites. It's really fascinating. I could do the same thing for you."

Gregorio's vocabulary is surprisingly good, but this is too much information, too early in the morning. "Give me a price on the sod," Lisa says. "And write up your other ideas too. I'll have to talk to my husband first, of course." The purpose of a husband, to use as an excuse not to commit to anything. She'll need to research this and get more estimates. A minimum of three is what she recommends to her clients.

She heads down the driveway and out into the neighborhood. The plumeria house is in escrow, sold for over the asking price to a corporation that has already ripped out the trees. Another terrific commission, but still frustrating. She loved those plumerias. Further down the street there's a painter's truck in front of the Gormans' house. The stinky carpet was torn out yesterday, and vinyl flooring will be installed as soon as the painters are done. Over on Hillside West, she sees Bob Larsen's Mercedes in their driveway. Eric and Bob have gotten very friendly lately. Bob told Eric about their son. Lisa feels terrible for both of the Larsens. No wonder Jeannette is so standoffish.

She's halfway done with her walk when Keith Nelson comes around the corner pushing a man in a wheelchair. Lisa nearly drops her entire stack of newsletters. She's never seen Keith outside of that Honda Accord before, and in person he's a huge man, much stronger and more terrifying than she'd realized. She never should have challenged him about where he was parked that day. Of course, she didn't know then that he was a criminal, capable of violence and destruction. Thank goodness he's not looking at her right now. She wonders why he isn't still in jail.

She's so shocked to see Keith, it takes her a second to recognize that the man in the wheelchair is his father. Jim Nelson is thin, pale, and fragile, and he can't be long for this world. Poor man. Poor Peggy Nelson too, dealing with this. Lisa makes a mental note to stop by CVS and pick up a sympathy card and then realizes Keith is looking right at her.

She wheels around to get away from him, her pulse quickening, her throat suddenly dry. She waits until she's halfway down the block before glancing over her shoulder to see if he's following her. The wheelchair has stopped. Keith is leaning forward, listening to something his father is saying. There is so much tenderness in Keith's face that Lisa nearly stumbles over a broken place in the sidewalk.

I was wrong, she realizes. Keith wasn't looking at me at all. He's worried about his dad.

A shadow blocks the sunlight above. She looks up at a blue heron, wings spread wide. Her eyes burn. *There's so much tragedy in this world*, she thinks, wishing she had a Kleenex instead of these ridiculous newsletters that no one reads or cares about and more than likely make no difference at all to her sales. What a waste of paper and energy. If it were trash day, she'd recycle them right now.

The heron lands gracefully on the framework of the fourth floor of the hateful new Riptide building and perches elegantly against the blue sky. Lisa takes a deep breath in and out and turns around. The wheelchair is heading in the opposite direction now.

"Hey neighbors," she says.

Keith glances over his shoulder.

"Wait up," she says. "I'll walk with you."

THE END

ACKNOWLEDGMENTS

Thank you to all the writers, teachers, editors, and friends who read early versions of this novel and offered suggestions and encouragements—especially Kate Anger, Sarah Rafael Garcia, Peter Gerrard, Anara Guard, Bryony Leah, Andrea Leeb, Sara Flannery Murphy, Eduardo Santiago, Alice Toth, Mary Volmer, and Diana Wagman.

Thanks to the Womxn's Write Inn (liz gonzalez, Stephanie Barbé Hammer, Ruthie Marlenée, and Mary Anne Perez) for getting me and this story idea through the pandemic. Thanks to Samantha Dunn and her memoir workshop group (Catherine Cooper, Jody Forrester, Andrea Leeb, Mirella Zolli, and Cheryl Jacobs) for making a fiction writer feel welcome.

Thank you to the sisterhood at She Writes Press— especially Leslie Rasmussen, Suzanne Simonetti, Shelley Blanton-Stroud, and Debra Thomas. Thank you, Brooke Warner, for publishing my novels, Samantha Strom and Lauren Wise for managing my projects, Julie Metz for designing my covers, and Tabitha Lahr for designing my pages, and Cait Levin.

Thank you, Krista Soukup and Blue Cottage Agency, for marketing and promoting my stories.

Thank you to my family and friends for reading and supporting my work.

Thank you to Professors Shank and Alvarez, who published a version of the story about Ray and the possum in Volume 20 of *The Ear*. Thank you to the *Corona Book of Horror Stories* for including a version of Ringo's misadventures in their second edition. Thank you to the *Sunlight Press* for including a version of Jeannette's story in their November 2020 issue.

Thank you, Riley, for listening to me read and sitting on my lap when you feel like it.

Thank you, Steve, for reading, road managing, celebrating, commiserating, listening and everything else.

About the Author

Mary Camarillo lives in Huntington Beach, California with her husband, Steve, who plays ukulele, and their terrorist cat, Riley, who makes frequent appearances on Instagram. Her debut novel *The Lockhart Women* won multiple awards. To learn more about Mary and her work, visit her website at www.MaryCamarillo.com.

Author photo © Creel McFarland Limerick Studio

SELECTED TITLES FROM SHE WRITES PRESS

She Writes Press is an independent publishing
company founded to serve women writers everywhere.
Visit us at www.shewritespress.com.

Nothing Forgotten by Jessica Levine. $16.95, 978-1-63152-324-3. In 1979, Anna, twenty-two and living abroad in Rome, is involved with a man already engaged to be married. Decades later, she is contacted in California by the Italian lover she knew decades before, reminding her of their affair and the child she gave up for adoption—and threatening the life, and marriage, she's built since.

The Sleeping Lady by Bonnie Monte. $16.95, 978-1-63152-387-8. Rae Sullivan's comfortable existence as a shop owner in a small northern California town is upended when her business partner is murdered in Golden Gate Park. Frustrated with the avenues the police are pursuing, Rae embarks on her own investigation, which eventually leads her to France and puts her marriage—and her life—in jeopardy.

Bittersweet Manor by Tory McCagg. $16.95, 978-1-93831-456-8. A chronicle of three generations of love, manipulation, entitlement, and disappointed expectations in an upper-middle-class New England family.

Appearances by Sondra Helene. $16.95, 978-1-63152-499-8. Samantha, the wife of a successful Boston businessman, loves both her husband and her sister—but the two of them have fought a cold war for years. When her sister is diagnosed with lung cancer, Samantha's family and marriage are tipped into crisis.

Eden by Jeanne Blasberg. $16.95, 978-1-63152-188-1. As her children and grandchildren assemble for Fourth of July weekend at Eden, the Meister family's grand summer cottage on the Rhode Island shore, Becca decides it's time to introduce the daughter she gave up for adoption fifty years ago.

Hard Cider: A Novel by Barbara Stark-Nemon. $16.95, 978-1-63152-475-2. Abbie Rose Stone believes she has navigated the shoals of her long marriage and complicated family and is eager to realize her dream of producing hard apple cider—but when a lovely young stranger exposes a long-held secret, Abbie's plans, loyalties, and definition of family are severely tested.